A KEPT WOMAN

by

AUDRA GRAYSON

CHIMERA

A Kept Woman published by
Chimera Publishing Ltd
22b Picton House
Hussar Court
Waterlooville
Hants
PO7 7SQ

Printed and bound in Great Britain by
Cox & Wyman, Reading.

A KEPT WOMAN

Audra Grayson

This novel is fiction – in real life practice safe sex

Chapter One

'Come on, boys.'

Jael Alistair's soft, honey-veneered voice drifted through the night. She continued walking through the whispering grass as it swayed in the dark's breeze. The crumpled tops of her butter-soft leather boots made a pleasant sound as their folds brushed against each other with every step.

The two Irish Setters caught up to Jael, even though her pace was mindful of how late it was and how far she had yet to go. The hounds appeared together from one side of the dusky field, their bodies jostling against each other as they ran at full stride, in tandem.

Jael looked down at one noble red head and smiled as the dog put his nose into the cuff of her thick wool sweater. 'Yes, it's still me,' she said, rubbing the rolled edge of the sleeve against his muzzle. He moved off then, following the fast-moving shadow that his accomplice had become. The pair trotted out in front of Jael, noses low to the ground.

Her fingertips brushed her long, fine, black hair back behind her ears as she raised her glance to the speck of light that shone in the distance. The granite-coloured clouds sped away from the waxing moon at that instant, and its pearl light reflected off Jael's milky forehead and chin. She walked behind the dogs, listening to them circle back closer to her, then lope still farther ahead. She pulled each sleeve back from her slight wrists and briskly rubbed her cheeks into an apple redness.

It was colder than it looked, she thought. She lifted her face to gaze at the luminous moon, the glistening stars around it. The night had a New England, mid-autumn clarity. Jael darted the tip of her tongue out to moisten her full lips, then slowly pulled both lips into her mouth and bit them gently. Brushing her hair back again, she bent her head and quickened her gait.

Jael's destination was the set of doors underneath the light in the distance. She walked on without thought and heard only her own steps crack and rustle in the tall grass, felt only the bracing vigour of the wind's gusts. The air's chilling vitality stimulated Jael. She felt strong, hale, restored by its sharpness.

The field inclined gradually to support the house that perched at the point of greatest height. Jael leaned into her steps and walked up the hill effortlessly. She emerged from the moon's glow into the incandescent harbour of light that welcomed her home. The Setters came from around the house and waited as Jael pulled her keys from the pocket of her brown corduroys.

She held the red leather fob in one hand and found the heavy key that would let them in. Jael turned it in the lock, pulled the wide glass door open, and smiled as the dogs jostled her aside in their haste to enter.

She went in behind them, closing the door firmly after them all. She turned and went into the conservatory and bent down to pull off her boots, then placed them on the rush mat that lay against the wall. Her forest green sweater came next, and her hair fell down her back in a feathery cascade as she drew the sweater over her head. She hung the wool jumper on a hook. The sheer, long-sleeved silk undershirt she wore smelled of neroli and jasmine, and its ivory colour contrasted with her crimson cheeks and scarlet lips.

Jael went back into the hall and walked down the flagstone floor. Her grey wool socks made a minute scratching sound as she turned on the ball of her foot and went into the library.

She smiled to see the blaze that danced in the fireplace greet her cheerily. Vanilla-scented candles glowed in corners, illuminating the gold lettering on the dark leathers of the bound books. It was kind of Thomas, she thought, to consider her coming in from the cold, even after his friends had come over. She bent her head and surveyed the leaden crystal liquor carafes that stood on the mahogany table just inside the door. Another smile came to her lips to see that Thomas had placed a large cognac snifter on the silver tray, next to them. She poured herself a cognac, and sauntered to a flame-lit corner to turn the big-bottomed glass in the candle's rising heat.

As she warmed her drink she put her other hand on the back of her head, her fingers twining in her silken hair, and stretched. Her narrow back arched, her slender shoulders drew back, and her shapely breasts were tautly outlined under her shift. Jael ran her fingertips over one nipple, then the other, circling them absentmindedly as she watched the candle's flame play through the burnt amber colour of the cognac.

Jael crossed to the fireplace and smoothly lowered herself into the leather wingback chair that squatted there. She threw one calf over the chair's arm and traced the wale of her brown corduroys as she breathed the cognac's scent deeply and stared into the fire.

The two dogs joined her. One leaned against the chair, and Jael glanced down and smiled to see him gazing up at her as her skin warmed before the flames. The other stretched out on the richly patterned carpet at her feet. Jael put the sole of her foot onto the dog's exposed side

7

and wriggled her toes against his ribs.

The trio sat there as Jael grew accustomed to the silence
that filled in the spaces around the pops of burning wood.
As the night wind left her ears, she heard other sounds,
somewhere in the house.

Men's laughter. Clinking glasses. Men's voices raised
in joshing argument and more laughter. Then quiet.

'The poker game is on,' she said to the dog sitting
next to her. 'Is that where you two visited before you
came in here?'

The dog blinked beseechingly at her. Jael passed her
cognac to the other hand and petted the smooth auburn
fur of his big-boned head. An impulse filled her reclined
body. 'Let's go see them,' she whispered.

She swung her leg off the arm of the chair and slid her
other foot from the reclining dog's side. She stood up,
sinking almost imperceptibly into the Oriental carpet.
The dogs rose to their feet to follow, then halted behind
her as she stopped before a candle for a moment to heat
her glass again.

Jael walked back down the flagstone hall, past the
century-old, framed theatre bills, and turned to go through
the house. She walked through the main hall, lit as if by
torches with evenly spaced lamps that threw their dimmed
lights onto the high, sapphire blue walls. The kitchen
opened before her.

Smoke floated from several lit cigarettes and hung in
the doorway. Jael walked through it, into the stunningly
bright light of the room.

'Hiya,' she said softly as Thomas looked up from his
cards. He gave her a tiny wink. Jael watched as her
husband's azure eyes trailed down her body, lingering
for a moment on the dark nipples that showed under her
gauzy shirt. His lips parted and he moved his jaw just a

8

small degree, first to one side, then the other. Without meeting her gaze again, his eyes dropped to the five cards in his hand.

She felt desire build in the sweet knob nestled between her vulva every time he looked at her like that. This time was no different. Jael side-stepped until her back was against the wall of the kitchen, just inside the door. She put her cognac on the counter and placed her hands behind herself. That tilted her pelvis out, and she crossed her thighs. Jael looked at Thomas, wishing that the intent glare he had fixed on his cards was still on her. She lowered her chin and watched him. Placing the tip of her tongue between her lips she flexed the inside muscles of her legs, rubbed her thighs together, and clenched and released her vagina rapidly and potently, over and over. Her nipples tightened in concert with her efforts, and Jael took a deep breath, filling her chest. The excitement of standing before six other men and her husband, bent on enticing him away from the game, filled her mind.

She exhaled slowly. Something to the left caught her eye. Another man's stare adhered to her body.

Jael's jaw dropped, her lips parted. The words 'Who is that?' flooded her mind. Her breathing quickened, and she felt the wetness that had started between her legs turn to a gush.

The man's wolf-grey stare was resting on her hips. She felt like his eyes were pinning her in place. And she knew that he fully realised what she was doing with the tight ring of muscle that opened into her secrets.

Jael's nipples had been taut, but now they were stiff peaks. The betting on the hand of cards passed around the table and finally came to this man. Without taking his concentration from her body, he tossed some chips into the centre of the table and muttered something. Her

9

hearing was dampened by the rush of blood in her ears, and Jael couldn't hear what he said. She only heard the rumble of his voice, the words coming out as if rock-tumbled through black treacle.

Thomas sat next to this man. They were the only two angled to watch Jael stealthily. The sudden tilt of Thomas's head drew her attention, and she glanced at him.

Jael froze. She knew by the forbidding tenseness that crossed his face that Thomas saw her pouting lips and flared nostrils, and the intense sensations built by this other man, surge out of her eyes. She watched Thomas look at the other man, and Jael knew that her husband saw the same thing that she recognised: a greedy hunger for the charms that she displayed.

Thomas's eyes flicked back to Jael's. She felt shame at her own transparent arousal fill her throat. No words came to her mind, only the dead certainty that she would feel his icy anger for days over this. There was no way to explain that at first she'd had her lecherous look and pose directed at him, but this interloper had caught her silent seduction. She knew Thomas had seen only her smouldering eyes focussed on the other man's face, and the other man fixated on her lustiness.

She would never know him. The thought deluged Jael's mind and filled her with despair. She felt sure that Thomas would never invite him over again. He'd be a closed subject, all of this something that never happened. She would never be able to ask his name because Thomas would know that she wanted him. She would never see him again. She dropped her gaze from Thomas's and tried to collect herself, to gain control over the unaccountable sorrow that filled her over the loss of this stranger.

10

Jael risked another glance up at Thomas, hoping he would ignore her long enough to let her skulk from the room.

What she saw shocked her.

Thomas leered at her. His face wore half a sardonic smile. His Arctic blue eyes were narrowed knowingly. He squinted at her, dropped his gaze from her face to her hips and still-crossed legs, and nodded his head just a fraction of an inch, his chin pushed out. Jael understood what he wanted her to do, and a carnal pleasure filled her mound with blood and excitement.

She began thrusting her hips, just a fraction of an inch at a time to match Thomas's slight nod. Her husband wanted her to make the other man want her. Jael half closed her eyes, still gazing at Thomas. A smirk played at the corners of her lips. If Thomas knew that this other man wanted her, it would make him want her more. She began fluttering her hidden muscles again. Words melted into sensations.

Jael rested her head back on the wall. She felt the almost painful need for a man as it flowed from her clenching tightness forward to her swollen clitoris and around the engorged skin of her labia.

The sound of the men's deep voices at the table made Jael drop her head and look at them. Thomas was speaking to someone across from him, but his gaze darted back to Jael again and again, as if trying to capture her attention. When Jael centred on him and the message he was conveying, Thomas gave her another shock. And she couldn't explain this one away.

Thomas held her gaze in his own for a long second, then slowly turned it towards the other man. Then he glanced back at Jael and nodded.

Jael understood, but Thomas's meaning unsettled her.

11

She looked hard at her husband. She could pursue that man, not just tease him, she thought. Thomas wanted her to do it. But why? Jael turned her husband's possessive character over in her mind. He was a jealous man, she thought, furrowing her brow at him. Why did he pick tonight to turn her loose?

Then she glanced at the other man. From the look on his face, she could tell that he had glimpsed at least part of this transaction of glances between herself and Thomas – and he, too, understood what it all meant.

Jael looked back at Thomas. His attitude was still permissive, to the point that he turned his attention back to the card game. Although she was baffled, Jael knew now that she could take in this other man's face, body and character with no guilt.

What she saw set her ablaze with flames hotter and wilder by far than those in the tame fireplace she had left a few short minutes ago – before she had ever laid eyes on him. He was, in fact, one of the most handsome men that Jael had ever seen. The lips she could imagine on her tight nipples were almost feminine, their contours so perfect, his mouth so wide. She wondered if his tongue were as agile as his lips were kissable. A shiver ran up her spine as she imagined the feeling of his beard between her thighs as he licked and suckled her steaming urgency.

His chin jutted forward, strong. Jael spied his Adam's apple just under the hairline of the beard. She yearned to open her lips and teeth over the skin of his throat and pull it into her mouth, to leave marks of how she felt about the way he bewitched her.

His skin, everywhere that she could see, was tanned to an even brown. She decided that his sexy darkness was no doubt the result of a yacht, and she smiled faintly. He looked like a man who spent a lot of time on the ocean.

He was lean, athletically thin, and the movements of his body under the thick cotton of his polo shirt were the smooth, controlled ones of muscles accustomed to use.

Her eyes travelled from the obviously expensive shirt to his forearms. They were tough looking, not as she would have expected from the leanness of his frame. They were sinewy, with thick wrists, and ended in solid hands and broad fingers that looked capable of handling anything. Jael knew that if she had him between her legs, the heat from those hands would sear her, and their power would grip and inscribe her with the passion he felt as he exploded inside her.

She rocked her hips back and forth, thrusting as she fancied the effectiveness of his palms on her skin, his fingers slipping through her wetness, mixing it with his saliva, spreading it all over her pussy.

As Jael's eyes grazed over him, she knew he was watching her. She knew he looked at his cards only long enough to factor his chances, and then, he watched her as she craved him.

She didn't care. Deftly, she hooked the back belt loop of her trousers and pulled it up hard. The seam of the khakis gave her something to rub against. Crotch to crotch, she thought, tightening her bottom and moving against the material. Her eyes were half closed, and she looked at the other man.

She felt his predatory eyes fasten her to the wall again, and she loved that she was performing for him. Jael dropped her head to stare at him directly, willing him to know that she wanted to share the breath from his open, panting mouth, wanted to run her fingers through his short, thick, dark brown hair, needed to trace her lower lip across his wide cheekbones, had to run her thumbs over those dark eyebrows as she kissed his eyelids and then sat back to make his shaft fill her. She concentrated on her soaked depths again, encouraging the building pulse there, knowing that her body was meant to swallow and stroke his impossibly stiff cock, to take every inch he had to give.

As if he heard her thoughts whispered, the man stood. In one easy motion he reached back to swing the chair away, raised himself, and turned to face her. Jael glanced at Thomas, who was gazing up at the other man.

'I need some matches,' she heard the other man say calmly.

'Here's a light,' someone offered.

'No, I'll get my own,' he said.

And he walked towards Jael.

His strides were long and even and firm. His hips were narrow, his thighs and waist not one whit wider. Jael locked her eyes onto his packet as he walked across the room's expanse to her. She licked her lips to see how closely his jeans held his firmness. She chanced a look up into his eyes.

He appeared to be amused.

As he walked out of the room, he swerved ever so slightly towards her. He lifted his hand, and his knuckles brushed against one of Jael's hips that she knew had held his sober fascination for so long. He continued decisively on his way, leaving Jael to shudder in his wake. Her head throbbed with an appetite grown to a fervour with that touch. She looked at Thomas and found he was looking back, his expression one of absolute composure.

Should she follow him? she wondered, and raised her eyebrows in question. Thomas raised his chin in half a nod. Jael spun on one foot to go after her quarry.

Just as she stepped into the hall the man came walking towards her again. Jael lifted her hand to touch his chest.

But he didn't look at her; instead, he turned his muscular torso and paced past her, his chest barely sweeping against her outstretched fingertips.

He was wearing his coat, and once inside the kitchen doorway, he announced, 'Hey, sorry to be a spoilsport, but I have to get going.'

Groans of protest greeted him. Jael stood in the hall and bit her lower lip, hard, at the sound of his deep, pebble-filled voice.

'See you later.'

He turned back, then, and paced past Jael. She looked at him, begging him to turn another glance in her direction, to let his hand stray near her body one more time.

He whisked past her and walked up the hallway, his perfectly proportioned legs developing into his lean, manly bottom.

The rear view perspective did nothing to extinguish the furnace that was stoked in Jael's belly. Without a thought of looking back to Thomas, she too was pacing up the hall.

She broke into a jog and rounded the corner. As she did, the glass door closed.

Was she to follow him outside? Did he want her to? Did he want her? Her questions were a torrent. Her instinct to chase him provided the answer. Jael flung the door open and found herself outside in the frosty air.

But he was gone. He had transformed into night. Not even a shadow of him remained. Another well of extraordinary anguish bubbled up inside her at the idea of losing him.

Jael folded her arms across her chest and took a few tentative steps towards the walk that led around the house. He had to be in the drive, she thought. But she hadn't heard his receding footsteps when she darted outside, and she heard no engine start now. Where was he?

She looked down towards the field she had passed through on the way home. As she surveyed it under the radiant moon, she felt a change take place in herself. 'I'll never be the same again,' she whispered, and knew that even though she didn't understand why, the thought was a conviction. Seeing that man had brought her to a new page and chapter in her life. Marrying Thomas, an established, accomplished older man while she was finishing university last year had changed her life – made it more stable, more secure. But this man, this man who had disappeared into the night... he disrupted things.

Underneath her palms, Jael felt her ice-hard nipples protruding. She began rubbing her breasts, kneading them in her palms. She stood under the dark yellow light from above the doorway and pushed her fingers into her nipples, squeezing them up against her thumbs. Her fingers ground away at herself, and she felt her excitement, forgotten for a moment in pursuing that man, rise again.

She slid one hand down her stomach, pushed her fingers into the thick material of her corduroys and pressed against her clitoris. Standing under the light with her legs still tightly together against the cold, Jael squeezed one breast and rotated her hips in a circle as she manipulated the soft folds of skin that encased her throbbing jewel.

'This is for you,' she said as loudly as her soft-spoken voice would allow. 'All for you.'

But her trousers were interfering with the sensations that she had to have. Jael longed to dip her fingers into her saltiness, to taste herself, to lie on her back and climb towards an orgasm as she thought about him. Turning, she pushed the door open and went back into the warmth.

She ran down the hall past the library and office, up the stairs and threw herself onto the bed. Lifting her hips, Jael wrestled her corduroys and kicked them and her plum-coloured silk panties off. In her grey wool socks and thin undershirt, she rolled onto her belly and opened the drawer under her nightstand. Her butt was elevated in the cool air, and she pumped her hips against the mattress before she rolled onto her back to bring her treasure with her.

It was a simple vibrator that fit her exactly and always helped her to find her sweet spot. Spreading her legs, Jael spun the vibrator's dial with her thumb and set it on maximum motion.

She closed her eyes and tilted her head back as she traced the dildo's head down through her split. It slid along easily on the slickness that had run all over her by now. Jael moaned softly and teased her clit with the ridge under the phallus's circumcised head. The busy vibration shook the hard toy against her own little hard-on.

With one slide, Jael ran the dildo's length between her labia and then pushed it up into herself. She arched her back as it sank deep, taking its humming sound and attendant pleasures into her body. She pulled its broad base up against herself and pushed her clit down hard against its vibrating bottom.

Her fingertips holding it by the base, Jael pumped the dildo in and out. 'Oh,' she grunted, then began swivelling it. It was grinding inside her.

'Fuck me,' she groaned. She rolled onto her stomach, still holding the dildo far up inside. She pushed up onto her knees, her chest on the mattress, and held the dildo in place with her trained vaginal muscles. Oh, what would he be like pounding against her bottom? She could feel

17

the skin of his legs, thin over his lean muscles, hot against the backs of her thighs. Jael imagined him holding her tightly by her hips, his cock thick, thicker than this dildo, spreading her open and taking her.

She was a maelstrom. She bent her head and braced herself against a pillow, then reached down with both hands and began frantically pulling and rubbing at herself. She put her fingers around the dildo's width, then slipped the tip of an index finger in beside it. 'Mmm,' she groaned, 'you're so big.'

Jael grabbed her pubic hair in one hand. She pulled it up, bringing her clit's hood with it, then put two fingers around her button. She rubbed, pressed, circled the centre of her frenzy. Her vagina clutched the vibrating dildo, and its rumbling filled her just as that man's voice had.

'Oh God, yes,' she hissed, her teeth clenched together. Quickly, she rolled onto her back. Jael grabbed the dildo and began driving it in and out of her grateful body, still pulling her pubic hair to expose her clit. The vibrator's course ran along her wet avenue, and Jael pumped her hips to keep up the pace.

The crisis was building. Her eyes were screwed shut, and her lips snarled to express the agony so acute before the release. Jael sucked in her breath and held the vibrating dildo up against herself, shoving her mound up and down in rabbit-quick strokes.

'Yes!' she called, welcoming the orgasm. It burst through her clitoris, through her pelvis, and rocked back into her vagina. The muscles spasmed and released in strong even attempts to suck the shot out of the plastic dildo pleasuring her.

Jael tossed her head back and forth on the pillow and groaned her satisfaction. Her fingers released their now-unconscious grip on her pubic hair, and she gently pushed the dildo in and out. She held it there for a few moments, relishing its willing, never-ending vibrations.

Smiling drowsily, Jael pulled her ready-hard lover out and held it up to see it in the moonlight streaming through the window. Her juices had baptised this serviceable toy yet again. She dashed her tongue out and licked its head, tasting the wet that came from the deepest parts of her. It tasted briny, like the Atlantic Ocean that washed onto the shores just a few miles east, where her fantasy fuck from downstairs spent his time.

Jael felt as if her climax had come in full-tide, after the night spent exhibiting her desires before a man who wasn't her husband. She held the dildo into the light again.

And to think. She didn't even know his name.

Chapter Two

'Good morning!' Jael said brightly as Thomas walked into the kitchen. The clear sunshine poured into the room from the skylight. The stained glass panels at the tops of the windows splashed their hues onto the tiled walls and stainless steel appliances. Jael stood in a puddle of the coloured light, looking down at the way her hands were tinted a rosy shade, as she chopped up fresh fruit for their breakfast.

Thomas walked behind her and put his hands on her shoulders. She felt his fingers grasp her through the thick terrycloth of her robe. 'Good morning, beautiful,' he said.

Jael tilted her face up to him and smiled. Thomas kissed her lips and moved off to the cafétiere of coffee that stood next to the stove.

He poured himself a cup and turned around to sip it, leaning back on the edge of the counter. 'You looked a sight when I walked in last night,' he said, his twinkling blue eyes smiling at her over the rim of his cream-coloured mug. She knew he was holding his cup there so she couldn't see his full expression.

'Fast asleep in your shirt and socks, no bottoms anywhere in sight, and your vibrator beside you.'

Jael blushed, her skin heating up all over her body. She bent her head to the task of slicing a kiwi, and said nothing.

The silence between them was electric. Jael could tell that he didn't mean to let up on her until she made some kind of answer.

'I don't even remember your coming to bed,' she murmured. 'It must have been late.'

'Not too long after Cole Trevor left,' Thomas said. He took another sip of coffee.

Jael started and looked over at him, and knew that her eyes were wide in spite of herself. But Thomas was looking into the contents of his mug, and outwardly paying her no attention at all.

Was that his name? She mulled over the syllables silently. Cole Trevor. Cole. Her eyes flitted back to her work.

'Is that the guy who left right before I went to bed?' she asked. To hide her fluster, Jael put a spoonful of cottage cheese into each bowl and placed them on the mats on the round oak table, turning her back to Thomas.

'Yeah, that's Cole,' Thomas said. 'He lives in Framingham.'

'Oh,' Jael said, desperately trying to find a way to lengthen this discussion. She sat down as she thought. 'He's not from Marlborough. That might explain why I've never seen him before.'

'I guess you'd remember him if you had.' Thomas's voice still lilted as if he were kidding her over her lewdness in the kitchen last night.

'Yeah, I knew everybody but him,' Jael volunteered. Now she wished Thomas would stop this talk as it neared the borders of interrogation.

'No idea why he quit when he did,' Thomas said, pressing on. He finally walked over to the table and sat down. Jael jumped up like she'd forgotten something. Foundering, she spied the pepper mill on the island where she'd prepared the food, and moved to pick it up.

'Seemed that he was on a winning streak.' Jael nearly flinched as Thomas's words winged into her back.

Dammit, she knew he was going to be upset. She adjusted her features to calmness as she turned back towards him. She glanced at Thomas as she put the pepper on the table and sat down again. He was watching her from the corner of his pale eyes. 'I wasn't paying attention to who won what. Did you win much?' she asked.

'I didn't think you were. And no, I didn't have much luck. Not even when I came to bed.'

Jael smiled shyly at him, then looked down at her fruit salad. 'Sorry about that. I took care of everything myself. Didn't know when you were going to make it upstairs.'

'It's all right.' Thomas's tone was back to the affectionate one she was accustomed to.

'You should have woken me.'

'I didn't want to disturb your dreams, dearest. I figured that if you'd fallen asleep without hiding the evidence of what you were up to, it was all a very pleasant interlude for you.'

Jael put her elbow on the table and placed her chin in her hand. 'Maybe I wouldn't have had to be completely awake. Maybe you could have had your way with me while I drifted in and out. It's exciting that way, in the middle of the night, all that hardness and movement.'

Thomas reached under the table, and Jael knew his hand was in his navy-blue robe, stroking at his half hard cock. 'I like doing you like that,' he said, leaning back in the heavy oak chair. He put one elbow on its thick arm and leaned a little to the side, and Jael saw what he was doing. 'I like getting you to roll onto your side and pumping away at you from behind.'

'And to think that I was still soaked from my own little games.' She stabbed a piece of strawberry with her fork and held it to her lips, then sucked it into her mouth.

'I have an early morning today. Got to get to the office,' he answered after a long scrutiny of Jael's lips.

'There's always here and now. This table has seen lots of action,' Jael said. She reached down to the knotted band around her waist and began loosening it.

Thomas pulled his hand out of his robe. 'I'd love to, honey, but let's keep it. It'll make me groggy, and I have to deal with a tough tax case, first thing.'

Jael's robe slipped open, and she pulled its top away from her breasts. Her ripe nipples were there for him. She brushed her fingertips across one of her breasts, then trailed her fingers down between them. 'You sure?'

'It'll be better if we wait until tonight,' Thomas answered, fixing the knot on his own robe to ensure that it stayed closed. 'We'll have all day to think about it.'

Jael reached for the tie of her robe and drew her cover closed again. She felt vaguely humiliated by her inability to seduce Thomas, even after a conversation that continually alluded to her behaviour last night.

'All right,' she said. 'Whatever.'

Thomas picked up the pepper mill and ground some onto the cottage cheese on his plate. His gusto over the salad restricted any more talk. Jael ate half-heartedly, and when Thomas stood to leave, she picked up his plate and hers and pushed her own food down the disposal. 'All those starving children in Africa,' Thomas said on his way out of the kitchen. Jael watched him walk up the hall. And that was it, she thought, going to the table to gather the utensils. She rinsed them under the faucet and bent to put the silver spoons and china into the dishwasher. They'd been together an entire year, and he'd lost interest. They were an old married couple now. Pretty soon, this whole thing was going to be about companionship, and horniness would be a memory, she knew for a fact.

The top rack of the dishwasher caught her attention, and she pulled it out. It was filled with the beer and highball glasses from last night.

Jael reached for them. 'Did your lips touch one of these, Cole Trevor?' she whispered as her fingers slipped over their weighty bottoms.

The ashtrays were stacked between the wires at the washer's very back. Jael took the pair out and held them up. She knew he touched one of those. She could picture him pulling an ashtray towards himself, taking the cigarette from his perfect mouth and flicking its ash away, even though she hadn't seen him do it. He was paying too much attention to her to smoke, she thought, and the memory made her insides ache.

Thomas came around the corner at the end of the hall. 'Inspecting your household goods?' he asked, pacing towards her.

Jael shoved the ashtrays back into the dishwasher and closed it as he walked into the kitchen.

'I have to worry,' she said. 'A bunch of half-drunken louts, messing around with some of my best drinking glasses and the only two ashtrays I have.'

'They're careful,' Thomas said. 'Tie this for me.'

Jael reached up and skilfully knotted her husband's tie. He pulled his jacket over his shoulders and turned to walk out of the room again.

Jael smoothed her still-damp hair back behind her ears and watched his broad back retreat towards his study, where she knew he would pick up his briefcase, prepared last night after everyone had left, and leave, perhaps shouting a 'Goodbye' to her on his way out.

'See ya!' he yelled after a few seconds passed.

'I was wrong about that part,' she said aloud.

Walking up the hall to the conservatory to let the dogs out, Jael considered going upstairs and playing with the vibrator again.

The thought left her cold.

She was sick of getting herself off, she thought, as the dogs rattled by her and stood in anticipation at the wide glass door that opened onto the fields she and Thomas owned. She was tired of that plastic thing, tired of artificial stimulation, tired of the only orgasms she'd had lately coming from a dick that wasn't attached to a man.

Jael opened the door with a jerk and let the dogs race. She watched their chestnut bodies fly across the ground. 'I wish I were neutered like you guys,' she said, then laughed ruefully, shaking her head.

'You know what's wrong with you, girl?' she asked herself, making her way back to the staircase. She was feeling like she had lost her chance to be promiscuous, to explore. Thomas was a middle-aged man. He had sown his wild oats. But she had settled down with him when she was only twenty-one. Now she was twenty-two, and she felt as if she should have spent the last year having fun, not becoming domesticated.

She had the seven-year itch, she decided. Thomas was losing interest in sex, but feeling content with home life, and she was gaining interest in her snatch and feeling dissatisfied. With everything.

Jael walked to the wardrobe in their bedroom and opened its heavy doors. The smell of her home-made neroli and jasmine perfume wafted out and permeated her senses. She pulled out a pair of old jeans and a paint-splattered, V-neck T-shirt and tossed them onto the cast-iron bed. Walking to the dresser, she rummaged through her underwear.

She would try to think about him all day. She'd feel

25

sexy for him when he came home that night, she thought. She'd put on a pair of G-string panties, and then when he wanted her to, she'd feel hot for him. She pulled out the purple pair, the ones that captured the deep lavender that the sun shed across the sky when it set over the ocean. Jael bent and stepped into them and tugged them up around her waist. She looked at herself in the mirror over her dressing table, then turned around to catch a glimpse of her bottom over her shoulder. Both fair cheeks were exposed, and the purple strap up the back was nestling between her buttocks.

Jael liked how she looked and smiled at herself. She reached into the dresser drawer again and found a pair of thick white cotton socks. Then she went back to the clothes on the bed and pulled on everything. She sloppily tucked the T-shirt into her trousers as she skipped down the stairs.

A pair of steel-toed work boots that Jael grabbed in the conservatory completed her ensemble for the day. She reached up onto a shelf and pulled down a welding mask and a pair of work gloves, tucked them into the mask and the mask under her arm, and walked out the door to go to the rambling barn where she created.

At six o'clock, Jael walked back into the house and put her things away in the conservatory. The smell of baking fish floated in the air, and she patted her stomach as she recognised how hungry she was. She walked to the kitchen and found Thomas already tucked into his meal.

'Hey!' Jael said. She walked to the sink and washed her hands under tepid water. 'What you got there?'

'Lisa's almond and broccoli thing, some kind of fish…'

'"Some kind of fish,"' Jael said mockingly. 'All these years living in Massachusetts, and you still don't know what kind of seafood you're eating.'

'If it's not shrimp or lobster or crab, it's an unidentified swimming object.'

Jael laughed. 'So how did Boston treat you today?' She finished drying her hands and sat down at the table.

Thomas heaped a serving of the vegetable dish onto her plate and shrugged one shoulder. 'All right, I suppose. Landed another client.'

'Excellent!' Jael said.

'Everybody's happy,' Thomas answered. 'So did Lisa take off already?'

Jael frowned as she manipulated the serving fork to put a piece of fish onto her plate. Quickly, she pulled her face smooth with an effort, hoping that Thomas didn't notice her frown. 'I guess,' she answered. 'I was working all day, so I didn't even see her get here.'

Jael glanced at him as she took a bite of the paprika-seasoned fish. She chewed purposefully, then decided to get into the subject that had been niggling at her for two weeks. 'Why do you keep asking about her, wanting to know where she is all the time?'

'No particular reason. It just seems odd to me that she comes here every afternoon, but the two of you never cross paths. Don't you have any special instructions you want to give her?'

'No, I'm happy with the work she does and the dinner she fixes. You always seem to want to check on her whereabouts when you get home, though.'

'Ah, yeah, I guess I have been asking after her, haven't I?' Thomas bounced the tines of his fork on his plate, and the sound made Jael cringe a bit. 'It's just that Robert's wife noticed things going missing from their house, and their housekeeper is from the same agency.'

'Oh,' Jael said, relieved. 'Nothing's gone missing here.'

'How would you know?'

'I can see! Everything's exactly where it always is.'

'Yeah, but you're not a person who's really aware of her surroundings. Your mind tends to be a million miles away whenever you're around the house.'

'You're probably right about that,' Jael said, smiling.

'So what did you do today?'

'Not much. Had every intention of working on that big piece for the gardens that the city commissioned, but something about it strikes me as not right. So I sat down and sketched a bunch of ideas.'

'Why don't you try to sell some of your sketches and drawings?'

Jael wrinkled her nose. 'I don't like working in two dimensions.'

'I know, but you have a lot of really good stuff that just comes out of you. Why not see if you can get somebody to take them off your hands for a price?'

'Maybe someday,' she said.

'Well, I'm finished,' Thomas said, standing up and taking his plate to the sink. 'I have some papers to get ready for tomorrow.'

'Okay.'

As he was leaving the kitchen, Jael turned towards him. 'Hey, Thomas?'

'What, love?'

'Are you going to be using your computer?'

'No, not right away.'

'Mind if I surf the net? I think I'll look up some galleries in Boston and see if I can talk to somebody tomorrow about having a look at the sketches I did for this sculpture.'

Thomas grinned at her. 'That's a fantastic idea. Take all the time you need.'

Jael cleaned up the table and followed Thomas's steps through the library and into his study. He sat at his huge mahogany desk, papers spread all over its glass top. Jael went to the small computer desk and sat down in the high-backed chair.

As she waited for the computer to boot up, Cole Trevor's face came to mind, just as it had all day. She peeked at Thomas from around the chair's black leather back. He was absorbed in his reading. She clicked on some icons, and when she was on the search screen for the white pages of the telephone directory, she quickly typed in Cole's name and hit the enter key.

There was only one in Framingham. He had an e-mail address, as well. Jael smiled and reached for her leather-bound address directory in the drawer. She began writing on the first page that fell open. Glancing at the letter, she saw an S.

Appropriate, she thought. Sexy, seductive, salacious, sensual, stimulating…

Her mind was running on adjectives for Cole Trevor when she heard Thomas clear his throat, right above her.

Jael grabbed the mouse and struggled to make the arrow land on the minus sign up in the corner of the screen. Desperately, she clicked on it and made the screen disappear.

'What are you doing, sitting there with one hand rubbing yourself?' he asked. He began to pull his fingers through her hair and massage her scalp tenderly.

Jael glanced down at where her fingers were. 'I didn't realise I was.'

'Want to find something more interesting to look at while you do that?'

She turned and looked up at him, her libido spiralling suddenly. 'Let's,' she whispered.

29

Thomas turned to his desk and walked back around it. Jael took the opportunity his retrieving a chair gave her to leave the site she'd been at for Cole Trevor's information. Thomas wheeled his chair next to her and sat down, leaning back, his long jean-clad legs stretched in front of him.

'Go up to "Favourites" and take your pick,' he said softly.

Jael did as she was told and chose one of the adult-orientated sites listed there. She typed in the ID numbers from the tab of yellow paper stuck on the monitor, and they began browsing.

'Download whatever you like,' Thomas said.

Jael clicked on thumbnail pictures, and without looking at them more closely, gave the computer instructions to get them. The hard drive buzzed and whirred, and she felt her yearning increase sharply with anticipation.

'That's enough,' Thomas said, his voice tight in his throat. 'Put up the picture viewer and let's have a look.'

Jael logged out and followed her husband's instructions. The first one to greet their eyes was a picture of a woman leaning back, turned slightly away. She was pulling her plump, hairy labia up to show her bare pinkness. A man's meaty cock was inside her, and kneeling on a platform at her face, another man had his long, thin, hard prick in her mouth.

'Put them in a slide show,' Thomas said gruffly, unbuttoning his jeans.

Jael clicked through the menu, and each picture appeared on the screen, stayed for a few seconds, then disappeared as another took its place.

The second one was a woman in ankle-high white socks and track shoes, lying on her stomach underneath a net hammock, facing away from the camera. Her fingers were in a V on her pussy, pulling the lips apart. She had a rock-hard penis in her mouth and a man's strong hands on the back of her head. From the hammock above, a huge sturdy cock descended and stuck in her anus.

'Look at him take her,' Thomas said. His voice was deep with craving. Jael looked over at him, her face hot and reflecting the burn between her legs.

Thomas stared at her. 'Take off your trousers,' he muttered. He unzipped his fly and pulled out his stiff rod.

Jael looked at his hard-on, licking her lips, wanting Thomas to grind away at her until she was full of the spunk that would extinguish her fires. She stood and quickly undid her jeans and kicked them away. She stepped on the toe of each sock and pulled them off, as well. Now, as she posed before her husband, she was very glad that she had chosen to wear G-string panties this morning.

The look on Thomas's face told her that he was gratified by her choice, too. 'Take off that shirt,' he growled. Before the shirt was completely off, she felt Thomas's broad palms pressing against her breasts, flattening them. He was standing before her, and as she dropped the T-shirt on the floor, he picked her up and sat back down on his chair. Jael put her legs over its arms and began thrusting her hips, rubbing herself against the firm length of Thomas's cock that was tight against her.

He bent his head forward and took one of her stiff nipples into his mouth. His teeth scraped her areola, his tongue played havoc with the hardened tip. Jael arched her back and laced her fingers together behind his neck.

Thomas ran his hands down her back and hooked his thumbs in the top of her panties. He pulled his mouth off her breast and kissed her chin. 'These were nice to look at,' he said, 'but I want them to disappear.'

He helped Jael to stand, and she slipped them down her thighs. When she righted herself, she pushed out her hips and made her neatly trimmed, black hair greet Thomas at eye-level.

'Sit down,' he ordered, gesturing towards her chair. Jael did so.

Thomas stood up and pushed the chair with her in it back against the side of his desk. Without another word, he knelt and buried his face between her legs.

Jael slung her legs over his shoulders and melted into the strokes of his tongue searching in her still-empty hole. Thomas pushed two fingers into her, and she began tightening the muscles in her buttocks to swivel her hips around. She danced on those thick fingers, and Thomas darted his tongue like a snake's against her nub.

Jael put her hands on his head, longing to press Thomas's face closer. 'Hm mm,' he murmured from deep in his chest. So she stretched back and put her hands on the top of the chair. Then she pumped her hips in his face.

Thomas put his arm across her stomach, controlling her movements as he rode her with his mouth. He reached down and opened up her lips with his fingertips, his tongue tracing and exploring every nook. Jael tilted her head back and shut her eyes.

He raised his face and looked up at her. When he stopped like that, Jael looked down sharply. His lips were covered with her sugar, but he said sternly, 'Look at the pictures.'

Jael fastened her eyes on the screen as it rotated the horde of pornographic riches before her. There was a woman eating another woman as yet another woman fisted the first. Jael drove down on Thomas's probing fingers. His tongue was delicately stroking at her clitoris, pushing her on towards oblivion.

A kneeling, naked woman with a pert body like Jael's looked imploringly up at the camera, a massive shaft lodged between the candy-red lips of her mouth. 'I want to suck your balls,' Jael groaned to Thomas.

His answer was to bend his knuckles and twirl his fingers inside her. With his other hand, he reached up and began pinching her nipples.

Jael moaned at each dull pain. Her thighs tightened around Thomas's head, and she felt her womb quiver as it toiled at the inevitable climax. His tongue worked at her clitoris, and it burnt under the friction of his technique.

She gripped the back of the chair and raised her hips as the orgasm built. Thomas drove on relentlessly with his fingers inside her, caressing her cushioned walls.

Jael began the low keening she used to tell Thomas how close she was. He sucked the swollen bump in between his lips like a grape and fluttered his tongue against it. Jael grimaced. Her back arched. Thomas's big hand held her ribs as her arms tightened and pulled her upwards. She held herself suspended half-off her seat as the raging wave crashed over her. Jael rocked, her inner muscles grasping at Thomas's fingers.

And just at the height of her prolonged coming, Thomas bared his teeth and sunk them into the entire structure of skin around her clitoris. The extra pressure, so perfectly timed, so deliciously painful, made Jael scream. She shook, the muscles in her arms ached, and she came and came. She squirmed on Thomas's thrusting fingers. He pulled his mouth off her, but quickly replaced it with the heel of his hand. Jael ground against it, welcoming the steady pressure, and gasped a 'Yes!' as another orgasm

33

smashed into her.

When the tidal wave rolled away, Jael collapsed. Her arms were limp and useless, and she lay back stunned in the chair.

'Still haven't had anything proper inside you,' Thomas said, standing up. He grabbed the other chair and wheeled it in front of the computer, turning it to face him. He pulled Jael off her seat by her wrists and gently pushed her shoulders to make her bend over.

Thomas's actions renewed Jael's eagerness. She turned her head and laid a cheek on the chair so she could see Thomas when he pumped away at her from behind.

He opened his jeans and pulled them down just enough to unfetter his cock. He stared at the computer screen, and the glow from its pictures illuminated his face with a ghostly white in the now-dark room. Thomas centred himself behind Jael.

She pushed her bottom out willingly, exposing the place where he would plunge. Thomas sunk his fingers into the flesh of her hips and bent his knees. The rough denim against the backs of her legs excited Jael, and she began thrusting back at him, begging him with her body to fill her up.

The wide head of his cock butted against her bottom. Then it slid down the scorching, dripping front of her body. Jael squeezed her eyes shut and began rubbing at him greedily, tightening her thighs to hold him in place. Thomas drove his penis back and forth in short strokes. Jael knew it was wet from her efforts when he pulled back and rammed into her.

The force of his entry slammed the chair against the desk. Jael grunted, 'Uh,' then synchronised the movements of her bottom with the shoves of his hips.

'Oh, Jesus,' Thomas groaned. 'Stop it.'

Jael froze in place. He pulled out of her, then grabbed her hips and dragged her away from the chair. He shoved her down onto the floor, and Jael caught herself. She pushed her buttocks into the air again. Thomas was on his knees behind her. He spread his legs around the outsides of her thighs and pinched them together.

Jael tightened her inner thigh muscles to give Thomas as much resistance as possible. He penetrated her again, his wet cock leaving a trail where he dragged it between her thighs.

Thomas put his hands on her shoulder blades, pressing her down into the floor. Jael pushed her bottom up even higher. He groaned and grunted and ground and swivelled his cock inside her. She heard him draw the air sharply between his teeth, and she smiled lasciviously. He was going to pump her full.

And Thomas cracked his palm against one of her buttocks. Jael quaked and jammed her bottom against him in quick, come-sucking strokes. He smacked her again, and Jael responded by grinding herself against his hips, holding him inside her with her tight ring of muscle.

'Make me come, you little bitch,' Thomas said through clenched teeth. He gave her another sharp slap, and Jael reached behind her. She sank her fingers into the tops of his thighs as she massaged his cock with her pussy muscles. She drove herself back on it repeatedly, barely pulling away before slamming back again.

He grunted in unison with her efforts. He leaned forward again, pressed his hands into her back, and came, moaning, cursing a string of foul words, his fingers sinking into her shoulders.

Thomas swung his leg over her close-pressed thighs and lay down on his back next to her. Jael relaxed onto her stomach and rested her cheek on one forearm, gazing at his profile. After a few minutes passed, she said, 'You never hit me or called me names before.'

His eyes were shut. At her words, he opened them, turned his head and looked at her. 'We haven't had a lot of contact lately. I thought it might be fun to start things off in a new direction. But I'll never do those things again if you didn't like it.'

Jael inched over and put her chin on his chest. 'I really liked it,' she whispered.

'Then we'll remember that.'

She smiled and placed her cheek on him. Her gaze travelled to the computer desk and rested on the images still parading across the screen.

Suddenly, the edge of something lying on the desk caught Jael's eye. She realised what it was.

The address book was open. Had he seen what she'd written?

Chapter Three

Jael raised her head from her work when she heard the dogs bark. A glance at the alarm clock that sat on her work surface – a piece of plywood perched on cinder blocks and covered with a huge mirror – told her it was only four o'clock.

She wondered what was going on and put down her fountain pen.

Jael stood up and walked across the dirt floor of the barn, around the immense piece she was in the long process of welding and forming. She slid back the heavy door and emerged into the bright orange sunlight of the autumn late afternoon.

Up on the driveway she saw Thomas's sports car. 'Now what is he doing home?' she said. The Setters raced towards her, panting with excitement to let her know the news.

Jael ran towards them, and they increased their speed to bear down on her more quickly. At the last possible moment each dog veered off to one side, then slid to a stop and turned and raced in front of her. Jael laughed, throwing her head back and feeling her ponytail drag against the thin cotton of her shirt over the small of her back.

'Let's see what he's up to,' she called to the dogs. All three ran towards the house.

Thomas was in the kitchen, leaning against the stove, drinking a beer.

'Hey, my honourable friend,' Jael said, smiling at him.

'What are you doing here?'

'Early poker game tonight.'

'Oh?' All she could see in her mind's eye was Cole Trevor sitting at the round oak table in her own kitchen. 'Where?'

'Fred's place.'

'Can I go?'

Thomas looked at her, then turned the beer bottle back and forth in his fingers and examined the label. 'You don't play poker,' he finally said, barely hiding a smirk.

'No, but Anna will no doubt be home.'

'I didn't know you and Anna were great friends.'

'I never get out, Thomas. Usually, you're the one prodding me to go with you.'

'I like prodding you,' he said, grinning at her. 'All right. You can come along. Maybe you and Anna will hit it off.'

'So what time are we leaving?'

'Six-ish.' Thomas walked around Jael to open the doors under the sink. He put the bottle into the coloured-glass recycling bin. 'Do me a favour, will you? Dress up.'

Jael narrowed her eyes at him slightly. 'For a poker game?'

'Just dress up.'

'How do you mean?'

He smiled at her. 'I mean, don't pull on a pair of jeans with holes burnt in them from soldering and some old faded sweater. Wear… I'll tell you what,' he said as a thoughtful looked crossed his face. 'I want you to wear something special. Put on that tight, long, straight burgundy skirt you have. The one that buttons down the front. You know what I mean?'

'Yeah.'

'And then on top, wear that dark blue shirt, the low

38

cut one with the pearl buttons. That one buttons down the front, too. And those really high heels you have. The ones with the straps and gold buckles, that kind of look like brogues, but with a... a sadistically feminine touch. And do you still have that pretty green lace garter-belt I bought you?'

Jael nodded.

'Good, wear that with tanned stockings. And wear the matching green bra and panties.'

Jael gave him a quizzical look. 'Any particular reason for this choice?'

'I like it.' Thomas pulled her to him and wrapped his arms tightly around her. 'And I want everybody there to know that when we come home afterwards, I just have to undo those buttons in order to have you. That outfit screams accessibility. But with a classic touch.'

'Okay.' Jael inclined her face towards him, and Thomas kissed her lips. 'Now, no more questions. Just go get ready.'

Jael turned and left the kitchen.

Two hours later she walked through the house, pulling on her ivory cashmere coat and looking for Thomas. He was nowhere to be found. The dogs were in the conservatory and all the lights were off, as if he had already gone.

She wondered if he'd left without her; it hadn't taken that long for her to get ready.

She paced through the kitchen and the dining room, through the TV room and the sunroom to the front door. She looked outside and managed to just glimpse Thomas sitting in the driver's seat of his car.

Jael opened the door and closed it firmly behind herself. She got into the car and said, 'Hey, what are you doing out here?'

'Waiting for you. I wanted to see what you looked like from a distance.'

'And? The verdict?'

'Stunning. One thing, though. Go back in there and pull your hair up. Pull it all up in a twist at the back of your head and pin it there.'

Jael unsnapped her small leather handbag. 'I wanted to ask you what to do with my hair, so I brought what I need with me.'

'Very good.' Thomas smiled at her and nodded. 'Let's go then.'

He coasted the car around the circular drive, but stopped before they went onto the road. Thomas looked at her and tilted his head sideways. 'I very much like the make up. It's glistening in little flecks across your nose. And the blush looks gorgeous on your cheeks, really brings out the cheekbones. The black eyeliner around your eyes works, too. You're the only woman I've ever seen who can wear black eyeliner well. You did a beautiful job. You look like chiselled porcelain, the way the sun's playing across your face.'

'Thank you.'

They drove in silence the rest of the way. Jael used the mirror under the sun visor on her side as she did her hair. When they pulled up in front of Frederick and Anna's house, her throat and neck were completely exposed.

'Dazzling,' Thomas said. He made a purring sound low in his throat before he spoke again. 'Follow me.'

Jael walked several paces behind Thomas. He flicked his index finger towards one luxury sedan and said, 'Cole Trevor's here.'

Jael stared at the car. 'I guess he's a regular now,' she

said in her low tones, their smoothness belying the jitters she felt at knowing Cole was so near.

Thomas didn't answer. He turned and walked up the sidewalk to the front of the sprawling brick house. Jael kept behind him, her high heels sounding hollow on the concrete. Thomas pulled open the door and held it for her. She walked in before him and stopped in the hallway.

'Go through,' Thomas said from behind her as the door thudded shut.

Just then Anna stuck her head around the corner. Her dark eyes glistened as she looked at Jael, then up at Thomas.

'Welcome!' she said. 'Come on in. The boys are back in the game room. You know where, Tom. Honey, you come with me and help get the drinks ready.'

Jael took Anna's outstretched hand and rounded the corner with her. She heard Thomas's footsteps recede down the greater hallway as she took off her coat.

'Sorry,' Anna said, taking the coat and folding it over the back of a chair, 'but I've never known quite how to say your name. Is it just like "gaol"?'

Jael smiled. 'Yes, that's it.'

'Wonderful! Conjures up images of imprisonment, dungeons... sweet torture.' Anna glanced knowingly at Jael, but Jael had no idea why.

'Anyway,' Anna continued. 'Let's get these things ready and take them back to the men.'

She sat down at the table.

'Go ahead, Jael, get the beers out of the refrigerator and put them on the tray. Frederick has glasses chilling in the freezer.'

Jael took the bottles and lined them up, then got the tall pint glasses and put them on the tray.

'Go ahead and carry that back. I expect they're going

41

to keep you busy tonight. Thirsty crowd. And they'll keep wanting to take looks at you, too.'

Jael ducked her head to hide her embarrassment and lifted the heavy tray effortlessly.

'You have some muscle for such a little thing,' Anna said.

'It's the sculpting. I climb around and work with metal all day.' Jael walked expertly on her high heels and carried the drinks in the direction that Thomas had gone.

With one glance, Jael spotted Cole Trevor the moment she walked into the room. He was staring at her, as if he had known she would appear in the doorway. The sight of his eyes devouring her made Jael's knees wobbly. She felt beads of perspiration break out between her breasts, and her hands started to shake, clinking the bottles together.

'What do you have there, Jael?' Frederick asked when he noticed her.

Jael smiled at him weakly. 'Hi, Fred. Looks like a bunch of Samuel Adams and some iced glasses.'

'Bring one of each over.'

Jael put the tray down on an unused card table and took Frederick's request to him.

The men's voices rumbled in their separate conversations as she worked her way around. Jael went in a cycle that would make Cole Trevor the last man she served. It gave her time to collect herself.

When it was his turn, she walked slowly to the tray. Turning her back to the men, she picked up his glass and surreptitiously pressed her bottom lip against its rim, leaving a print in the frost. She angled the glass in her hand so that the mark would face him, picked up the bottle of beer and turned around.

She saw Anna watching her from the doorway. Anna's

eyes brushed over the table, and Jael knew that she saw who was the only player without a drink. Anna put the tip of her tongue against her upper teeth and smiled lecherously at Jael.

Caught, Jael could only smile back. She narrowed her eyes in a suggestive way and shrugged slightly. Anna nodded a little and withdrew from her watch.

Jael carried the beer and glass to Cole. When she was standing next to him, he sat back in his chair and turned to face her.

'Jael Alistair?' he said in his molasses voice.

'Yes, good to meet you.'

'Mmm. Good to meet you, too. Is that for me?' His wolf's eyes slipped down to the glass with its lip print facing him, then back up to Jael's face.

'Yes.'

'Thank you.' He took the glass from her, his hand enveloping hers for a moment. Jael thought she would swoon as his callused palm pressed tenderly against her knuckles. She still held the bottle of beer. She brought it back closer to her hip, in hopes that his knuckles would press against her there.

Cole held his hand out for the bottle. Jael was forced to place it in his fingertips. He looked up at her and smiled a thin smile that told her he was aware of her purpose.

'Come here, Jael,' he said, raising his bearded chin and pulling her close to his face with an intent look. She bent at the waist and leaned towards him, using the table for support.

'Put your hands behind you,' Cole whispered towards her ear.

Jael pulled her fingertips along the felt surface of the card table, then reluctantly removed the hand that hung dangerously close to his thigh. She clasped one wrist with her other hand, resting them just above her behind.

'You're not close enough,' Cole said in a low, rumbling voice; almost a whisper.

She leaned closer.

He looked into her eyes. Then his gaze traced up to her forehead. Jael counted the moments as Cole took his time in measuring the angles of her face. She watched his pupils dilate as his eyes rested for a long time on her mouth. He spread his thumb and index finger over his own mouth and folded his other arm across his chest.

As his surveillance moved down to her chin, Jael felt a slow growth of needy tension start in her depths. She was intrigued by his examination of her, especially as his eyes trailed down her throat and glowed as if he needed to devour her. Her reaction began to build, creating its own energy that drove on at a dizzying speed. She felt exposed, dangerously so, but she needed this detached investigation of her body. She only wished that she weren't clothed right now.

Cole's eyes stopped at the V of her blouse that descended to her chest, and that she knew drooped open as she was bent over next to him. Jael knew she was showing Cole the emerald-green bra that cupped and squeezed her breasts. But his eyes raked back up to hers.

'Come here,' he whispered, pushing his strong chin out.

Jael put her ear next to his generous mouth.

'Do something for me,' he said, turning his head just a minute degree so that his lips brushed the hindmost ridge of her ear.

Jael's nipples stood solid and her panties grew more damp. 'Anything,' she whispered.

'Get me a whiskey.'

Cole leaned away from her abruptly and put his arm

nearest her up on the table, effectively pushing her away. Jael straightened her back, mortified at how cruelly he had removed his attention from her. A hot blush washed over her torso and tears swelled in her eyes.

She felt stupid. Did she think she was going to seduce him right now? She'd leaned so close to him, hoping he smelled the heat from her. Right there, in front of everybody. What had she been thinking?

In an attempt to cover her tracks and stop her thoughts, Jael inclined herself towards the man on her other side. 'Would you like anything else?' she asked.

'No, thanks. Well, maybe some pretzels,' he said.

'Right,' Jael answered. She walked behind him and leaned over the next man's shoulder.

'Anything else?' she asked.

Just as he opened his mouth to answer, Cole's voice reverberated through her.

'Jael, I meant now.'

She bent her head and turned around, only to catch Thomas's stare. Jael looked closely at him. Somehow, she wasn't surprised to see the pleased expression he wore.

She walked to the kitchen and found Anna standing there, holding out a filled highball glass for her. 'Cole always takes whiskey,' she said.

'Gee, you're a regular mind-reader,' Jael answered.

'Don't get snappy with me, just because you're hot for him.'

'Who said that?'

'Did he fluster you so much that you don't remember me standing there, watching you make love to his glass?' Anna leaned forward and said in a conspiratorial tone, 'He is drop-dead gorgeous, isn't he?'

Jael grinned at her, relieved at a moment of lightness

45

in all this, and said, 'Yeah, he is something.'

'Take him his whiskey,' Anna said. 'Maybe you'll get lucky and he'll talk to you later.'

Jael left the room, carrying the single drink. She walked back into the poker den, her back straight and her chin held high.

'Pardon me, sir,' she murmured to Cole. She moved his pack of cigarettes out of the way at his elbow and placed the drink on the coaster there.

'Thank you, darling,' he said. 'That was fast.'

She bent her head and turned to walk away.

'Jael, come here,' he said.

She turned back to him.

'Come here,' he said in a businesslike tone, motioning her to come closer. She leaned down once more. 'You're absolutely beautiful. The most perfect creature I've ever met. Tom Alistair is a lucky man.' Cole watched her, and as she felt the blush creep up from her cleavage, Jael could see in his eyes that he was enjoying the effect of his pronouncement. He lifted his hand and brushed a few stray hairs away from her ear. Then he leaned back and caught the cards that the dealer tossed his way.

'Thank you,' Jael said. She stood straight and walked away again, her confident footsteps resounding through the room.

'Come on, let's go sit down and have a drink of our own,' Anna said when she saw Jael. She had two big glasses full of red wine, one in each hand. Jael followed her to a room on the opposite side of the house from the men.

'What did he say to you?' Anna put the wine glasses on the coffee table as she asked her question. She curled up like a big cat on the overstuffed settee and patted the cushion for Jael to sit next to her.

Jael picked up a glass as she folded her frame and relaxed. 'What makes you think he said something?'

'Because you were there a bit longer than you should have been, if you just gave him his whiskey and walked away.'

'He didn't say much.'

'I think he said a lot. Look at you! You're beet red at the thought of it.'

Jael lifted her glass to her lips and took a long draught. She could feel Anna watching her and knew that Anna was waiting for an answer, but Jael didn't make any. Anna finally spoke again.

'I have no doubt that Cole wants you, you know. If I know Cole Trevor, I know that he'd just love to give it to you on the sly.'

Jael raised her eyebrows. 'And how well do you know Cole Trevor?'

Anna laughed. 'He's been friends with Fred for a while. And he's pretty open about his conquests.'

'If he kisses and tells, then I'd better not let him anywhere near me.'

'He never just kisses, sweetie.' Anna picked up her glass and took a swallow. 'Why not take him on, even if he does brag a bit?'

The thought crossed Jael's mind that she shouldn't be having this conversation and couldn't believe she was having this conversation. But she felt reckless. 'Thomas,' she answered.

'Thomas? Oh, I get it,' Anna said, nodding. 'You think he'd get jealous.'

'Not get jealous. He is jealous.'

'Have you ever thought of messing around?'

'Not really, no. It's just that Cole Trevor is unusually attractive.'

47

'I think "foxy" is the term for him. It fits him in lots of ways. But nobody else, you've never thought about having fun with anybody else?'

Jael pursed her lips, then quaffed her wine again in thought. 'No, not really. I see good-looking men every now and again, but I usually don't give it another thought.'

'That's because you're so luscious, you don't have to chase after them. They come to you.' Anna looked hard at Jael. 'In fact, I'll bet you scare half of the ones that would like to try their luck. But you don't scare me.'

Jael returned Anna's searching expression. What Anna had just said could hardly slip by unnoticed. Jael lowered her voice and traced the rim of her wine glass with the tip of her index finger.

'What do you mean?'

'Oh, I just mean that I'm not intimidated by a beautiful woman. Some women are, you know, those of us who are average looking.'

Jael glanced over at Anna, then dropped her gaze to the gently rocking, dark surface of her wine again. 'You're not "average looking". You're very pretty, Anna.'

Anna laughed, a short pulse of a chuckle. 'It's okay, Jael, really, I'm not digging for compliments. Just telling it like it is. Women who are jealous of beautiful women wish they could look like you all. I don't think like that, though. In fact, I like looking at you. Maybe as much as Cole does.'

Jael felt confused, unsure of her footing. There seemed to be a game going on here, but one whose rules were a little unfamiliar.

'Well, thanks, Anna. I'm not sure what to say, but thanks for the compliment. I'm not digging for them, either.'

Anna smiled and took a drink of wine, looking down into her glass. Jael watched her as she swished her mouthful around before she swallowed it, and then found herself looking into Anna's smouldering eyes again.

'So tell me, how does it feel to be a sex symbol?' Anna asked.

Jael fidgeted a little, certainly uncomfortable now. 'Anna, I don't know what you're on about. Why are you saying these things to me?'

'Just trying to make conversation. You and I don't have much in common, except that we're both a little overheated right now.'

'Overheated?'

'You want Cole Trevor, and I want... Well, never mind what I want.' Anna took another long drink of wine.

'Are you hot for somebody back there, too? Don't tell me it's Cole. Or Thomas.' Jael tried to smile, but the tension in her stomach crushed whatever joke she thought she was trying to make.

Anna snickered and shook her head. 'Not back there, no.'

Jael averted her eyes, staring down into her glass. She tipped it and held it up to watch the legs of the wine trickle back down. As they merged with the body of burgundy again, she said, 'I think I know what you mean, Anna. I'm flattered...'

'But you're not a dyke.'

Jael smiled involuntarily. 'No, that's not what I was going to say. I was just going to say that I've never really had a woman come on to me before, so I don't quite know how to act.'

Anna snorted. 'You might not have realised that a woman was coming on to you before, but I really find it hard to believe that nobody has.'

49

Jael paused, then wiggled a little against the still-wet panel of her scanty underwear. 'Well, actually, no woman has ever come onto me, but I've... I've done some things.'

Anna unwound her legs and spread them a little as she lay back against the pillows. 'Like what?'

'What would you like to have happen? I mean, what would you do with another woman?'

Anna narrowed her dark eyes. 'I don't want to tell you something and have you feed it back to me, like some kind of psychic fantasy line. Tell me the truth. What have you done?'

Jael shrugged her shoulders and put her glass down on the coffee table. She ran her palms down her thighs. 'Not much. Messed around with a roommate at university.'

'Regularly?'

'Sort of. It happened a couple of times. When we were drunk.'

'Did you come?'

'No. But she did. I made her come every time. I've always been serviceable that way.'

'Oh, I'd make sure you came,' Anna said. She stretched out her leg towards Jael, and Jael examined the graceful arch of her foot and the black straps of her sandals over her olive skin. Anna whispered her next words. 'I'm particular about that.'

Jael's eyes traced up Anna's voluptuous form, lingering on the swell of her breasts, before coming to rest on her full mouth. Anna's tongue slipped out and the tip protruded a little before she parted her lips to speak in a low voice. 'So would you like to try? Having another woman make you come?'

'I don't know. Thomas...'

'Right. Thomas. He worries you. Do you think he'd really mind another woman, though?'

'I don't know. It's not something we've ever talked about. But we are married, and messing around... you know, with you... well, that would be messing around with another person.'

'He's really the jealous type, then.' Anna turned her wine in towards her breast, her wrist curling elegantly, her long fingers holding the bottom of the glass. 'And you know him better than anyone. If he found out, I guess you'd have trouble.'

'Maybe.'

'Maybe? I thought you meant he took your marriage vows as seriously as you obviously do.'

Jael smiled nervously and folded her arms over her chest. 'I don't know that I take them all that seriously. After all, I am lusting after Cole Trevor, aren't I?'

'Yeah, that you are. He's worth a second look in any case, though. You know what, Jael?'

'What?'

'You could pretend that I'm him.' Anna's voice was quiet, secretive; that of a woman engaged in girl talk.

'No, that wouldn't be right.' Jael found herself whispering like part of Anna's secret. 'What would be the point of having another woman, only to pretend she's a man?'

'Are you sure you never came with your girlfriend? You seem pretty hot to me.'

'No, I didn't.'

'And you're sure you wouldn't want to try? Right now? I think a good, prolonged orgasm would tune you up nicely. I'm another woman, so I know exactly what to do. I can make you come as quickly as a man gets himself off. But then there's Thomas...'

Jael glanced around the room. She gauged her own horniness, the improbability of Cole satiating it, and then

51

let her gaze rest on Anna's. 'Wouldn't need to tell Thomas, would I?'

'He'll probably find out on his own.'

'I can take that chance.'

Anna's fingers played with the flap over the button on her white trousers. 'Think you could come with a woman in control?'

'I'm a quick study.'

'You make some pretty interesting decisions on the fly, too,' Anna said. She pushed her tongue out between her lips and ran it over her upper one. 'But you're used to men, aren't you? So let's start with something easy.'

She leaned forward and put her wine on the table. Then, quickly, she pulled Jael into her arms. Turning her head sideways, Anna pressed her lipstick-coated mouth against Jael's.

The lushness was unbelievable, incomparable to anything Jael had ever felt from a man's kiss. She moaned low in her throat and parted her lips. Anna's tongue invaded expertly and began darting about with Jael's, beguiling her to revel in this foreplay.

Jael took the initiative. She slid her hand down Anna's arm and onto her chest to cup a full breast in her hand. It was Anna's turn to moan, and she began pulling off the short-cropped, white jacket that was over her sleeveless black shell.

'Jael?' Thomas's voice came from just the other side of the doorway.

Anna threw herself back into the settee. Jael felt robbed of the soft globe that had been in her grasp and irritated by Thomas's intrusion. When he walked into the room, Jael turned to face him. 'What?'

She glared at him as he watched Anna straighten out her jacket and then look at her. His eyes centred on her lips, then darted back over towards Anna's mouth. He smiled broadly. 'Nothing,' he said. 'Just wondered if you were going to bring any more beer out. I'll grab a couple myself.'

'She'll be right along,' Anna said to his back.

'He gave you his permission,' she said to Jael when he was gone.

Jael looked at her. 'I don't know, Anna. The kiss felt great, but if he knows what's going on here I could be in trouble.'

Anna's voice was husky when she answered. 'It's up to you. The kiss did feel great, though, didn't it? And I can still feel your hand on my tit. Such a pretty hand...'

Jael leaned hungrily towards Anna again, her lipstick-smeared mouth ready to accept more suckling. Anna bit her lower lip gently, and without letting it go, slipped off her jacket. Jael pulled the blouse out of Anna's trousers.

Anna pulled back. 'I'm thinking, Jael. We should do something you're accustomed to, since you've never really been with another woman before. Since another woman never made you come.'

'Like what?'

Anna stood and walked to a cabinet placed diagonally across the room from the settee. She bent down and opened one drawer and reached back into it for a moment. When she turned around, she was holding an enormous strap-on dildo.

'Let's ball,' Anna said breathlessly.

Jael stood up and slipped her skirt down over her hips. 'That thing's going to split me in half,' she said, her voice cracking with lust.

'I intend to,' Anna said. 'You are hot. Just fucking hot. Unsnap that garter, take your panties off, and put the garter back in place. Lift up your shirt.'

Jael did so.

'A matching bra. Lovely. Take the shirt off, too. And leave the shoes. I love them.'

Jael did everything that Anna told her and watched as her soon-to-be partner slipped off her white trousers and panties and black bra. Anna slipped her strappy black sandals off, stepped into the harness and fastened it around her waist.

Dressed in her emerald-green bra and garter belt, her tanned stockings and brown heels, Jael slid her hips to the edge of the settee and lay back.

'You know the way you want it, don't you?' Anna said, her voice husky with anticipation. She stood between Jael's legs.

Jael wrapped her calves around Anna's hips. 'I want it any way you want to give it.'

Anna took a mouthful of wine, then leaned over and kissed Jael. The red juice spilled down Jael's chin and throat. Anna licked it off, spilling some wine on the settee. She straightened herself and put the glass on the table, then looked at Jael devilishly.

'Ready?'

'Ready.'

Anna smiled and leaned over Jael, putting her hands on the settee's back. Jael reached up and took Anna's swinging breasts, one in each hand. She looked at the dark nipples, the small bumps of pink around them, and squeezed the breasts together. Raising her face to them, Jael opened her mouth wide and licked both nipples in one long, slow, sweeping lash of her tongue. She sucked a nipple into her mouth. Anna groaned and reached back to take the permanently hard cock hanging off her. She rubbed its head between Jael's legs. Jael moaned to tell Anna how she appreciated the concentration on the rise of her clitoris.

Jael caressed Anna's other breast with her fingertips, circling its roundness with spine-tingling slowness. Slowly, she slipped her grasp down to the nipple and began pinching and squeezing.

Anna's breasts hovered over her, dangling and moving under Jael's ministrations and Anna's actions. Anna bent her knees and put them on the hard edge of the settee, just under the cushion. She kept the shaft of the pussy-rending dildo in her hand, but slid its glans back to Jael's eager opening. Jael jerked her hips, grunting around Anna's breast, her sounds muted by the flesh in her mouth.

Anna looked down at Jael. 'Here it comes, little girl,' she said, her voice low. Jael pulled her mouth off Anna's rigid nipple and pulled her chin up so that its swollen salmon-pinkness slid off her lower pouting lip and down her face. Jael's eyes were shut tight. Her fingers were pulling and squeezing Anna's other nipple.

Anna began pressing her hips forward, guiding the length of the cock into Jael.

Jael froze. The dildo was wide and long, bigger than anything she had ever taken up between her legs. She grimaced as Anna pushed the last inch into her.

'Ahhhh,' Jael groaned.

'Words fail you?' Anna asked mischievously.

Jael began humping against the hard-on that was so big.

'That's it, get yourself off,' Anna said. 'Take what you need, honey. We can do this all night.'

She began oscillating her hips, rotating the cock around as it stayed lodged in Jael's depths. Jael felt it rubbing and opening places that had never been treated to this kind of business. Streaks of pure pleasure swept through her as Anna ground around inside. 'Thank you, thank you,' Jael sobbed. She gripped Anna's hips and matched her pumping against Anna's expert motions. Jael pushed her high-heels up into the air above Anna's back, then spread her legs wide.

Anna repositioned herself slightly so that she was driving the phallus straight down into Jael's begging tightness. Jael grunted. 'Work your muscles, honey,' Anna said. 'It'll feel so good.'

Jael stopped her machine-like strokes and squeezed her walls around the cock. 'Oh,' she grunted. Her words were slurred when she spoke. 'I need to play with myself.'

'Go ahead,' Anna answered. 'I'll keep fucking you.'

Jael slipped her fingers down onto her wide open wetness as Anna began sliding in and out. 'Oh,' Jael managed to gasp. She felt back over her hairy vulva and found that her body was divided in two around the dildo's pumping proportions, her lips stretched tight to encompass its size.

Jael pooled her efforts onto her clitoris. The effects of Anna's massive rod pulling and pushing at her hole, massaging her soft wet walls from the inside, while she squeezed and stroked her clit on the outside, were all too much. Jael locked her ankles around Anna's back and grunted her way to a mind-blowing orgasm. It felt as if portals to another way of being were opened to her as the sharp pains of pleasure rocketed through her, then eased into long, drawn-out spasms that brought heaven into a place deep in her pussy.

Jael's hand slid down her own hip, trailing her juices over her garter belt and skin. But it wasn't like finishing with a man, who began thrusting his way to a good fuck when he knew that Jael's need was satisfied. Anna kept banging Jael, but there was no hint of a crisis, of another's imminent orgasm and come-loaded insides, and then no more. Anna's strokes were as measured as ever, slipping into Jael and parting her body to make way for the dildo's width, then withdrawing just enough to let her walls relax before taking the hard-on again.

Jael started moving her hips. 'I want to come on it,' she whispered between gritted teeth.

'Come all you want,' Anna said breathlessly. 'Need some help?'

Without waiting for an answer, Anna put her hands behind each of Jael's knees and pushed Jael back until she was folded double. Expertly, Anna slipped Jael's calves onto her shoulders, all the while stroking patiently and hard.

Jael arched her back so that her clit was in contact with the big lover between her thighs. She wrapped her arms around Anna and began shoving herself back and forth, building to another explosion.

This one came even more quickly than the first. Jael felt her pussy muscles gripping and holding the dildo with strength, milking it for pleasure. This climax was centred in the high, hidden regions of herself. As it ebbed away, taking with it the red stars that had showered down behind Jael's tight-shut eyelids, it left her wanting more.

'Get on me,' she groaned. 'Do me.'

Anna pulled out of Jael, and Jael gasped. Her eyes popped open as Anna grabbed her ankles and slid her around so that she was lying on her back. Anna mounted Jael and put her own feet flat against the inside of the settee's arm. Her knees were bent. She grabbed Jael's hips and pulled them closer, then slid them up over her smooth thighs.

'Climb on,' Anna said gutturally. Jael pushed her entrance down on the cock's never-fading head and found that she was stretched and ready for it again. She struggled against the angle that had her hips up in the air as she tried to make herself get poked. Anna leaned forward to help, and the phallus slid easily into Jael's heated wetness.

'You're going to get a good pounding,' Anna muttered. 'I want to fuck you till you squeal.'

'Please, yes,' Jael moaned.

Anna laid down on Jael, her breasts crushed against the lace of Jael's bra. Jael ran her hands up and down Anna's back and sides, loving her curves, the generous softness of her hips, the slight sway of her lower back that gave onto the sexy, juicy, biteable cheeks of her bottom. Anna's skin gave into the pressure of Jael's insistent fingers and hands, yielding a soft warmth that no man possessed.

Anna's long dark hair fell down over Jael's face. Jael ran her fingers through it and rubbed it against her lips. Keeping the cock still as it rested in Jael's secret place, Anna bent forward and kissed her. Anna's soft full lips quivered against Jael's chin, up her jaw, to her ear. Anna nibbled there, furtively licking, until Jael was wriggling. Jael's body was begging to be balled.

Anna opened her mouth over Jael's and sucked Jael's breath out, then blew it back into her. Their tongues twisted and slipped back and forth, first one mouth, then the other. Jael's hands were lost in Anna's hair – and Jael lost herself. She was no longer conscious of where she was, what she was doing. Making love with this woman's body felt like making love with her own reflection. Jael saw her own face hundreds of times every day on the mirror that lay under her hand as she drew at her workspace in the barn. Anna was that form come to life, come to serve Jael, to discover her needs and satisfy them until Jael was left spent and panting and hoarse from crying out her coming.

Anna lifted herself over Jael and put her hands on the cushion under Jael's shoulders. She began sliding the dildo in and out. 'You'd look beautiful with a black velvet band tied around your throat,' she said. 'Would you like that? Would you like me to put it on you? Would you be mine?'

'Yes, yes,' Jael moaned. 'Just fuck me.'

Anna bent her head low and went to work.

With the leverage Anna gained by placing her feet against the settee, she was able to pump in and out of Jael passionately. Jael rubbed the length of her slit against the length of Anna's cock, and the feeling soon became more necessary to her than her own heartbeat. Jael crested the wave of desire that had never fully receded, and she rode it expertly – as ably as Anna rode her. Throwing her legs back and forth, the insides of her thighs rubbing Anna's soft flesh and the straps of the dildo's harness, Jael came again. And again. And again.

'More, more, make me come more,' she moaned. She was almost incoherent, her lips and tongue dry with her panting and groaning.

'That's all for now,' Anna said clearly. She cruelly yanked the hard length from Jael's heat. 'You'd better get to that game room and see what the men want. With any luck,' she said, chuckling and standing up, 'they'll want to bend you over the card table and take turns ramming that hot little cunt from behind. Would you like that?'

Jael was running her slim fingers in and out of her pussy and frantically rubbing herself towards another climax.

'They're going to smell you all over your fingers when

59

you give them their drinks,' Anna said, standing above Jael and watching.

Jael tossed her head back and forth, her once neat hair spilling out, and pushed her hips into the air. Her hand dipped maniacally, her fingers rubbed rapidly, and she greeted another orgasm with a spiked cry.

'Get yourself dressed,' Anna said, shaking her head and stepping out of the harness. She walked back to the still-open cabinet. She bent down and reached in, then tossed the dildo towards the dark recesses. Anna shut the door and stood up. She slid open a drawer at the top, took something out and turned around.

When she looked at Jael, she smiled. 'You obey orders very well,' she said as Jael finished straightening out her clothes and went to work on her dark hair. 'As a treat, I'm going to let you call yourself one of Anna's Girls.'

She walked over to Jael's side. 'Lift up your hair,' she said softly.

Jael did so. Anna took the inch-wide black velvet ribbon she held and tied it at the vertebrae of Jael's slender neck.

'Do you fuck a lot of women?' Jael asked softly as she pinned up her dark ponytail.

'Are you jealous?'

'No. I'm asking because I'd like to be with some of them, too.'

'I'll invite you over some time,' Anna said. She pushed Jael's chin up with her thumb and kissed her throat. 'They'll eat you alive,' she whispered.

Jael turned to wrap her arms around Anna, but Anna pushed them down. 'Go get another tray of drinks and serve the men,' she said.

Jael did as she was told. As she walked down the hall, she felt a throb begin again in her clit. Maybe they would bend her over the table. Maybe Thomas would take her first, then watch as the other men lined up and gave her their cocks; thin ones, thick ones, sturdy ones, meaty ones. Balls slapping against her ass and thighs, come spilling out of her over-full reservoir...

'There she is,' a deep voice said as she walked into the poker game. All of the men turned around and looked. The room was well-lit, and a red flush slipped over Jael's face like a mask as she looked at them and realised what she had just been thinking.

'Jael, come here,' Cole Trevor said, and pushed his chair away from the table. Her eyes snapped to him. She put down the tray and walked to within inches of his knee. He looked at the black band around her throat and smiled. Then he picked up her hand and held it to his mouth, inhaled deeply, and kissed the back of it. 'Thanks for bringing some refreshment,' he said. He winked at her, then motioned for her to get the drinks.

Jael served Thomas first, Cole second, and worked her way around the rest of the table. The game picked up where it had left off when she walked in, but both Thomas and Cole watched her closely.

In their eyes, she could see the knowledge they had of her.

Chapter Four

'We haven't seen much of each other these past couple of days,' Thomas said as he walked into Jael's barn.

She looked up from her drawing, startled. She could make out the silhouette of him as he walked through the darkness towards her where she sat in a pool of bright light. 'No, I guess we haven't.'

'I was going to take the new saddle over and try it out on Tiptop. Want to come with me?' Thomas stood next to her desk.

Jael wrinkled her nose and shook her head, then looked back down at her sketch. 'Nah, I'm hard at work here. Besides, it's almost dark.'

'Come on, it's Saturday night, for crying out loud. Give it a rest. The arena's lighted, and it's not too late. Bet you some folks are still at the stables, as a matter of fact.'

Jael shrugged a shoulder and tossed her hair a little as she turned to a blank sheet of paper and made a few black strokes. 'No, really, Thomas, I'm in the middle of something.'

'How's it coming, anyway?'

'It's all right. I'm finding a new source of inspiration from somewhere, so things are pulling together.'

'Maybe it's because your inhibitions are falling away.'

Jael glanced involuntarily towards her husband, but jerked her eyes back to her drawing paper before she met his gaze once again, in a more measured way. 'I'm not inhibited about my sculpting.'

'No, you're pretty handy with a blowtorch, that's for sure. Come on, Jael, let's go to the stable. I really want to find out if this saddle suits me and Tiptop.'

'Go without me,' Jael said, beginning to feel harassed. 'I'm not bothered about your saddle.'

'I want us to spend some time together, honey.' Thomas walked behind her and sat down on an Army cot where Jael often napped. 'I've been meaning to talk with you about this. Don't you feel that we're drifting apart?'

Jael put down her pen and turned towards her husband. She took in his touchy expression and hunched shoulders. 'Yeah,' she said in a gentle voice. 'I've noticed it for a little bit. We don't feel very close. It's like we're not on the same page any more.'

'Good, I'm glad you feel the same thing. That means we can fix it, if we both see it. And I have an idea for us to get on the same page. We need to have some new things to share and talk about.'

'Yeah?'

'Yeah. Let's get together with Anna and Fred.'

Jael blinked, stymied for an answer straightaway. 'That's hardly new,' she said, settling on something. 'We already know them.'

'I mean, let's really get together with them. Get to know them a lot better.'

'What are you talking about?'

Thomas looked at her stealthily, and Jael wasn't sure if she liked the way his expression was changing from concerned to cunning.

'Let's see if they'd like to play with us,' he said clearly, as if he were discussing which movie to see tonight. 'I was thinking that we could start off making love in the same room, then see if they want to swap partners. I'm sure Fred wouldn't mind.'

Jael had closed her eyes in the middle of Thomas's talking, and now she shook her head back and forth. 'Wait, wait, what? I'm not hearing you right, am I?'

She opened her eyes to see Thomas grinning at her, but he was also jiggling his leg up and down, like he was agitated.

'Anna's sexy. If you wouldn't mind Fred, I wouldn't mind her. It'd be really different for me, grabbing onto her big boobs and having all that soft flesh to slap my balls against, after sleeping with slender you all these years.'

Jael's mouth dropped open. 'Excuse me, but I look a helluva lot better in clothes than she ever could. And you can just forget about skeletal me the next time you get a hard-on.' She shook her head in slow amazement. 'Listen to yourself, Tom! Do you know what you're saying? You want to be with Anna, and you want me to be with Frederick? Well, you might like her, but I can't imagine enjoying him. Ever. Oh, I can't believe this!' She threw her hands up into the air. 'I can't believe we're actually talking like this. All the years I've known you, Thomas, I would never even guess that you, with your jealousy and constantly keeping tabs on where I am, I can't believe – I can't believe you're the same man, that's all.'

Jael fell silent as Thomas stood up and paced over to the massive sculpture she was creating. 'I've constricted you in the past, it's true. Put a damper on a lot of the things you wanted to do with yourself because, well, you know why.'

'No, I don't.'

'Sure you do. I can admit it now, but it took me a while to figure it out. I always knew how much other men wanted you, and I was always afraid that you'd decide to take on somebody else. To take him into your bed, or what's worse, leave with him.'

'You're such a fool, Tom. You knew before how much I loved you. And I still do.'

'Yeah, well, knowing that doesn't always make it easy for me to accept the fact that you might need to have a life of your own.' He wheeled on her. 'I know you have a life of your own, Jael.'

Jael nodded. 'That's good, Tom. I guess I do. Doesn't everybody?'

'No, I mean that I know what's going on with you.'

'What do you mean?'

'Follow me.' Thomas paced to the barn doors and slipped out. Jael suddenly felt a chill creep over her. She stood quickly and jogged after him.

Thomas was already halfway to the wide glass doors of the house. He stopped to wait for her when he reached them, and Jael and he walked through in single file. Roughly, he took Jael's hand and pulled her towards the TV room. When they were there he shoved her towards the settee, and she plopped into it, looking up at him with a puzzled, worried feeling.

'Tom, why are you getting physical with me like this? I don't understand anything that's going on.'

'That's all right. It'll clear itself up. Here's what I'm getting at, Jael. I want to screw Anna, all right? I want to get with her. I have this fantasy about inching my shaft into her and making her squirm. And it's only fair that if I have her, I should offer you to Fred.'

'Along with all the other problems I have right now, there's the small one I already pointed out. I can't imagine being with Fred. He does nothing for me. I don't find him attractive in the slightest.'

'So what? If you don't like him, you can use him. Let

him dip his wick, which he'll enjoy, but get yourself off, which is even better. Am I right?'

'Never mind that.' Jael looked at him with all the alarm she was feeling ringing through her. 'There's also the issue of your sanity. Tom! Do you know what you're saying? I'm serious, I want to know if you're all right. It's like you've turned into somebody else, and you're scaring me.'

'The thought of messing around with somebody else scares you?'

'No, the idea that you would encourage it. You're scaring me, Tom, not the thought.'

'I didn't think the thought would. It doesn't seem that actually being with somebody else scares you, let alone the mere thought.'

'Would you stop being so legal minded with me, like you're putting me through a cross-examination?'

'Fine, Jael. I just think it's funny, you being shocked to hear me suggest that you go ahead and lay somebody else. Especially Fred. When you've already had your legs over Anna's shoulders.'

'Sorry, I don't know what you're talking about.' Jael folded her arms across her chest and looked towards the window.

Thomas stepped into her line of vision and leered down at her. 'Don't tell me it slipped your mind, how Anna turned you into a squealing pig in a couple minutes flat.'

Jael snapped her gaze up to Thomas's tense face. 'What the hell, are you already arranging things with her, Tom? And that's what she's saying about me? Because she's lying. Oh, wait, no, I get it. The two of you are already screwing, and now you're trying to accuse me of being with her to make yourself look better. Because she's threatening to tell me. Some shit like that.'

Thomas walked across the room and picked up the remote control from the top of the television. 'Seeing is believing,' he said. He backed up, pushed 'play', and sat down next to Jael.

She felt exhausted. The blood drained from her gut and pooled in her feet so she couldn't run away, no matter how much she wanted to fly from this room.

The video, shot from inside the cabinet where Anna got the dildo, was surprisingly clear. There was Anna, crouched over Jael. Anna's hips were oscillating as she stirred Jael's sex and made her moan. Jael's thighs quivered around Anna's hips.

'Was it that hot? Were you faking any of it?' Thomas ran his hand over the back of the settee, around Jael's shoulders.

'It felt good,' she whispered.

'Anna really knows her stuff, then?'

'Yeah, I guess.'

'Don't be ashamed, baby. I'm more upset about how you tried to lie to me than how you begged her to do you. In fact, that's my favourite part.'

Thomas pressed 'stop' and then 'fast forward'. Jael turned her head and looked at him press the buttons. 'You seem to really know your way around this tape,' she said quietly.

'We had a fun time with it.'

'Who's "we"?'

'Fred and Anna and I.'

'Jesus Christ, Thomas. I feel...' Jael turned her head away, biting the insides of her cheeks to control her rising tears.

Thomas pressed 'play' again. Jael heard her own passion-torn voice crying, '*Yes, yes, just fuck me.*' Jael looked back at the television. There was Anna driving into her body, propelling her towards yet another obliterating climax. Even now, Jael could feel her pussy drizzle its thick juice. Her entire lower body held one gasping memory of that series of orgasms bursting.

Thomas unbuttoned his jeans and put his hand on the back of Jael's head. She licked her lips.

'*More, more, make me come more,*' her voice moaned in the video. Her legs were thrashing rhythmically, working her pelvis against Anna.

'Now you make me come,' Thomas said. In his voice, Jael heard the anger and jealousy he'd felt since he'd learned of her flat on her back under somebody else, well and truly impaled.

Jael turned towards him and pushed her fingers down into his jeans. She rubbed his erection through the cotton of his Y-fronts.

'I'm sorry you had to find out like that,' she whispered.

Thomas turned down the volume so that she and Anna were fucking silently in front of him. 'I knew what was going on between the two of you when I was back there.'

'Yeah, but to have it shown to you like this.' Jael took his penis out and bent to kiss its head.

He pushed 'stop', and without warning, grabbed Jael's hair and dragged her up to a sitting position. 'You don't deserve to have your dignity,' he said. 'Not after the way you acted under Anna. You've never come like that with me, crying and begging and sobbing "Thank you". You little dyke bitch. Who knew you liked pussy? I thought you liked cock, Jael, and now it seems I should have been watching you around women. Who else's tits have you sucked?'

Jael sat perfectly still, her face turned away from Thomas, but her head inclined towards him as he held her hair tightly. 'I haven't been with anybody else since we got married,' she said.

'Get down on the floor.'

He let go of her hair and gave her head a shove. Jael didn't dare look at him, but slid down onto her knees.

'Crawl over in front of me. Turn the other way. I don't want to look at you.'

She did so.

'Pull your jeans and panties down. Let out that white butt of yours.'

Jael pulled her clothes down around her thighs, then held up the bottom of her long sweater so Thomas could see everything. She bent her head and looked at the exposed tops of her legs and took a deep breath. He was angry, but now it seemed like a staged sort of anger, like he was pulling it up from inside himself in order to make a point. Judging from the feel of his cock, he was more turned on by the sight of her and Anna than disturbed by it.

Thomas's cowboy-booted foot pressed into her back and smashed her facedown on the floor. Jael barely caught herself before he was sitting astride her bottom.

'I've never done this to you, Jael. Believe me, I've wanted to. At a certain time of the month, you know. You were always too finicky, you moved away. But the time has come, my dear, for me to make you bite the carpet. And this is going to hurt.'

'No, Thomas, please!' Jael tried to twist onto her back, but he had all his weight on her. 'Not that, please! I'm frightened of it! It'll hurt!'

'You seem to like big things shoved into little places. I can't compete with that dildo pounding like an oil rig. But Anna didn't put it in your rear, did she? That's what's left for me, baby. You made sure of that yourself.'

Thomas put his hand firmly on her shoulder and pushed

until she was facedown again. He took her hair in his hand and wrapped it around his fist before he swung his leg off her and knelt beside her. Just as Jael struggled to get onto all fours, he put his knee into the centre of her back and pinned her down.

He yanked her hair back with one hand and smacked her exposed buttocks with the other. 'Dammit, Jael, why are you making me punish you?'

'I'm sorry, please, I'm sorry,' she cried out. Her back was bowed as he dragged her head backwards and she shoved her hips against the floor from the pain.

'Now you have my handprint on your bottom.' He smacked her again, pulling her hair at the same time. 'I should have done this long ago. I should have marked you so you wouldn't forget where you belonged when you were out whoring around.'

'I've never whored around, Thomas, please, I'm so sorry, you know I'm a good girl.'

'No, I don't.' He smacked her again, the hardest one yet.

She cried. Thomas let her hair go, but Jael just lay there, breaking down. 'I'm so sorry,' she said in choked sobs.

'Why'd you try to lie about it? Stupid girl.' Thomas smacked the side of her left buttock. 'I can't stand being treated like a fool, Jael. You're not going to fuck everybody I know like an animal and deny it to my face.' He smacked the side of her right buttock. 'Do you understand me?'

'Please, don't.' Her voice cracked with her tears again, but she didn't try to move.

'Relax, sweetie, and it won't hurt so much.' Thomas pushed her jeans down a little further and swung his leg over her thighs. 'I was going to ride Tiptop today, but riding you is a fuck of a lot more fun, don't you think?'

She felt him drag his underwear down so that his cock stood out, bobbing and free against her bottom.

'On second thought,' he muttered and stood up. 'Don't move.' Jael heard him pull off his shirt. It landed next to her face. She grabbed it and buried her face in it to wipe her tears before she spoke again.

'Thomas, I'll do anything for you. Just don't make it hurt, okay?'

'Humph,' Thomas grunted. She heard his boots hit the floor, one after the other, and his jeans sliding down. 'You don't have anything to negotiate with, Jael.' His jeans landed on her other side, the belt buckle clinking. Then she heard the noise of the soft brown leather belt sliding from the loops, like a snake slithering from the burrow of a freshly killed mouse. 'But I'll make you a deal. Are you listening?'

Jael nodded her head.

'All right. Here it is. I'll be very careful with your butt if you agree that I can lash you before I sodomise you.'

'I bought you that belt, Thomas. I love that belt. Please don't use it...'

'Shut up. Either you agree or you don't. Something bad's going to happen to your rear, Jael, whichever you choose. But you do have a choice.' He knelt beside her.

She knew from his cutting tone that he was dead serious. 'I'll take the beating,' she eventually whispered.

'What do you want?'

Her low voice came out strong. 'I said, I'll take the beating.'

'That's what I thought you said.'

She screamed when the belt struck her bottom. Its inch and a half width was more vicious than Thomas's bare palm. It cut her to the soul.

'You act like I'm tormenting you, but I want to check something,' Thomas said, still in his badgering tone. Jael felt his fingers root into the crack of her bottom and down through her pussy.

'I thought so.' He was chortling. 'I really, really thought so. My, my, Mrs Alistair, but you're positively drenched. It feels like a tropical rain forest down there, you're so steamy and wet. I almost believed that you needed mercy, but now I think you need the strong arm of the law again.'

Before she could take a breath to disagree, the belt scourged the tops of her thighs. She bit the balled-up shirt that she held in her fist, and the tears squeezed out of her tightly shut eyes.

'Mmm,' Thomas groaned. 'Let me check you again.'

He flung the belt aside and kneeled over her prone body. His cock was so rigid and Jael was so soaked, it slipped into her vagina unbidden as he pressed it against her. Jael began pumping her hips with her husband and torturer inside her.

'Oh,' Thomas groaned and began pumping too, his hips synchronising with hers in their dance. 'That's it, baby, get me good and wet so there's some lube on my cock when I jam it in your other hole.'

'I'm begging you, Thomas...'

'Jael,' he said breathlessly. 'You don't even know from begging yet.'

And with that, Thomas pulled his stiff length from her pussy and lodged his wide glans between the cheeks of her bottom. He pushed.

'No, lower,' Jael shrieked. 'Go lower, please, Thomas.'

He pulled back slightly, then straightened his torso and dropped down onto his knees, repositioning himself. His big hand slapped down on her left buttock and squeezed it to the side. She could tell he had his cock in his hand from the sureness with which it butted against her anus.

'Bullseye,' Thomas rasped, breathing hard. He ran the head down between her sticky folds again, grazing just inside her vagina as he travelled back up towards his real goal. He leaned forward and plunged in.

'Oh, God, no,' Jael groaned.

Thomas's knuckles were still against her bottom. That must mean he was hardly inside her, she thought. He was hardly inside her at all. A whimper escaped her and she kicked her feet against the plush carpeting.

'Be still,' Thomas growled. He inched his cock in another fraction.

Jael pressed her forehead against the floor. 'I'm going to die, Thomas,' she said softly.

'One more word, and I stop taking my time.'

'Then let me push myself on at my pace, okay?'

'That sounds good, Jael. That's the spirit. Take my cock at your leisure.'

Now that he was firmly in place, Thomas leaned forward, his hands on either side of her head. He pressed down steadily. Jael pushed her hips up and back and his manhood, swollen to bursting, slid in another notch.

'This is tighter than I ever imagined.' Thomas's voice was strained, and Jael knew he was barely keeping himself from abusing her with everything he had.

She slid herself back again. He was filling her now, and she knew she was taking almost his whole prick.

'How's it feel?' Thomas whispered.

'It hurts, but in a good way,' she whispered back.

'Tighten your… oh, yeah, that's it. Oh my God.'

Carefully, Jael began driving herself back and forth on him. The thrusts opened her body, letting him go deeper each time, until Thomas said, 'I'm in. Now let me fuck you.'

His thighs tightened around her narrow hips and the soles of his feet slipped under her thighs. Jael stilled herself, finding a centre down inside where she could balance his need and her pain.

'Fuck, fuck, in, in, in,' Thomas chanted to himself as he took his first strokes. Jael sucked her breath in sharply and bit her lower lip. Then she parted her lips, concentrating on making the pain flow through her and out of her mouth. 'Aaaaah,' she moaned.

'Quiet,' Thomas ordered.

Jael turned her head to the side. She could hear the sound of his skin slapping against hers. She could feel his engorged rod stuffing her completely, in a way that having him in her vagina had never filled her. He was slamming in and out of her, a pain rocketing through her nether regions, then subsiding into a dull hurt, a pain, a hurt. Thomas was fucking her so hard that she was moving along by inches, the carpet burning her cheek and breasts and knees.

He stopped ramming her long enough to wilfully shove her jeans further down and out of his way. He pulled himself up higher onto her bottom again, and his pounding started all over.

'Yes!' Thomas spat the word out. Jael cried out too. He ground his hips against her, as if he wanted to cram every part of his body inside every part of her body, to flow into her with his semen and become part of his woman. He pumped his hips and ground them some more before he exhaled with a moan.

'Thank you, Jael,' he said softly. 'Thank you for letting me do this to you. Even though you did deserve it.'

He pulled his softening penis from her bottom and stood. Jael rolled onto her back and looked up at him.

Thomas looked down at her like a conquering hero. 'I

feel like a... a subjugated slave. Just like a slave,' she said.

'Subdued, maybe. But not subjugated, just from that. You needed to be brought into line, Jael. Now go to the bathroom and get a warm washcloth to clean me.'

Jael got to her feet unsteadily. Her bottom felt as if it were on fire. She pulled up her panties and her jeans. Without fastening them, she teetered off towards the bath.

The warm water ran over her hands as she dampened the cloth and wrung it out. She looked up at herself in the mirror. There was a completeness blooming in her features that she had never seen before.

Chapter Five

Thomas climbed into bed as Jael was in the bathroom, cleaning herself from their encounter.

'Did you bring the dogs in and carry my clothes up?' he asked.

'Yeah.'

'Good. I'll want that shirt washed tomorrow, since you cried all over it.'

'Don't pick at me, Thomas.'

'You pleased me.'

She paused and glanced out at him. 'I'm glad.'

Jael washed her hands, then her face, brushed her teeth, and pulled her soft hair back into a plait. She started to put on her pink silk pyjama top when Thomas stopped her.

'Get into bed naked with me. I want a little contact.' She obliged him. 'Tell you what else I want. I want to know more about what goes on in that head of yours.'

Jael laughed, a self-deprecating, quiet laugh. 'Not much, Tom, you should know that by now.'

'That's just my point. I should have an idea about what you think, but obviously, things are going on with you that I'm the last to know. So while you're feeling subdued, I want you to do something for me.'

'Which is?'

'I want you to write out a fantasy for me by morning.'

'Honey, I'm completely shattered. I don't think I could even hold a pen.'

'I told you what I want, Jael. Now I'm going to sleep.

Your essay's due by the time I get up.' He rolled onto his side, facing away from her, and snuggled into the eiderdown duvet.

Jael looked at his sandy hair, tousled on his pillow. She ran her hand over his head and rubbed his temple with her fingertips until his breathing became shallow and even. When he gave his customary little groan, she knew he had passed the threshold into sleep.

She swung her legs back out of bed and put her feet on the floor. Sighing, Jael stood and went back to where she had tossed her silk pyjamas over the chair next to Thomas's wardrobe. She put them on, then fished her slippers from under the bed and sank her feet into their teal-green, velour closeness.

He'd asked her to write out a fantasy, but what should she write? She thought about it on her way down the stairs.

Jael turned and went back through the hallway and into Thomas's office. She sat down in his deep wooden chair that rolled along on castors, and tugged the cord on his banker's light. Its glow reached into the corners of the room, not very successfully, but it lit the entirety of the dark green blotter in front of her. Jael opened the drawer of his commanding, mahogany desk and reached inside. A legal tablet greeted her fingers, and she pulled it out and dropped it on the desktop. Fumbling around for a pen, she found one rolling loose.

She slid the drawer closed with her stomach, bit the end of the cheap ballpoint, and looked at the yellow expanse of blank paper in front of her. She was stuck. She glanced over at the computer. Maybe if she went up on the net and looked around, she'd find some stimulation. But she knew that the staged photographs in the porno sites could never come near the sweatiness of her imagination. If only she could concentrate, she chastised herself.

She wriggled in her seat, her bottom still stinging from Thomas's assault.

She told herself to think about her body. What did she want done to her body? She looked back over at the computer's dark screen. She wanted Cole Trevor done to her body.

She bent her head and began to write.

Thomas was already out of bed when Jael awoke. She had propped the tablet against the cafétiere. Now, she envisioned Thomas leaning back against the counter, the cafétiere standing next to him as he held the paper in his hand and perused her most intimate thoughts about another man.

He wasn't going to like it, she thought, and rolled over. She should have thought about Cole, but put Tom's name in it. If he was that violent over Anna, how would he react to what he read? Oh, why did she write that? She put her hands over her face and lay there for several long moments. 'Might as well get up and face the music,' she said softly.

Jael descended the same stairs that had taken her to Thomas's office and her fantasy about Cole last night.

As she walked into the kitchen, Thomas began reading aloud:

'I want Cole to pin me to a wall. First with those coyote eyes. Then with his hands on my shoulders. Then with his chest and belly to mine. And his hips. He's well hung and has big balls that swing when he pushes himself against me. I can feel his great rod against my pubic hair. He picks me up and tells me he likes how supple and small I am.'

Thomas's eyes darted to Jael's. Through her trouble and embarrassment to hear her words come back at her, Jael could still see Thomas's amusement that his crack about Anna's breasts worried her.

'I spread myself around his hips. I want to get stuck on his cock. I want to hang onto his shoulders and see the tendons in his neck stand out while he works himself in and out of me. I lock my legs around his waist. He lets me slip down. My cunt engulfs him. He slams me back against the wall and grunts. He wants to thrust into me more than he can, standing like this. It's driving him crazy. I bounce on his big dong. I squeeze my legs around his waist and move him around inside me. He slides me down the wall slowly. He sits back onto the floor. I'm astride him. I ride him like an unbroken stallion while he pinches my tits and tells me how he wants to rip me apart with his cock. I come. He lies down on his back. I swivel my hips around and around. I go clockwise and then counter-clockwise. His dick is like a spoon, stirring up my horniness and dipping into my honey. He grabs my wrists and pulls me towards him. I pull back and we suspend each other. He comes. I leave after I'm full of him and my pussy stinks like his sperm.'

Thomas carefully placed the tablet on the countertop behind him. Jael stood leaning against the island in the centre of the kitchen. Her arms were folded over her chest, and with wide eyes, she stared at the floor across the room.

'Pretty abrupt ending,' Thomas said.

'I was tired,' she answered softly.

'And pretty straightforward stuff. I thought you had something more complicated in you.'

'Isn't it bad enough as it stands?'

'Cole Trevor, eh?' Thomas took a deep breath and

moved to pick up the cafétiere. Jael noted that he wasn't looking at her. He pulled the coffee canister towards him and spooned the dark crystals into the glass pot.

Jael went to put on the kettle for him, but as if on purpose, Thomas reached for it before she got there. Her hands dropped to her sides.

'I'm sorry, Tom. I shouldn't have named him.'

'Yeah, you should have. I told you to write out a fantasy. Though I have to admit, I didn't consider what I'd do if you did name somebody. I thought you'd just write out some scene that you and I could act out.'

'Oh, Tom, it was late. My judgement wasn't what it should have been. I should have thought more about the effect I was going to have.'

'No, Jael, I'm glad you were honest with me. I broke you down a little last night, and the result is that I'm learning more about you. It's all right.'

But he still hadn't looked at her.

Miserably, Jael plunked herself down into a chair at the table. Thomas placed a cup in front of her, then one at his usual place.

'Thanks,' she whispered.

They didn't say anything else until Thomas poured their coffee and seated himself.

'Right then, Jael, let's talk about what this fantasy reveals. I know you want Cole. I've known you wanted Cole since the second I saw you looking at him. It was a rude awakening for me, to see you staring at him with that hungry look in your eye. But there was no use denying it to myself. And there's no use in pretending it doesn't exist now.'

'Aren't you upset?'

'You're not going to believe me when I say no. But I'm really not. You want him. I like to see you get what you want. You know that. If you want him that much, that he makes his way into your fantasy life and you're willing to confess it to me, then you should have him.'

'Thomas, you're really saying some provocative things lately. Why are you getting so kinky?'

'Is it kinky to tell your wife that you want her to be happy?'

'It's kinky when it has to do with her and another man. We've had a relationship of good, athletic sex, and now, things are getting all... I don't know, they're getting deep.'

'I notice the way you're making yourself available to other men, Jael. At least as eye candy.'

'What do you mean?'

'Come on, Jael. It came to a head on the night of that poker game when you saw Cole for the first time. You never, ever came into the kitchen on one of those nights before. But that night, you appeared. And do you think it was completely unconscious that you were wearing a see-through shirt? You wanted somebody to stare at you and think dirty thoughts.'

'I wanted you to stare at me. I tried everything to get you to leave that game and come have a quickie with me. I thought it would be a lot of fun for you and me to run off together and ball while everybody was there.'

'And you don't see how that's some kind of performance for all the men at that table? Everybody would have known what we took off to do, and everybody would have had the same thoughts about doing it to you themselves.'

'I honestly didn't think about it that way.'

'Maybe you didn't. I don't know if you really did or not. But you sure looked like a lusty, ready bitch that night. And you turned it on full-steam for Cole Trevor. Ah, don't look so shocked. I knew all of this that night, and I know it now.'

'I'm attracted to him, yes.'

'You nearly dropped your head in his lap and blew him during the game at Anna's. She was back there, giving it to you with a fake prick, and the only reason you did that with her was because you were starving for the real thing from him.'

'Okay, so I won't go anywhere near him ever again.'

'No, that won't work. I'll tell you why, Jael. I think you just need a bellyful from another man. Look at this fantasy you wrote. The whole thing ends when you have a steaming, stinking pussy from Cole Trevor's come. If it weren't Cole Trevor right now, it would be somebody else who crossed your path. You need some new cock. But I'm not going to let this drive us apart.'

'How can't it? If I go after him you're going to know what's going on, and I can't imagine you letting me have an affair. With him or anybody else.'

'Tell you what, Jael. The thought of you with another man used to get me nuts. But it doesn't any more. The thought turns you on, and it turns me on. It used to drive me crazy because I knew I'd really like it if you went out and got your bun buttered, and I couldn't understand why I liked it. I don't care any more about why it gets me solid, though. Especially now you're showing how much you want to do it. There's just one thing.'

'What?'

'You can ball anybody, but there are conditions. First, I have to agree to let you think about it. Second, it has to happen by my design. Third, when it happens, it can happen only with my permission. No knee-tremblers, no blow jobs, not even any frigging on the side.'

Jael's breath caught in her throat. 'Thomas, it sounds wonderful.' She stood up and turned around to sit on his lap. She caught the clean smell of her own tea-tree-scented hair as he pulled her onto him.

'I have to be involved constantly and nothing happens without my permission. You have total freedom, Jael, but freedom as I define it.'

'Can I go after Cole Trevor?'

'Yes.'

Jael slid down Thomas's legs and under the table. She turned around and began tugging at the cord to his robe.

'No, just wait, Jael. Honestly, I'm not in the mood right now. I've been thinking pretty hard about all of this since I came down here and read your work. I can't say that picking apart my feelings and analysing you has turned me on.'

Jael looked up into his sober blue eyes. He was regarding her in a distant manner, as if he were seeing a complete stranger for the first time and finding her interesting, but unapproachable.

'Don't let it come between us, Thomas.'

'It won't.'

Jael heard Thomas's car in the drive that night as he came home from the stables. She walked down the hall inside the house as he walked parallel to her outside, and she greeted him at the side door.

'So how was Tiptop?' she asked, reaching up and putting her arms around Thomas's neck.

'In fine fettle. Worth every penny, that horse. Some time with him and my mind is perfectly clear.' Thomas leaned down and kissed Jael's mouth.

She closed her eyes and accepted him with upturned eagerness. 'Good, I'm glad,' she said as he patted her on the butt and moved to walk upstairs. 'I like it when you come in, smelling like horse and leather.'

Thomas looked back and smiled at her. 'Come upstairs in about a half-hour.'

'Will you have something for me to ride?'

'Just come up and see.'

Jael paced downstairs for twenty minutes, watching the clock. Finally, she determined to go up and see what awaited her.

As she was ascending the staircase, Thomas called, 'Jael, come here.'

'On my way.'

She bounded up the steps lightly on the balls of her feet. When she strode into the bedroom the door slammed shut behind her.

Jael spun around. Thomas stood against the wall, behind the door. He was naked, and his penis was already half-hard.

One thing caught her attention after she surveyed Thomas's body. A pillow lay in the middle of the floor, in front of the large dressing mirror. A dildo stuck up from the centre of the pillow, held there by the straps of a harness.

Jael's head dropped down slightly in amazement as she looked at the toy. 'It's exactly like Anna's,' she said softly.

'I bought it after I saw that tape for the first time.'

'How'd you hide it from me?'

'You don't know the kinds of things I keep in my briefcase.'

'Seems that we have a lot to learn about each other.'

Thomas took a step towards Jael and tossed a tube of lubricant at her. She caught it in one hand. 'Get undressed and grease him up,' Thomas said, his voice already throaty with desire.

Jael pulled her clothes off quickly, kicking them across

the floor when they landed at her feet. She knelt down next to the pillow and unscrewed the tube's cap. With gusto, she squeezed a blob of gel into her hand and grabbed the dildo.

'Easy, take your time. That's my proxy. Treat him right,' Thomas said. He reached over Jael to the top of the dresser and picked up a pack of cigarettes and matches. Jael watched in amazement as he put a smoke in his mouth, and the smell of burning sulphur filled the room as he lit the cigarette and took a long drag.

'You're smoking.'

Thomas squinted at her through the smoke he exhaled. 'Is this something about Cole Trevor that turns you on? I smoked when we first met. You always said you liked it.'

'I do like it.'

Thomas held the cigarette between his forefinger and thumb and took another drag. Jael watched him savour it before he exhaled through his nose and grinned down at her. 'I'm getting a buzz.' A stern expression replaced his smile. 'You get back to work.'

Jael turned her attention to the dildo again. Gently, carefully, she started at its head and worked the lubricant down the shaft. When she was finished, she looked at Thomas.

'Your nipples are hard,' he said.

'I know.'

'Straddle that thing. But don't sit down on it. Just keep it ready at your hole.'

Jael spread her thighs over the pillow, her upper body erect so that the dildo's glans just brushed the hair on her vulva. She gazed up at Thomas.

'Look at yourself,' he said.

Jael looked into the mirror and smiled at her reflection.

There she was, nude, her nipples hard, coloured like two rosebuds. Her hands were at her sides, and she saw the lubricant glistening on them. She looked at her face and pleased herself with the sultry expression she wore. Her lips were pursed into a little smile, her eyes were shadowed with lust. Her gaze scanned down, and she saw the light flesh of the dildo contrasting with her black pubic hair. She glanced up at Thomas, looking for his approval.

He took another drag on his cigarette and leaned over her to put it out in the ashtray on the dresser.

'Play with yourself,' he said in a low voice as he exhaled. The puffs of smoke coming from his mouth punctuated his words, and Jael felt her pussy contract with heightened desire.

She slipped her fingers in between her soft labia and lingered in the hot slick of juice. The tent of skin over her clitoris was smooth with running wetness. She pressed the pad of her index finger up against the little hard nub that was the cause of all her pleasures, and circled it.

The delicious feeling sent a furore of excitement through her sex. 'Please, Thomas, can I fuck it?' she asked.

'No.'

Jael pinched her clitoris between her middle finger and thumb and began rubbing herself, circling, teasing, revolving her fingertip around and around her jewel. Her hips began rolling in circles above the dildo, and her stickiness dragged against its head, pulling it this way and that in her motion.

'I want it in me,' she moaned.

'Get yourself off,' he said. She looked up at Thomas. He stood in the shadows that had fallen through the bedroom. He reached to the wall and turned the light on. 'I want to see you,' he said. 'Now come.'

Jael fell forward and caught herself on her hand. Bent over, still with her slit butting against the dildo, she rubbed the lengths of her fingers through her salty heat.

'Look up at yourself.'

Jael raised her face until she met her eyes in the mirror. She scrutinised the woman before her.

There she was, abiding by a man's instructions. She was doing things to herself that he demanded. These were not the things she wanted to do. These were the things he wanted her to do, but because he wanted her this way, she too received pleasure from her obeisance.

The luxury of having a strong man to whom she submitted washed over Jael. Her lewd delight in the warm, lush, pleasurable ache she was causing herself spread through her body. She closed her eyes and stopped thinking about her submission. All of her energy focussed down on her snatch.

The moan built in her chest and rose. 'Now!' Thomas said. He grabbed her shoulder and rocked her back onto the phallus sticking up under her.

Jael grimaced as the hard-on filled her. It really was as big as she remembered it being with Anna. But now, Jael was in control.

'I'll fuck you,' she muttered, not caring if Thomas understood her meaning or not. She held the pillow tightly between her knees and threw her weight forward. She pulled her fingers from her pussy and grabbed onto the top of the pillow with both hands. 'Cunt,' she grunted. She began jouncing up and down, hard. The dildo struck deep, and she winced. 'Bitch.' Jael squeezed her breasts together with her upper arms and looked at herself in the mirror. Small beads of sweat stood on her upper lip, and her lower lip was red and full with engorging blood. 'I'll come all I want.'

She fucked the dildo, fucking herself. Jael threw her head back, and the ends of her long hair dragged against the top of her bottom. Her eyes were shut tight. She pulled the pillow up against herself, and the dildo was at a new angle. Now she had to slide back and forth, not just pump up and down. This brought the hard-on more onto her fat clit. The top of her pussy dragged along the dildo with every stroke she took. Her clit was pushed and pulled. Jael shoved herself down onto the dildo and fucked it hard. Her clit was smashed against it, and then it felt like a torpedo launched in her cunt.

The cry tore from her throat. She bared her teeth and tossed her head violently from side to side. Her pussy convulsed around the dildo, seizing it over and over as Jael rode her orgasm to its finish.

Before she was fully finished, Thomas said, 'Show me your ass.'

Jael crouched down, bending forward, but loathe to give up the dildo from her recesses. She slid her hands back under the pillow and held it to her crotch. The plastic cock was stuck inside her. In the mirror, Jael saw Thomas bend down and look closely at her bottom. He raised his hand a few inches above her fair posterior, and she saw the short stocky dressage crop in his fist.

'Thomas,' she moaned.

He struck her. The braided leather tool popped against her skin. 'That's beautiful,' he whispered, and Jael knew that a weal had risen instantly.

Thomas stepped back a few inches, and Jael, mesmerised, watched him raise his hand again. The crop's length came down on her other cheek. She jerked forward. 'Oh, perfect,' Thomas said.

When he righted himself, she saw his arrogant erection. He threw the crop onto the bed. 'Get off that cock and onto your back,' he ordered.

Jael did as she was told, even though she missed the way the dildo stretched her walls and packed her full. She pulled her knees up, expecting Thomas to hammer into her in its place.

But he stepped over her prostrate body and put one foot on each side of her chest. Looking down at her, a haughty expression on his face, he began jerking off.

He pulled the skin of his penis back tight with one hand and rubbed briskly with the other. Jael pulled her arms to the insides of his ankles and reached down to her pussy in order to masturbate with him.

'Tell me what you're thinking about,' Thomas said.

'I'm thinking about how hot and sticky your come's going to be when you blast it all over my tits,' Jael answered breathlessly.

'I always knew you were a slut. Stop fingering yourself.'

Jael pulled her hands up her body, trailing her wetness up her belly, and reached up to Thomas's balls. She sat up slightly and handled him with her fingertips, stroking the wrinkled skin, tugging at it, rolling each testicle around as he pulled at his prick.

Slowly, Thomas knelt down. Jael slid her hands up his thighs and onto his hips. He pressed his knees into her armpits. And she saw that the eye of his cock was pointed straight for her face.

Jael opened her mouth. Thomas moaned and slipped his length in between her lips. She clamped her jaw, holding his shaft firmly. Her tongue pressed hard against the underside of his penis, and she held her lips just over her teeth.

She relaxed her facial muscles and kept her gag reflex at bay through the strictest mental application. Jael concentrated on deep-throating him as Thomas fucked her face.

Her moan was smothered by his ramrod driving down into her mouth. His hands were cupped under her head, and he was stifling her nose against his pubic hair. He smelled like sweat, and Jael twisted under him, desperate to touch herself again.

'God, yes,' Thomas groaned. Every muscle in his body was tense, and Jael knew that he was on the cusp of barrelling his semen down her throat.

But he pulled out. He yanked his cock from her mouth and glared down at her. He dragged his hand out from under her head and grabbed his shaft, and with five sharp strokes, he ejaculated in her face.

'You're my property, Jael. Do you understand that? No matter who I let in your cunt or in your ass or in your mouth, every bit of you belongs to me.'

Jael nodded in silent affirmation. She could feel Thomas's shot all over her lips and cheeks and nose. He had come copiously, marking her face with scorching tracks of white potion.

'Thank you,' she whispered.

Chapter Six

Jael was astride a plank of wood that sat on the scaffolding next to her sculpture. She leaned over, tipping precariously, to use a file in order to create a sharper edge and a gleam on the metal at this height.

She saw the barn door open and glanced over. Thomas walked in, still in his suit.

'It's late,' she said. 'Are you just getting home?'

'Yeah.' He shoved his hands in his pockets and looked up at the sculpture.

Jael placed the file on the plank and swung around to crawl down. 'How's it look?' she asked, gesturing back towards the sculpture.

'Good, looks good. I like how it's reaching for the sky. Every time I see it, it seems to grow taller, but at the same time it seems stronger, more rooted somehow.'

Jael stood beside Thomas and squinted up through the bright floodlights at her work. 'Yeah. And this one's designed to weather, to rust, you know. So I'm hoping it'll take on a really organic appearance in the garden and become an example of how…' She glanced up at her husband and, smiling, stopped herself. 'Never mind.'

'No, really, I'm interested. You never talk about your work.'

'Well, I just want it to be an example of how art enhances the natural world. How humans can positively impact nature. How we can take impulses from biology and dress them up, refine them, make them better.'

Thomas smiled down at her. 'You're a stunning

woman.'

Jael looked away, the heat of her blush making her even more self-conscious. 'How'd your day go, then?'

'It went all right. I kept thinking about you, though.'

'Yeah?'

'Mm hm. I was wondering if you'd be up for a bit of fun tonight.'

Jael raised her eyebrows and smiled cautiously as she looked at her sculpture. 'What do you mean?'

'Why don't you set off in pursuit of Cole Trevor this evening?'

'Oh? And just how would I do that?'

'I know you have his number. Give him a ring.'

Thomas turned around and walked away. Jael watched him recede into the darkness near the door, out of the reach of her work lights. She sat down at her mirrored desk for a moment, then got up and shut down everything in the barn. She sauntered up to the house.

'How should I do this?' she asked when she found Thomas in the TV room.

'I told you. Call him.' Thomas looked at her closely, his eyes trailing up and down her body before resting on her face. 'Talk dirty to him.'

'Do you mind if I do it in the office? I'd probably need some privacy. In order to not be too shy.'

'Yeah, go ahead. I trust you, Jael. But you have to tell me everything that happens.'

'Agreed.'

She walked to the office and dragged the phone over to the high-backed, black leather chair that sat in front of the computer. When she took her address book out of the drawer of the desk and let it fall open, it spread its pages at the letter S, and there was Cole Trevor's number.

Jael took a deep breath as she stared at it and memorised

the digits. How could she do this? She'd never had phone sex before. She reached down and pulled her boots and socks off. She slouched down in the seat and put her feet up, yanked the phone cord until the phone fell into her lap, and picked up the receiver.

Strains of Mozart's *Mass in C Minor* reached her ears from the other side of the house. 'Great, he's got that on at high volume,' she said to herself. 'That means he's in a mood.' Jael plopped the receiver back onto the phone.

When she walked into the TV room again, Thomas looked at her quizzically. 'Nobody home?'

'I just wondered if you really wanted me to do this.'

'You haven't called yet?'

'No. I thought maybe another time...'

'I know my own mind, Jael. I told you to call him. Now get back there and do it.'

'All right.' She turned and marched through the house, the flagstones cold under her bare feet.

Jael resumed her position in the seat. She brutally scratched the top of her head with her fingernails, then rubbed the back of her neck fitfully. Her neck was hot, and she realised that she felt a little nauseous, as well.

'The fear is part of the kick,' she told herself. 'Now get to it.'

With wanton casualness she tucked the receiver under her ear and held it in place with her shoulder. She jabbed Cole's number out on the keypad and listened as the phone began ringing on the other end.

'Hello.' The power that his gravel-filled voice had over her was not muted by distance.

'Hi. Um, is this Cole Trevor?'

'Yes, it is.'

Jael took a deep, shaky breath. Her ribs hurt. 'Mmm. Good.'

'Can I help you with something?'

'You sure can. My pussy aches for you.'

He paused for a moment, and when he spoke, his voice was quiet and the slight background noise she had heard was gone. 'That's no doubt something I'd love to help you with. Who is this?'

'That's not important. It's enough that I have your undivided attention. I need to do things to you, Cole, and to have you take me to places inside myself where I've never been.'

'Damn,' he whispered, then spoke, still in a low voice. 'Listen, I want to talk to you. I really do. Just not right now.' He paused, and Jael could tell he was thinking. 'Call me back in an hour. I'll be ready for you then.'

Jael glanced at the nautical clock hanging on the wall above the desk. 'All right. An hour. Bye bye for now.'

'Bye.'

She hung up and held her head in her hands. 'An hour,' she sighed. 'How am I going to live for an hour with this hanging over me?'

The smell of pot roast reminded her that she hadn't eaten since early that afternoon. Jael walked to the kitchen and found Thomas standing in front of the microwave.

'Hey,' she said.

'Don't tell me you still...'

'No, I did it. But he couldn't talk. I'm to call back in an hour.'

Thomas glanced at his watch, and Jael smiled to see him have the same reaction to the news that she'd had. 'Right, well, I'd might as well have some dinner with you,' she said.

She made herself a plate of food as Thomas sat down. When the microwave beeped, she put his food in front of him with his utensils, and put her own in the oven afterwards. Hers heated in a few minutes, and she turned around with the plate in her hands to find that Thomas had waited for her.

Jael got some silverware for herself and sat down. 'What should I say to him?'

'What did you say so far?'

Jael pulled her upper lip in between her teeth and bit it sharply before she answered. 'I said that my pussy aches for him.'

'He answered the phone, and that's what you said?'

'No, I asked if it was Cole, he said yes. I said good, he said can I help you. I said my pussy aches for him, and he said he'd like to help me with that, but he can't talk right now, I should call back later.'

'All right. That's the kind of detail I want when I debrief you. Remember that. You're going to have to make mental notes when you go through your little experiences from now on.'

Thomas took a bite of braised celery and mushrooms. Jael nodded and picked apart some strands from the beef. 'I'm not really hungry,' she announced, stabbing the meat with her fork and leaving it sticking up as she put both her elbows on the table. She spread her fingers across her face and looked at Thomas through the V formed around each eye by her pinkies and ring fingers.

'Why don't you have some wine and go lie down? You look stressed out,' he said.

'I think I'll just go lie down. I can't afford to have my head muddled at all when I call him.' Jael stood.

'Good idea.' Thomas's appetite didn't seem diminished at all by the forecast of the night's activities. He bounced his fork in time with the music drifting through the dining room and into the kitchen from the TV room. She heard the metal hitting the crockery as she found her way down the hall towards the steps.

Thomas woke her with a kiss on the cheek and a gentle shake. 'Your hour's up.'

'Let me alone,' Jael mumbled. She pulled the duvet halfway over her head.

'Come on, little one, rouse yourself and call him.'

Jael didn't answer. Her slumbering mind materialised images of her sculpture. She saw it from above, as if she were hovering over it.

'Time to get up, Jael. Come on.'

'No, Thomas, don't. I'm tired.' She was coming around enough to know that she absolutely did not want to get out of bed at all this evening.

'Jael, I'm waiting.' She heard Thomas's footsteps take him out the bedroom door.

'All right,' she said. A few seconds later, she rolled over and pressed her head into the pillow. She stretched her back by grabbing onto the iron rungs of the headboard and pulling against them. She kicked her feet under the cover and remembered that she hadn't taken off her clothes before she'd nestled in for her nap. 'Climbed around that scaffolding all day. Worked like a dog. Now he wants me to do this,' she said thoughtfully.

'I'm really tired, Tom,' she called feebly.

No answer.

Jael sighed and groaned simultaneously as she sat up and pushed the thick warm duvet down around her legs.

'Can I call him from up here?' she called.

No answer.

'Shit,' she muttered, and got out of bed.

In Thomas's office, the phone was sitting where she'd left it. On the computer desk, though, Thomas had placed the 'worry stone' that Jael fondled in her palm sometimes when she was nervous. It was a small coping mechanism that Thomas had found for her when he took her to meet his family for the first time. She smiled to see it appear again, at another juncture in their relationship.

Jael dropped her bottom into the seat and slung one leg over the arm of the chair. She scooped the worry stone up at the same time that she grabbed the receiver in her other hand. Holding the stone tightly, she punched out Cole's number.

The phone on his end gave one half of a ring. 'Hello.'

'Hiya.'

'You waited longer than an hour.'

'Wanted to build your anticipation.'

'I was thinking, maybe you were winding me up before.'

'No way. I couldn't wait to hear your voice again.'

'My dick's like a stick at hearing yours.'

'Really? Can you take it out for me?'

He must have moved the phone down near his zip because she heard him pull it. When the phone was back near his mouth, he was breathing hard. 'I'm stroking it for you. Describe yourself.'

Jael thought desperately for a moment. 'The truth or not?' She decided to plunge ahead and let herself be herself. 'I'm about five-two. Around a hundred pounds. Long, dark hair...'

'Yeah, you're very petite. Your hair's very long. Very dark. Very silky.'

Jael's eyes darted around the room as different responses flew through her mind. Cole was describing her exactly.

'Yes, sure, if you want me to look like that.'

'You're telling the truth about how you look. I know.'

'Do you? What colour are my eyes?'

97

'A beautiful, clear, darkish blue. With a black ring around the iris. I told you before, you're beautiful.'

Jael raised her eyebrows and bit the inside of her bottom lip. He knew who she was. When she didn't say anything, he continued. 'It's only fair that I have a good picture of you in my mind. You know what I look like.'

'Do I ever.'

'What would you do to this big prick of mine if you were here right now?'

'It's not what I'd do to just your hard-on. I'd treat you like a god, all over your body.'

'Mmm. Go on, baby.'

'I'd straddle your stomach and reach up to that handsome face of yours. I'd run my fingers over your brows and make all the tension go away. I'd massage your forehead gently and make you forget about your day so you'd think only about me. I'd run my fingers back through your hair and down to your neck, and I'd rub from there down onto your shoulders.'

Cole's voice was husky and his words slurred when he spoke. 'I can feel your wet pussy against my belly.'

'Your stomach's so flat and hard, I can rub myself on you while I massage your shoulders and biceps.' Jael took the worry stone and pushed it up between her legs, massaging her own mound with it. As the waves of slut-pleasure rolled up through her pelvis with the pressure from the rock, she closed her eyes and tilted back her head.

'I swing my leg off you and have you turn onto your stomach. I spread my legs around your hips and rub myself on your ass now. I reach up and push my thumbs into those strong muscles on your back and find the pressure points that hurt you, but release you at the same time.'

'I'll bet you're good at releasing tightness.'

'One of the best. I knead your neck with my fingers while I twist my hips back and forth, grinding my snatch against you. Then I reach down and open up my pussy lips so I can get all my wet smoothness against your skin.'

'Play with my balls.'

'I lean back and drag my fingertips across the backs of your thighs while I slip back and forth. Oh, that steady pressure is so good…' Jael put her foot up on the desk and pressed down on her heel, making her leg muscles tense as she jammed the edge of the flat round stone against her clit.

'Are you touching yourself?'

'Yeah.'

'Are you naked?'

'No, I'm rubbing through my trousers.'

'Jesus, baby, put your hand down your panties and tell me how wet you are.'

'I can tell from how damp my crotch is on this side that I'm soaking.'

'I want to know how sticky you really are, not about your jeans.'

Jael palmed the stone, then mimicked Cole by putting the phone down to her zip so he could hear her go in. She brought the phone back to her mouth. 'I'm running my fingers through my thatch.'

'I'll bet your pubes are so dark, they're nearly blue.'

'They're crinkling under my touch.'

'Do you shave it to a strip down the middle?'

'No, I trim it really close to the lips, so you can see my vulva under it.'

'Sounds delicious. Are you rubbing back by your vagina?'

'Yes,' Jael moaned.

'Put your fingers in yourself. Then pull your hand out and taste. How do you taste?'

Jael put her fingers to her mouth and very deliberately suckled the three that had been dipped into her juices. 'My pussy tastes all-girl, salty and horny, but it needs a man's load shot in it to make it taste right.'

'I'd love to fuck you. Mmm. I'd love to have your footprints on my ceiling, I'd bend you in half and pound into you. I'd make you moan and beg me, "Oh, Cole, stop, no, don't, fuck me harder, no, stop, oh, Cole, Jesus, Cole, no, deeper."' He chuckled to himself and Jael laughed softly with him.

She slipped her fingers back into her panties and shoved the stone inside herself before she slid to her swollen clit to play. 'Sounds like you know what you do to women.'

'I make girls cry.'

His words sent shivers up Jael's back. 'I love to be kissed and then made to suffer,' she whispered.

'Do you like to beg for mercy and not really want it?'

'I'm learning to.'

'I'd love to teach you, baby. I'll make you writhe.'

'Make me come, please. That's all I want, is to come with you.'

'Keep rubbing your pussy on me. Now imagine I tell you to get off me, and I roll onto my back. You play with yourself with one hand and start stroking my cock with the other. Your fingers slip down to my balls, and you hold them in your hand. I tell you to climb on my shaft, to stick yourself on me. You do it. I tell you to lean forward. I brush my fingertips across your cheek and put my hand against the side of your face and tell you that I've never looked up and seen anything so lovely stabbed by my cock. Then I smack your other cheek, a good tap, for being such a greedy whore and turning all this around so now I'm doing the work.'

'And I gasp and begin wriggling on your cock, making it start up a hot current, like a plug shoved into a socket. But I want to feel your balls against my pussy, so I stand up over you…'

'And I look up and see your pink pussy, ready to drip…'

'And I turn around…'

'And I look at your pretty little ass and can't wait to sink my thumbs into your skin…'

'And I cram your thick cock into my tight hole and slip my fingers down under your balls and hold them up to my clit and rub my wetness against their soft skin. Then I put my hands on your thighs…'

'I bend my knees some to give you leverage. I want you to fuck me with everything you got.'

'And I start bobbing up and down with your erection packed into me. Oh, it's so good…' Jael sucked air in between her teeth as she felt her own orgasm get closer by the second. It was moving towards her with every word that Cole Trevor said. She pressed her first two fingers up into her vagina and pulled out the stone. It was heated and slick from sitting in a pussy that was running like a faucet.

Cole's voice rumbled through her as she pushed the stone against her clit and ground against it with all her might. 'And I slap you. I pull my hand back and slap your hip when you shove your ass up into the air. I grab both your hips and hold you down on my cock while I thrust up underneath you. Then I push you up, and you raise your bottom, and I slap you again. And we do it over and over. Your hip is fiery red, and every time you bring your bottom up, you know I'm going to hit you, but you can't stop yourself because you have to feel my prick sliding in and out of you.'

'Aaaaaah,' Jael moaned.

'Stop touching yourself. I don't want you to come. You called me, and you're going to get me off. Pull your hand out of your pants now.'

Jael groaned and hesitantly dragged the stone off her clit. She twitched when it slid off her button for good. Collecting herself, she licked her lips. They were dry from her panting. But she kept talking.

'I drive myself down onto your cock again, and you hold me there. You start shoving me back and forth on your hips like a fuck puppet, and I slide on your dick lodged in me. Then I lean back, and you reach up around my chest and grab my tits. You squeeze them and pinch my nipples and dig your fingers into them until I cry out. You keep hurting me, and I keep riding up and down on your hard-on, and I'm struggling under your hands from the pleasure and pain.'

'Fuck, yes!' Cole hissed. 'Ah, shit, come, yes…!' He groaned, then took a deep breath and exhaled slowly. 'I just made a mess. Thanks, baby, that was a good… I don't know what to call it. Fantasy?'

'It can come true,' Jael said softly.

'Mmm, yeah, I'd love to meet with you. I'd love to get together with you. But I'm seeing somebody right now. I don't want to complicate things; maybe risk the relationship.'

Jael felt jealousy rip through her over this unnamed woman in Cole's life. 'Oh, I'm happy for you,' she said dryly.

'Yeah, even a natural born bastard needs somebody to look after him. It's a steady fuck. But I want you to call me again.'

'That's as far as you're willing to go with this, though?

Just phone calls?'

'I'll be thinking about you.'

He hung up.

Jael threw the phone. It fell down behind the desk. She threw the stone at the wall, as well, and jumped up.

'Cad!' she said. She tugged her jeans closed and zipped them as she hurried up the hall.

'Thomas! You're not going...' Jael stopped when she paced into the TV room and saw his attitude.

He sat in his heavy, overstuffed armchair, in the dark, before the glowing stereo system in the dimness. Slow, dramatic harpsichord music filled the room.

'Bach?' she asked quietly.

Thomas nodded. 'Come stand before me.' Jael did so. 'Take off your clothes.' Jael unzipped the jeans she had just fastened and let them slip down. She pushed her panties down around her ankles and stepped out of her trousers and underwear at the same time. Her long-sleeved, purple, cotton Oxford came next. She wore no bra.

Thomas reached up and turned on the floor lamp next to him. He moved the shade so that the light fell fully on Jael and left him in darkness. She could just see his face and penetrating, cool blue eyes, then his hand as he moved it into the light and showed Jael the bamboo back-scratching stick he held. He let it dangle from his fingers as he spoke.

'Did you come?'

'No, I didn't.'

'Why not?'

'I was busy pleasuring Cole with my words.'

'Come here.' Jael took a step closer to her husband's knees. He lifted the bamboo stick and turned it so that the curved piece on the end was facing up. Leaning forward, Thomas pushed it between her legs and rubbed it back and forth. Jael parted her legs as he concentrated his rubbing on her knob.

He pulled the stick out from between her labia and brought it to his face. He looked at the edge that had pleasured Jael so briefly, then held it to his nose and sniffed it gingerly. He ran his tongue over it. 'You're very excited.' Jael nodded. 'Did you tell him who you are? Who was "pleasuring him with words"?'

'No.'

'Turn around.'

Jael slowly pivoted. She could hear the rustle of fabric as he leaned forward in his chair. 'I like this space between your thighs. And the curve of your bottom has always fascinated me. Now I know why. It's been begging for this kind of treatment.' The bamboo stick whistled through her air, then hit her cheek sharply. Jael winced and squeezed her eyes shut. 'Oh, that's lovely,' Thomas said. 'That's really something. Nice long weals. Two of them, from either side of the stick. Now let's make four.' He hit her other cheek. 'Turn around and look at me.'

Jael bit back the tears and moved to face him.

'Do you know why I'm hurting you?'

'No.'

'Because you're childish and timid. A childish and timid little slut. You're whore enough to call a man on the phone and have him beat off to your voice, but too much of a coward to tell him who you are. It's stupid, Jael. You're being stupid. How do you expect him to make any moves towards you if he doesn't know you want him? You have to be more aggressive and make Cole come to you if you're ever going to have him up inside you.'

Thomas passed the bamboo stick to his other hand and leaned forward, into the light. He turned his hand palm up and ran his middle finger between her legs. 'You're soaking. Turn around.'

Jael rotated slowly. Thomas stood. 'Give me your hands.' She put them behind her back.

'What are you doing?' she whispered.

'You act like somebody going through life with her hands tied. Now they are.' Thomas gave the cord a few turns and a few knots, and Jael felt her wrists firmly bound.

Then Thomas did what they both knew would drive her wild with unsatisfied craving. He brushed her hair to the side, off her neck, very gently. His fingertips grazed across the thin skin over her throat before he leaned down and began nuzzling the hollow of her shoulder. Without putting his hands on her, he turned his face towards her and sucked in the skin at the base of her neck. He drew it in between his teeth and nursed at it with long, slow sucks.

Jael trembled as the headiness took over. Thomas's mouth forced her to centre her mind and then her being around him. If her hands weren't tied behind her, she would reach back and push her fingers into his hair and pull his face against her neck. She would press her back against his chest and stomach and push her bottom out, arching her back and pushing her chest forward. He would take her breasts in his hands and roll her nipples between his fingertips as she gave over to the luxury of his lips and tongue and teeth bringing her to the height of yearning, stretched tight like a string ready for his fingers to pluck.

But none of that was happening. She couldn't respond as she wanted. Jael inclined her head far to the side, stretching the skin of her neck taut for him. She moved her arms and twined her fingers tightly together, and she knew that Thomas loved her useless grappling. He stopped love-biting her and trailed up with the tip of his tongue. She mewed helplessly. Right over the tendon on the side of her neck, he drew her skin into his mouth again.

'Oh,' Jael gasped. She closed her eyes and indulged in the feeling of being eaten from the top down, from the outside in. She moved her shoulder, trying to rub Thomas with it. He slipped out of her way cleverly, sliding back just enough to make his body inaccessible to her body's pleading.

He stepped behind her and picked up her long hair, running his fingers through it. Jael tilted her head back to him, encouraging him to pull her hair, to cause her pain, to give her any kind of feeling. He wound her hair into a coil and pressed it to the top of her head, then began kissing her neck. Jael bent her head down, and Thomas lingered over the vertebrae. He moved to her other side and left a trail of tiny bites from below her ear to the hollow of her shoulder there.

Jael shuddered under his soft, tormenting nibbles. 'Please, love me,' she moaned. Thomas took his face away from her neck, and she felt his hot breath on her shoulder for a moment as he floated above her, seeming to make up his mind.

He dropped the coil of hair and straightened his back. 'Bend over,' he said in a low voice.

Jael did as he ordered. She folded her elbows, sliding her constrained hands up her back in order to give him a better entrance from behind. She bent her knees and waggled her butt from side to side. 'Yes,' she said.

'No.'

Thomas spanked her. He hit her once for each word and said, 'Childish, timid, whore.' Jael held the sobs, but one broke out and shook her chest and shoulders with its ferocity. Thomas didn't move for a moment. Then he said, 'Now get out of my sight.'

Jael stumbled forward, unable to believe he could turn her on so thoroughly, push the buttons that he knew so well, then drive her away with such controlled rage. 'Thomas, please, I need...'

He pronounced each word clearly as he adjusted the lamp shade and sat down. 'Get out of my sight.'

Jael stood straight and slunk off to the side of the room. She stopped in the darkness, staring at Thomas. He picked up the remote to the stereo and made the CD back up to play the track he had missed because of her.

She turned and looked at the settee, and straddled the wide leather arm, one foot up on the cushion, the other on the floor. She jogged her hips back and forth a bit. The settee's arm was hard beneath her. Its firmness, solid against her, felt good.

Jael began moving back and forth on the arm, very deliberately. 'Mmm,' she moaned softly. Talking with Cole had built her desire to a fever pitch; his voice, making sex talk with him, the images of her body pierced by his. And her anticipation of making those pictures a reality. Thomas's treatment of her – shaming her for calling Cole, binding her, spanking her, suckling at her – his actions developed her desire into a fit of need. Now her desperate physical wants were cascading over and through her body. Every nerve was overwhelmed with a compulsion to get herself off.

But Thomas sat a few feet away, and although he gave every indication that he was involved in the music, Jael knew that his mind was back here with her. He was no doubt listening for some indication of her state of mind, some persuasive or entreating word from her. What would he think when he realised she was masturbating, humping away at the settee in her heat because of Cole Trevor's breathing in her ear? The thought of fulfilling her urge for Cole with Thomas so near and so seemingly detached embarrassed Jael.

'Thomas, I need you,' she said. Her lips formed the next words unconsciously. 'I need what you do to me.' He didn't even flinch. 'Thomas, I want you tonight. I want your strength. I want you between my thighs.' He wasn't moved.

He wasn't going to help, Jael thought piteously. He just fired her pussy up and dropped her flat, like that damned Cole. Oh, she'd like to take them both on at once and show them what she could do to them. She pulled herself to the edge of the arm and stood up. Then she turned to face the settee and mounted it like a horse, putting her pussy right on the arm's edge – the hardest part. She leaned forward so that her torso was just in contact with the smooth leather. She moved slightly to the side and leaned her forehead against the back of the settee, supporting her weight with her neck and making her back tense.

Jael jostled her hips to the side, opening her labia over the leather. Then she jerked back, closing her vulva and putting the side of her pussy against the hard surface. She tightened her legs, her toes against the floor like a ballerina's. With a grunt, she moved herself back and forth. And she began to grind away.

The gratification was constant. The perfect rhythm came instinctively. Jael's hips circled, and a pang of satisfaction went through her genitals, then receded slightly before the circle came full. Another circle, another sexy twinge, another moving away. 'Oh, yes,' she groaned. 'Make me come. I have to come.'

The music disappeared. Jael twisted her head around to look towards Thomas, but she could see nothing except his leg and arm. 'I need fucked,' she said, her hips still orbiting her climax. 'Please, Thomas, bend me over the arm of this thing and take me.'

He didn't respond. Instead, he turned the volume up. She heaved herself back into place and put her forehead against the settee, then picked up her cadence. Her arms were bound behind her, and all she could do was drag against the rope that held her. The pain of the pulled muscles in her arms was excruciating, and the steady pain right before the orgasm's arrival throbbed through her lower body. But she came. She cried out, choked moans and gasps. Thomas turned the volume still higher. A crescendo of harpsichord notes rose through Jael's wailing climax.

Her secret muscles gripped powerfully at the music's height. The crisis between her legs hurt. The never-ending hardness of the arm up in her thighs had no mercy, it didn't relax or pull back to let her feel her clitoris and labia twitch with her vagina's clutching. She grimaced, biting hard, groaning through her clenched teeth.

As the agonising delight receded, she became conscious of the harsh tension in her neck and back. A headache smashed into her, and Jael felt drained of the strength she'd need to right herself and climb off the settee. She fought to sit up, and toppling back, managed to catch herself.

She was dizzy from the effort it took to reach her strenuous orgasm alone and without her fingers to slip into her lips and bring it on. She shook her head and tried to coax her hair back behind her shoulders, away from the sides of her sweaty face.

She walked, slowly, to Thomas's side. 'Please, sir, I'm finished now,' she said softly. He didn't respond. 'I've given myself release, but you haven't been served yet.' She turned around and bent over, offering herself for him to feast his cock in whatever place he chose.

Thomas stood, and Jael's breathing quickened. Just do something to me, she prayed to him silently. Do anything, but stop ignoring me.

He untied the cord that held her wrists captive. Yes, Jael thought. Now make me lean into your chair and bury my face in the cushion to stop my screams. He shoved her forward with his hand on her bottom.

But he had pushed her away from his chair. Thomas sat down again. Jael stood and let her hands drop to her sides, her head hanging. Thomas threw the cord at her back, and Jael walked silently out of the room. She stopped in the hallway and looked back at him. Thomas sat impassively, eyeing the lights on the stereo. He picked up the remote from where he had put it on the arm of his chair and adjusted the music's levels. Jael turned away and walked down the hall, up the stairs, alone.

Chapter Seven

'Jael,' Thomas said in an important-sounding tone. 'The poker game's here tonight.'

Jael snapped to attention in the passenger seat. 'It is?'

'Yes.'

'It's Thursday. Isn't that an odd night to invite people over?'

'I'm not inviting "people". Only a few... close friends.'

Jael glanced over at him, barely able to keep the smile from taking over her lips. 'Can I ask who these close friends are?'

'Yes, Cole Trevor is one of them.'

Now Jael let the smile blossom across her face. 'We haven't mentioned him for days. This is good news.'

'Why? Did you think I'd forgotten all about him?'

'No, I just wasn't sure if you wanted me to forget about him.'

'So you'd leave off if I told you to?'

Jael looked out her side window at the guard rail racing by. 'Yeah, I think I could do that,' she answered.

'I don't believe you.'

She looked over at him. He was smiling wryly.

'I could, Thomas. I would never have started after him if you hadn't given your permission in the first place.'

'I don't believe that, either. You were so hot to trot, nothing would stand in your way.'

'Not true. Messing around with Anna was one thing. That... I don't know, that didn't count somehow.'

'Because it was another woman, and you thought in

111

the back of your mind that it would turn me on as much as anything.'

'Well, yeah, I guess. Sort of. I mean, I wanted to experience another woman like that, so I had a part in that decision-making process, too. And I never told you this before, but that wasn't my first time with a woman.'

'Really?'

'Really. I used to mess around with Robyn. You remember, that friend of mine from university?'

'My, my, now there's a pretty picture. Did you really?'

'Yeah.' Jael put her hand over her mouth and giggled. 'I used to eat her and masturbate her until she came.'

'She never did the same for you?'

'We were always sozzled when we did it, and I swear, every time, she passed out before I got my turn.'

Thomas laughed. 'Just like you, Jael. That's how you were when I first met you; willing to do anything between my legs and not caring about yourself. You're a different woman now.' Jael caught the searching glance that he cast her way.

'I guess it's just growing up. I've gotten more selfish. But, yeah, as far as Anna goes, I guess I figured you wouldn't mind as much if I went with another woman.'

'You know what?'

'What?'

'You were right.'

Jael laughed quietly. 'So it's the semen-shooting bit, then, is it? If there's no come left in there, you're all right with it?'

'No, I told you. I'm turned on by the thought of your coming back to me, freshly fucked.'

Jael wriggled in her seat. 'I'd like to be freshly fucked right now. By you.' She glanced over at her husband, hoping she could finally seduce him. 'You haven't had anything to do with me since Monday night.'

Thomas laughed. 'You act like three days is a famine.'

Jael could tell he was pleased, though. 'It makes me feel... less edible, if you don't want me for days in a row.' She settled her hand on his knee and slid up to stroke the inside of his thigh. 'I want you.'

'Between Cole Trevor and me, you're doing a lot of wanting.'

Jael paused for a moment, then slid her hand down to squeeze his knee. 'I could be wanting for a while. He has a girlfriend.'

'You didn't tell me that.'

'It was a little humiliating, to go through that entire phone call, offer him the real thing, and have him say thanks, but no thanks.'

'He refused to get together with you because of a girlfriend?'

'He said he's in a relationship.'

Thomas squinted at the road ahead. 'Hmm,' he said. 'All right. He's coming over tonight, at any rate. And I'll tell you what I want. I want Cole to go fuck his girlfriend with you on his mind. Make him want you. Make him want to slide into something that belongs to me. Put him on edge and leave him to blow a load that he should be pumping into you.'

'Yes,' Jael murmured. 'I'll do anything you say.' Secretly, she thanked him.

They drove the rest of the way home in silence. Thomas carried the groceries into the kitchen and Jael put them away while he watched her.

'Wear something naughty tonight.'

'I don't know if I have anything like that.'

'Sure you do. Put on that black leatherette teddy. You know the one I'm talking about?'

113

'The shiny lycra material?'

'Yeah, that's it. It has black lace over your breasts, right? But it's very low-cut. Wear that with your black leather suit jacket thingy over it. Your black leather trousers.'

'I don't have leather trousers.'

'Check your wardrobe. And your patent leather, black spikes.'

'That's a lot of different leather looks.'

'That's what I'm aiming at.'

Thomas walked out of the kitchen. Jael stood in front of the stainless steel refrigerator and watched his cocky, self-assured walk as he went up the hall. She opened the freezer and got out a pint of double chocolate fudge ice cream, retrieved a big spoon from the drawer, and sat down at the oak table.

Cole was going to be sitting there that night, she thought, looking around at her kitchen. She stood up and moved to the chair where Cole had sat the last time. 'I'll leave the imprint of my bottom here,' she said softly, and smiled. Jael opened the carton of ice cream and went to work on it.

Her mouth was satiated by the lavishly rich chocolate, and she was on the verge of an ice cream headache when Thomas came back into the kitchen. He was dressed in light grey gym shorts and a burgundy T-shirt.

'I'm going running,' he said.

Jael looked at his bulge. 'I'd wear a jock strap if I were you. Or some tighter undies.' She turned the spoon upside down and put it in her mouth, sucking the mound of ice cream off it. She narrowed her eyes at Thomas and jogged her eyebrows up and down a few times suggestively.

'They'll be here at seven. Let things get going, then appear around eight.'

'What should I do with myself until then?'

'There's a wide world of things to do. Choose one.'

Thomas smiled broadly at her and went towards the front door.

Jael cleaned up the kitchen and pushed the plastic grocery sacks into the recycling dustbin. She looked around the room one last time, assessing it through Cole Trevor's eyes as best she could, and went upstairs to check out her new leather trousers.

Jael paced to the guest bedroom that overlooked the front of the house at a quarter to seven. She kicked off her high heels before she ducked down and parted the curtains. She put her arm on the windowsill and her chin on her arm, and prepared to wait.

'Thomas said it's just a few guys tonight. One of them's Cole, but who are the rest?' A Jeep came up the cul de sac driveway, and Jael strained her eyes to see who was driving. 'He had a car the last time, at Anna's. A nice car.' The driver stepped out. 'Oh,' Jael said, and wrinkled her nose in slight disgust. 'It's only Fred.' She shifted her weight as she felt her feet going to sleep and watched as Frederick walked up to the front door. Thomas must have opened it immediately. As Jael listened carefully, she heard the two men laughing and talking downstairs.

She sighed. What if he didn't show? He knew that was her on the phone, so what if he decided not to come? He didn't know that Thomas knew. He might be uneasy around Tom, since he knew she wanted him. Or he might not want to be around Thomas and her together, for fear that Thomas would see what was going on.

Jael sighed again. If he didn't want to play with her, how was she going to make him want to? How could she make a man do something against his will? She heard

Thomas's words: "Make him want to slide into something that belongs to me." That's what it was all about, she thought. It was a little domination game between the two of them. Except Cole didn't know he was involved. So it was a domination game between Thomas and her, more like. He really was gambling that by controlling her urges, he could stop them from coming between them. But they were part of their relationship now. And if Cole had an idea of what was going on? She sensed at the last poker game that he knew something was going on between Anna and her.

'Ha!' Jael exclaimed, standing suddenly and spinning around. She slipped on her shoes and ran to the master bedroom. Cole *did* know that Anna and she made it. She remembered how he looked long and hard at the black ribbon Anna put around her throat. So she'd put it on again. Jog his memory, make him think a bit. She opened the side cabinet on her tall jewellery armoire and found the ribbon hanging on a small hook.

She lifted the top of the armoire's lid and tilted it back in order to see herself in the square mirror there. Jael ran her fingers back through her dark hair at her temples. She had curled it carefully, and it undulated in wide waves. She'd parted it on the side and arranged the length over her forehead with a downward turn so that now, brushed out and sprayed back, it framed her face at an angle as it fell down in a gentle surge to rest on her shoulder. Jael smiled at her cornflower-blue eyes, outlined with black pencil that curved up and out on the sides, to give her a cat-like look. Along with the coating of mascara, the glittering, baby-blue eyeshadow brought out the colour of her irises and made her eyes look innocently big. Her lips, though, were a vamp's. They were blood red, very dark, with just a hint of gloss in the lipstick. Her cheeks were blushed with a light magenta, a few shades lighter than the lipstick, but the same hue.

Jael ran the tip of her index finger along the outer line of her lower lip. She hoped Thomas would think to put on the low lights in the kitchen. She'd hate to walk in there with the fluorescent ones glaring. She'd look totally overdressed and overdone. But she knew Thomas would think of that.

She straightened out the ribbon and placed the shiny back against her throat. She tied its ends at the back of her neck, freeing strands of her long hair from the knot when she was finished.

The black velvet choker drew the eye straight up to her heart-shaped face, but at the same time, created a division between her features and the rest of her body below. Jael turned to the big dressing mirror. Her eyes moved between the black line of the ribbon and the curvy V of the tight lingerie she wore beneath her black leather blazer. Her skin, so milky white that blue veins were visible just below its surface, was exposed and breathtakingly fair, surrounded by the lines of black that her clothes and choker created.

She walked back to the armoire and grasped the tiny dangling handle of the uppermost drawer. She pulled it, and her collection of rings showed itself. Jael reached in and took out the one she had in mind. It was a simple ring, a big garnet. But the marquise shape of the stone and the curve of the wide, gold band echoed the cut of her bodice. And the dark red of the garnet matched her lipstick perfectly.

Jael slid the ring on and held out her small hand, admiring the theatrical effect of the large stone. Then another matter crowded into her mind. 'Oh, what time is it?' She spun and looked at the small crystal and gold clock on the cherrywood dresser. It was past seven! She'd got so carried away she'd forgot to watch! Jael ran back to her post, the spikes of her heels first clicking over the hardwood floor in the hallway, then sinking into the flokati rugs thrown throughout the guest bedroom.

She didn't bother to duck down or hide herself. Jael yanked the curtains open and stared down at the driveway, vexed that she had probably missed Cole's arrival.

But she hadn't. He was just getting out of his big sedan as Jael placed herself in the window. Jael knew that the movement she'd created caught his eye; he looked up, straight at her. A smile played about his lips, and he gave her a friendly salute. He took a few steps towards the house, but stopped and looked up again. Jael met his eye, absorbed in staring at his body and face, even from this distance. Cole gazed at her, shaking his head back and forth slightly. Then he brought his fingers to his mouth, kissed them, and blew the kiss to her.

Jael moved her hand away from the curtain. It fell behind her, and Jael knew that she stood as if a living portrait, against a field of dark forest green embroidered with gold. She caught Cole's kiss, and with her eyes half-closed and her mouth open, she pressed her lips to her palm. He wants me, she thought.

She looked down at him as her hand fell from her face. He stood with his hands hanging at his sides. The brown leather collar of his stone-grey field coat was turned up against the blustery autumn wind. His dark hair blew about. His stance was the proud, even conceited one that she'd seen twice before. This is the third time we'll be near each other, Jael thought. Third time's a charm.

She stepped back from the window and arranged the opulent curtains over it. The doorbell rang downstairs. Thomas wasn't so quick to open the door for Cole as he was for Frederick. Within seconds, though, she heard Thomas's baritone speech, and then Cole's voice, solid and touchable, like wet firm clay. Jael felt that if she went downstairs and reached towards Cole, she would be able to grasp his words from the air and hold them to her body.

She paced to her bedroom and looked at the clock. 'Quarter past seven,' she said. 'Forty-five minutes to go.' And with nothing else to do and no interest in watching out the window any more, Jael opened Thomas's wardrobe, took out the small ironing board and the iron, and began to cull out his best shirts.

At eight o'clock sharp, Jael walked out of the bedroom.

She knew there was a sheen of perspiration on her upper lip and chest from her work. Her arms and hands felt light from pressing down on the iron. She felt good, loose, focussed on the task of captivation that lay just before her. Thomas said to make Cole want her. But Cole wasn't going to be the only one. Every man there was going to get an eyeful, and if Cole Trevor wasn't interested after this, then there was no hope for him.

Jael strolled down the stairs slowly, feeling her hips sway with each step. She smiled to realise that she was making as much noise as possible with her heels on the wood. She wanted them to know she was coming.

The flagstone floor in the hall was her next venue, and she sauntered up it, the leather soles of her shoes and the taps of her heels clicking rhythmically as she got closer and closer to the kitchen. She smiled as she looked up the hall. Thomas had indeed made sure that the ambience would be as complementary to her look as possible.

The incandescent ceiling lamp that hung over the table was the only light on in the room. And there were only three men here; Thomas, Frederick, and Cole. The low-wattage bulb in the lamp illuminated them in a minimal way, leaving their backs in the shadows and lighting only their faces and hands on the table.

Jael stopped in order to take in the picture before her. It seemed that Thomas had consciously arranged things to include her perspective when she came up the hallway. Thomas sat facing her. The light caught the gold accents in his sandy hair, and when he raised his face to glance at her, he looked raw-boned and handsome from the dim overhead angle of the bulb.

He looked back down at his cards, playing the same wily game of glances he had played with her the first time Cole Trevor had been in their home. Frederick sat on the right as Jael looked. She discounted him quickly.

The man in question sat on the left. He was in the same chair he had used before, the same one that Jael had chosen this afternoon as she indulged herself in the decadent pleasure of the over-rich ice cream. Her delight in her sense of sight was as satisfied now as her taste buds had been then.

Cole's dark hair still looked windblown. It was short on the back and sides, but dishevelled on the longer top. If Jael didn't know better, she would think he'd just rolled out of a warm, sumptuous bed. Yeah, and left his girlfriend there, she thought with a harumph and a smirk.

Jael leaned her shoulder against the wall and folded her arms across her chest. She took deep breaths, feeling the swells of her breasts push against her arms. She pressed her tongue just out of her mouth and licked the centre of her upper lip as she surveyed his profile and reminded herself of the things that she liked best about him.

Everything.

Without unfolding her arms, she ambled into the kitchen and leaned against the doorframe.

Her knee nearest the doorframe was bent, the heel of her shoe just raised off the floor. Her hip was pushed out, and her black leather jacket opened to reveal it. The waistband of the trousers was just a little too big around her slender middle, and Jael knew that it left a gap that a man could think about nudging his hand into.

But her artist's perspective told her that she was illuminated only from the back, by the lights in the hall. To the men in the room she was an apparition; a black presence that had entered silently and stood watching them.

Cole didn't look at her immediately. He raised his cigarette to his mouth and took a drag. He looked straight across towards Frederick as he did so. His hand fell down at an angle to stop in front of his other shoulder. He stuck out his jaw and lower lip and blew the smoke upwards, over his eyes. It rose in a billow to the light overhead, then descended in a haze over the three men.

It seemed to Jael that he was steadying his nerve, finding the fulcrum inside himself from which he would have the greatest chance of standing his ground against her onslaught of feminine danger. Yes, he and his relationship were in jeopardy tonight, she thought.

The words forming in her mind galvanised her into action. She walked into the room and pivoted on the sole of her shoe to walk towards Frederick. He raised his eyes to her, and his jaw dropped. Jael bit the inside of her lower lip, but let the smile tug at the corners of her painted mouth. Well, Thomas was right about that; if they offered to swap partners with Frederick and Anna, it looked like Fred wouldn't mind one bit. She didn't meet Frederick's eyes. She let him take her in without having to admit to either of them that she was a person.

Thomas turned his glance up towards her as she approached him. Now she knew for sure that she had achieved the perfect look. His black pupils, so clear against the frozen blue of his eyes, dilated. Jael tossed her hair back over her shoulder and walked behind him, where she stopped and put her hands on his shoulders.

Thomas leaned back and put his head against her breasts. Jael pushed her shoulders back and forth, rubbing her body against him. She slid her hands down onto his muscular upper arms and squeezed his hardness.

Frederick still stared, gobsmacked. But she had walked around Frederick so that Cole could see as much of her as possible. Still, the darkness of the room, so necessary to her smoky appearance, was hampering her from showing herself off to him completely.

Jael could only hope that her entrance had put him on the spot; made him as unsure of himself as she thought he was. Slightly unsure, she thought. Nothing could make him actually nervous. As if in answer, Cole looked up at her with an apparent smile of greeting. Jael ignored him. She leaned her face down next to Thomas's, kissed her husband gently on the cheek and whispered, 'Hiya.'

'Hi, gorgeous,' he answered in his lowest registers.

Jael smoothed the ruby-red mark of her kiss from Thomas's stubbly cheek with her thumb. She glanced towards Cole, who was watching her, really quite coolly. But touching her husband's face like that made Jael remember when she had described rubbing another man's handsome brow and forehead to him. She set about demonstrating her technique for Cole Trevor now.

Jael stood behind Thomas and ran her fingers back through his hair. He pushed his head forward, into her hands and groaned a little. She took her fingers from his thick mane and smoothed it. Thomas tucked his chin down onto his chest as she pressed her thumbs into the back of his skull and rubbed in small circles.

'That's it, now do my neck,' he said.

'No, no, we'll do it my way,' Jael answered in her soft voice. She brushed her fingertips across his temples and let her fingers meet in the middle of his forehead.

She looked at Cole. He was watching her hands thoughtfully. Jael applied the slightest pressure to Thomas's skin and bone and worked outwards in small strokes. He closed his eyes and let his head fall back onto her body again. She looked down at Thomas and pulled him against her tightly, enjoying how big and masculine he was. She moved her feet apart until they were at shoulder width, and she bent her knees as she slipped her fingers down onto Thomas's eyebrows.

She started at the centre, on either side of his nose, and worked out in tiny revolutions of her fingertips. Thomas sighed, a breathy, satisfied sound. His eyes were closed, his chin tilted up. He was exposing his throat, and Jael couldn't resist bending down around him and taking a nip of it before quickly standing erect.

Thomas started a little. 'Sorry, was that a little sharp?' she asked. He smiled in response and settled his head back against her. Jael slid her fingers down onto either side of his jaw and rubbed. Then she moved up over his cheekbones and tapped gently along each one, systematically covering every millimetre of her lover's tender skin.

She was looking down at him, and realised that although Cole was in the room and she had started out performing for him, she was now only interested in Thomas's physical comfort and pleasure. Jael leaned over him and kissed one closed eyelid, then the other.

'Mmm,' Thomas hummed. Jael smiled at his upturned face and brushed her fingertips down to his throat. Then she put her palms against his upper chest and slid her hands down onto his flat, sexy stomach, rubbing him in long, slow strokes.

Jael was bent low over Thomas's shoulder. Her dark hair had fallen over her face on both sides as she concentrated on his lean body. Now, in this docile, serving attitude, she lifted her head, let her hair fall away, and looked at the other two men.

Frederick hadn't taken his eyes off her yet, she could tell from the glazed look on his face. His lips were parted, and the hand he had on the table was moving as if he were squeezing something. Part of her anatomy, Jael thought and smiled.

But it was all for Cole.

He, however, was examining his five cards.

'Good hands tonight?' she asked.

He glanced up at her as if surprised to find that she was still there. 'Yeah, very,' he answered. His eyes drifted down to her touch on Thomas's belly, and then Cole leaned back in his chair and tilted his head to the side, as if trying to look at her behind. Jael moved her bottom towards him. Slowly and silently, Cole leaned forward and reached for her jacket. She strained towards him, without losing her rhythm on Thomas. She watched over her shoulder as Cole took the hem of her jacket between his first two fingers and lifted it. She pushed her hip towards him. Cole looked across at Frederick, who was smiling broadly. 'Very good stuff tonight,' he said, raising his eyebrows at Frederick and nodding in approval.

Jael smiled boldly at Cole before aligning herself behind Thomas again. Then Thomas spoke. 'Jael, why don't you get us each a beer?'

'One for me, too?'

'No, none for you.' He smiled, his eyes still closed. Jael smiled too, and pulled her hands up Thomas's stomach and chest as she stood straight. She walked away from him, but let her one hand linger on his shoulder as she sauntered towards the refrigerator.

'Want anything special?' she asked, looking back at Cole.

'Something domestic. Home-grown. New England,' he answered.

'I think we only have exotic,' Thomas said.

Cole tilted his chin back and answered in a drawl, pulling each word out deliberately. 'Then I'll have some of that.'

'Red Stripe?' Jael asked.

Cole smiled. 'Jamaican beer? Strange choice.'

'Hot and steamy in Jamaica,' Jael said.

'Hot and steamy in here,' Frederick muttered.

Jael looked at the back of his head and smiled, then glimpsed Thomas. He was watching her, his eyes heavy with lust. Her glance seemed to draw him to her. Thomas stood and walked around the table to come to her where she was. He reached over her shoulder and pushed the refrigerator door closed. Steadily, Thomas leaned his weight against Jael until she was held firmly between him and the cool steel in front of her. She felt his erection rub against her lower back, and she pressed her bottom out for him. Thomas put his hands up on the refrigerator door, just above her head, and pressed his chest into her back. Silently, Jael thanked him. She put her hands up too, and looked back at Cole over her arm.

He had pushed himself away from the table and sat watching her and her husband. He was slouched down in his seat, his feet flat on the floor. When Jael looked

125

him in the eye, Cole gave his hips a thrust upwards. She knew what he was referring to: the mental image they both had of her facing away from him, impaled on his cock.

Jael shoved her shoulder against Thomas and he backed up. 'I'm going to put on some music,' she said in a low, throaty voice. Her eyes lingered inside Cole's as she walked out of the room.

Thomas followed her. As she walked into the TV room, he grabbed her shoulders and spun her around to face him.

'You're doing well,' he growled. He took her face in his hands and looked into her eyes. 'Do you still want him?'

'I was thinking of you when I was touching your body.'

'You didn't wish it was him?'

'No. I was glad it was you.'

Thomas greedily pressed his mouth hard against Jael's. She opened hers, and his tongue transgressed her lips. She clung to his neck desperately. Thomas put his hands on her hips and dragged her to him. Jael twined her leg around his and Thomas bent his knee. She rode on his thigh. He jammed his mouth against hers so hard that their teeth collided, and Jael moaned as Thomas scooped under her tongue with his own.

He pulled his mouth away from hers and trailed his fingers across her cheekbone. 'Is this what you wanted? You wanted me to slip you a quickie during a poker game?'

'Yes,' Jael whispered.

'You have me so hard, I can't believe it. But I'm going to wait to give you what you need, all right? I want you to concentrate on Cole right now.'

'You don't think it would turn him on to know that

you and I are doing it right across the hall, just through the dining room from where he sits?'

Thomas ran his fingers back through her hair. 'Beautiful,' he murmured as she tilted her head back and nuzzled his wrist. 'Beautiful animal. He'll see how you look when you go back in there. They'll both know I had a little of my way with you. Go back. I'll put the music on.'

Jael turned and went.

'Now, where were we?' she said when both men's gazes snapped to her as she marched in the doorway.

'Giving us something to satisfy our appetites,' Cole answered in a low voice.

'Mmm, right,' Jael said. 'I believe that was a couple of Red Stripes.'

'That would do it for me,' Cole said.

She got two mugs from the cupboard before swinging her hair back and looking at him. 'You take whiskey as well, don't you, Cole?' She let her lips go full around the 'O' in his name.

'Yeah, sure,' he answered. Then, softly, 'But I'm already intoxicated.'

Music flowed into the room. It was slow, sexy jazz, hinting at late nights and waking up, hair scented like cigarettes and cologne, stretched between love-stained sheets with a stranger in the bed.

Jael swivelled her hips in time with the high-hat cymbal taps. She felt the leather of her trousers rub against the cheeks of her bottom, exposed by the G-string panties she wore. She bent her knees and dipped down, letting her hand go behind her. She pushed up under her jacket and touched her bottom as it swayed. Then she side-stepped to the refrigerator and got out three bottles of beer.

Swaying from side to side, Jael got out the bottle opener and popped the metal top off each bottle. She could feel Cole's and Fred's eyes boring into her back. She pushed her bottom out a little and wiggled, then did some step-ball-changes with the bass line of the music. She poured the beers and turned with two in her hands.

Jael placed one in front of Frederick and walked towards Cole. She put it down as he reached to the breast pocket of his tight T-shirt for his pack of cigarettes. 'Let me do that,' she whispered.

Cole looked up at her, and Jael gazed into his gunmetal-grey eyes. Slowly, she reached towards his chest. As her fingers grazed him, as she felt his firm skin give slightly under the pressure of her grasping, aching fingers, the world stopped. Jael didn't hear the music any more. It felt as if a gale were rushing through her ears, accompanied by the shallow sound of her breathing. This kitchen, mundane, receded before the world that Cole Trevor offered her. Jael's shadow fell across Cole's face, but she could still see the gleam of his eyes, and the fire that burned there drew her like a moth to Cole's flame.

Her fingers slipped down into his pocket. She caught the top of the cigarette pack and pulled it out. Cole slid his hips forward and began reaching down into the pocket of his jeans. 'Please,' Jael whispered. 'Let me do that, too.'

Cole withdrew his hand slowly and let it drop. He slung his biceps over the back of the chair, and Jael had full access to the side of his body. She walked behind him and bent down as she slid her hand down his chest and stomach and veered off to his hip. From the inclination of his head, Jael knew he was watching her fingers as they crept down his torso. 'We're both enjoying this, aren't we?' she asked.

Cole took a deep breath and pushed his hips up into the air. Jael felt the rough band of his jeans, then the edge of his pocket. Cole pushed his hips up further. Jael shoved her hand into his pocket.

'Mmm, you're warm,' she whispered. She felt the body-heated metal of his lighter. She took it in her fingertips and pulled it out. With a few small, sauntering steps, she was standing in front of Cole again. She picked up the pack of cigarettes, took one out, and placed it between her lips. She tongued the end of the filter, just slightly, then lit it.

The flame leapt up, and Jael stared at Cole over it. He could climb on her right there, right then, she thought, and smiled to herself.

She lit the cigarette, snapped the lighter shut, and tossed it onto the table. Then she held the cigarette towards Cole. He opened his mouth slightly, and she gently placed it on his lower lip.

Fred's tense voice sounded from the other side of the table. 'I should have brought Anna.'

'Why?' Cole asked. His voice was unmistakably husky.

'Anna and Jael are close friends,' Fred answered.

Cole ran his fingertips over his own throat and gazed up at Jael. 'I know they are,' he said.

Thomas walked into the room, and Jael knew he had been standing in the dark on the other side of the doorway, watching her tempt Cole. Cole looked over at Thomas and lifted his beer mug. He took a long draught of it, then purposefully sat the glass back down on the table with a thump.

'I have to get going,' he announced.

'We hardly played!' Frederick said.

'I think we played enough,' Cole answered. He stood up.

'Come on, Cole, stick around,' Thomas said.

'I have to take off,' Cole insisted. He pushed his chair under the table and left the kitchen.

Jael winked at Thomas, and he smiled dryly. She knew she had performed her duty well; maybe a little too well, judging from Thomas's cloudy looks. Still, she didn't feel finished. Turning on the ball of her foot, Jael paced after Cole.

She found him in the sunroom. His jacket was already on, and he was fishing in his pocket for his keys before he stepped outside. He glanced at her and stopped preparing to go.

Jael moved close to him, closer than she had ever been. She reached out and pressed her knuckles into his bulge. Cole's body stiffened all over as she turned her hand to let her fingertips trace up the erection that filled his jeans. She stroked it, putting her fingers on either side of it, humming, 'Mmm…' when she felt its width. With her thumb, she felt the round head of his cock.

She looked up into his eyes. He was looking down at her, and she could read the questions he had: Did she want it now? And where could they fuck?

'She'll be a lucky girl tonight,' Jael murmured. She turned and walked away.

Chapter Eight

Jael lay sleeping.

Thomas stepped more quietly when he saw that she was out cold. He moved to the cane-backed dressing chair and small, ornately carved cherrywood table next to it, and turned on the little boudoir lamp that sat there.

The lampshade was navy blue, so Jael's features were indistinct at best in the dark glow. Still, she scowled in her sleep when the soft light came on. Thomas gazed at his wife. 'Look at you there,' he whispered, overcome with fondness. 'So beautiful. Perfect woman.'

His mind was clouded by the excess of gin he had drunk with Fred. The dry, sour taste of the quinine in the tonic was still on the back of his tongue. Thomas leaned over and pulled off his track shoes. He toppled forward slightly before he managed to get his socks off as well. When he stood and pulled off his jeans, he knew he was making too much noise, but was unable to stop himself.

'So why Cole Trevor?' he asked her quietly. Heavily, he sat back down in the chair to pull his shirt over his head. 'Bad ass, that guy. Fred, anybody, I could control him. But Trevor's tough. Can't pin that bastard down.' Thomas tossed his shirt towards the wicker laundry hamper. 'You sure made him want you tonight, though.' He examined Jael closely.

She lay on her side, facing him. Her expanse of dark shiny hair was spread out on the pillow above her head. He smiled, thinking of how she smoothed it back off her cheek and upwards off her temple right before she fell asleep. It was an unconscious gesture on her part, but it always filled him with a warm familiarity that things were as they should be before he drifted off.

'Ah, Jael,' Thomas said wistfully. 'Who'd have thought it'd come to this? I want you to do it. If it'll satisfy both of us. You know what I mean. But don't dare leave me for him.' The bare thought of her preferring Cole to him over the long run incensed Thomas. He stood up and left the room.

The Irish Setters were in the conservatory for the night, and they both jumped up and milled about his legs with worry when he appeared again in the dark. 'Settle down, you two,' he said. 'Go lay down.' They returned to their respective beds and turned in circles as he rummaged around.

'There you are,' he muttered. The dogs each thumped down onto their cushions as if emphasising his thoughts. Thomas lifted up his finds and glared at them under the autumn moonlight coming through the glass roof. 'Maybe I'll take Jael to the next Boston fetish fair,' he considered. He turned and paced back up the stairs, two by two.

By the time he reached the top of the stairs the feel of the weapon in one hand and aid in the other made him hard. The thought of what he was about to enjoy made him sober. 'You better be naked,' he said, as he pushed open the heavy wooden door and stalked into the bedroom.

The purposeful sound of his footfalls on the thick carpeting seemed to affect Jael. She rolled onto her back and threw her arms over her head. Her wedding band hit the thin iron rung above her and made a small chime. The sound was so normal to her that it didn't disturb her sleep, but Thomas stilled to hear it. He let its note die down before he continued his approach to the bed.

He stood above her and looked down. The rose-coloured duvet, so much like the blush that came to Jael when she was in the throes of lovemaking, had slid to her stomach. Her breasts stood up, as firm when lying down as they were when she was standing. The nipples looked like strawberries in this light. They were big and pliant and flushed to a shade of pink that worked in concert with her pale skin to make Thomas's excitement grow.

He flicked the deerskin flogger against his leg. Its tentacles were soft and yielding, but demanded respect. He couldn't imagine it hitting his genitals. 'But you'll soon find out, Jael,' he whispered to himself.

With one pull he yanked the duvet to the foot of the bed. Jael's sprawled body was exposed. Thomas leered at her, her petite frame, the mole on the side of her right knee, her left knee bent towards the centre of the bed. She moaned as the cool air washed over her body, and she grasped for the missing cover. Thomas was pleased to see that she stretched her hand in the direction where he slept before she relaxed again.

His hard-on grew more engorged with lust and blood as he gazed at her. His mind formed the words that his jaw was almost too drunk to say. 'Christ, you're gorgeous. Smashed as I am, just looking at you gets me hard.' Thomas held the flogger over the crotch of her golden silk G-string and dragged its softness up her belly.

Jael pushed her lips into a pout and tossed her head from side to side before reaching down and shoving Thomas's toy away. He thought about leaning over her and biting her lips, how it would feel to draw them into his own and suckle at them. 'This is better,' he told himself. He held the flogger over her, between her spread legs, then snapped its ends up against her pussy.

She started and groaned in her sleep. He hadn't disturbed her enough. Thomas pulled the flogger back just a little further from her body and cracked her snatch with it again.

Jael's eyes sprang open. Fright emblazoned her face. She stared up at Thomas. He knew his form, in silhouette against the dim light behind him, filled her sight. The smell of her fear cleared his mind completely. 'Enjoy him?' he asked.

'What? What d'you want?' she slurred in a whisper.

'Cole Trevor. You enjoy him?'

'I didn't... do anything with him. You know that.'

'You touched him.'

'You said to.'

Thomas stopped his interrogation for a moment to savour her wide, fearful eyes. 'Like the size of his cock?' he asked, hissing at her.

Jael seemed to sink languidly into the soft mattress under her. 'Yes,' she whispered.

Thomas pulled the flogger back and hit her silk-covered pussy with it, almost hard enough to cleave another slit into her, he judged. Jael gasped and drew her legs back, then shut them tight.

'Right idea first,' Thomas said. He dropped the flogger onto the bed and grabbed the top of her panties. Jael lifted her hips and pushed the G-string down. Thomas pulled the panties off and dropped them onto the floor. 'Why would you come to my bed wearing underpants?' he asked.

'I wanted you to know that I wasn't thinking about him.'

Thomas grunted and grabbed one of her ankles. He brought forward the coil of black fabric he held in his other fist.

He unravelled it, letting it drop onto Jael's stomach. She lay still as he found the loop at the end and fastened its Velcro hold around her ankle. Then he pulled the long band up over her body and nudged with his fingers at the top of her head. Jael lifted herself off the pillow, and Thomas strung it behind her neck. He pulled it down across her to her other ankle and caught that one in the cuff at that end.

He looked at Jael. His wife's legs were pulled back, her knees bent, and she was held open for as long as he chose to keep her that way. But it wasn't enough. Thomas wheeled towards her wardrobe and flung its doors open.

Jael's scarves hung from one wire hanger. Thomas reached into the closet and tugged two long silk ones out. He draped them around his neck, then pulled the hanger out and held it into the low light. He saw what he wanted and hung those on himself with the other two.

When he walked back to the side of the bed Jael looked up at him with wide, doe eyes. He saw her alarm, but her fright was the measure of his own excitement. Thomas leaned over her and, staring into her eyes, grasped one of her slim wrists. Jael's lips parted. 'Thomas,' she whispered. 'I don't want this.'

'I do,' he murmured.

'You frighten me. You're doing things I can't take.'

'We'll see about that.'

Thomas wrapped the end of one scarf around her wrist and tied it. He slipped his little finger between Jael's skin and the silk of her bind and was satisfied it was secure, but safe. He wound the other end of the scarf up around the iron rungs of the bed, and tied that tightly.

Jael lay there, her knees almost on her chest, her thighs spread wide, and one arm extended above her. Thomas growled low in his throat and walked around to the other side of the bed to secure her other wrist. Her legs trembled as he backed away to study his work. 'Are you cold?' he asked in a low voice.

'No,' she whispered.

'Why are you shaking?'

'Because of you.'

Thomas walked backwards to the foot of the bed and examined Jael's pose. Her pussy was open to his gaze. Thomas moved to the small lamp and pulled off its shade, then dragged the lamp as far as the cord would allow. He found he could hold it right over Jael's lower stomach.

He turned his head and looked at her genitals in the suddenly glaring light. The black thatch that she kept trimmed and well groomed was split to reveal the rose petals of her labia. The bump of her clitoris stood in opposition to the gulf of her vagina's opening. Thomas licked his lips.

He sat the light back on the table, then moved to pick up the deerskin flogger from where he'd dropped it. Her bottom was next to his hand. Thomas passed the flogger to his other hand and reached down. He pushed his index finger into her anus.

Jael squirmed and shut her eyes tight.

'You don't like anything happening to this little rear, do you?' he asked.

'No, it hurts.'

'Thought I widened that hole.'

'Please, Thomas, do what you're going to do.'

'I'm not even started yet,' he said. 'Be quiet. Don't tell me what to do. Open your eyes.'

Jael's eyelids flickered open. 'I want you to see what I'm up to,' he said. He tossed the flogger onto the chair behind him, then pulled off one of the two scarves left around his neck. Quickly, he put it over her soft, pouting lips. Jael gasped, and that gave Thomas the chance to push the scarf into her mouth.

She struggled uselessly, pulling her arms hard against the ties that constrained her. She tried to wrap her fingers around the taut silken fetters as she tossed her head to and fro.

Thomas stretched the gag tight across her face and put his fist on either side of her head. Jael stopped moving, like an animal that knows the trapper sees it in his snare. Roughly, he shoved one fist under her head. He passed the ends of the scarf into his opposite hand and tied them firmly.

She mewed. Thomas smiled. 'I'm really pleased to see you like this, Jael. I like this a lot.' He took the last scarf from around his neck. 'And I think you know where this goes.'

Jael blinked at him. Thomas glanced down. Her chest was covered with a film of sweat, her breathing was panicked and quick. His eyes raked back up to her face. Her eyes, so enchanting, so captivating, so capable of bribing him into anything with a promise of passion to come, were on the verge of terror-stricken. Thomas bent down and put the blindfold across them.

When he was finished tying it, he checked the security of all the knots holding Jael. 'Anything hurting you?' he asked. She shook her head. 'Good,' he answered. 'I want you to concentrate on the pain I cause.'

Thomas turned and put the flogger on the table before he sat down in the chair. He picked up the lamp and moved it back and forth in front of him, illuminating Jael at different angles, showing up different parts of her bound profile. There were her legs, open and high. There were her ribs, showing beneath her skin now that her arms were stretched above her head. Thomas leaned forward and held the light towards her chest. Her nipples were hard, tumid peaks of maraschino cherries on top of the vanilla single serving of each breast.

Thomas put the lamp down and moved to the bed. He leaned over her as quietly as possible and took a nipple in his mouth. Jael groaned. Thomas circled her pinkness with the tip of his tongue before sucking the nipple hard and then releasing it. 'Your pussy's hooked right into your tits, isn't it?' he asked. 'It's like a direct line between them. They let each other know what's going on.' He traced one fingertip from the nipple he had just sucked to the other. He pinched that one between his knuckle and thumb. 'Would you come if I played with your nipples?' he asked.

Jael writhed. Thomas left off squeezing her and retrieved the flogger from the table. 'Would it take a little more than that to get you off?' he said. She turned her face, two-fifths covered by a blindfold and gag, towards him. A low sound, like a warning snarl, started in her throat. Thomas smiled to himself. 'Getting angry doesn't help anything, Jael,' he said. She kicked her feet, but that did nothing except jerk the restraint against her neck. She tossed her shoulders back and forth, jostling her legs. 'Very pretty,' Thomas said as he watched. The way he had her trussed, everything she did caused some other part to move against her will.

He stepped forward and with a single flick of his wrist, snapped the flogger over her breasts. Jael arched her back and screamed, but the gag muted it. Thomas tilted his head and squinted at the red slashes that such a gentle flogging had caused. 'So fair,' he breathed. He hit her again.

Jael was moaning in short, rhythmic cries. Thomas leaned over and put his face close to hers. 'Shhh,' he urged her. 'Shhh. That's a girl. I want to talk to you.' He stood and waited as her heavy breathing calmed down. He placed the flogger on the pillow next to her. 'Jael, now I have you in this position, I want to say something to you. Honey, I really think...' Thomas stopped for a moment and bit back his laughter. 'I really think that right now, Cole Trevor is fucking somebody else.'

She turned her face away. Thomas lay down on top of her, his knees tight against her bottom and his hands on either side of her chest. 'He's out riding his girlfriend, you know. I saw you running your hands down him like you did to me. And you got in his pocket. I'm sure he liked that. Why didn't you go out to his car and ball him in the drive? You could have started to get him out of your system. But you did all that work, getting him tuned up, and he's out banging and sweating with some other woman. No, you know what? I'll bet he's giving her head. I'll bet her clit's twitching under his tongue right now. And he's slipping his fingers in and out.'

Thomas reached down and put two fingers inside Jael. He worked them around in her as he spoke. 'You're the jealous type, Jael, I know you are. I am too. That's why we get along. We both know that the other one won't put up with any shit. So I know that when you decided on Cole Trevor, you can't help but get jealous over him. You might submit to me, but I know you want to own him the way I own you. You want every drop of his come to belong to you – every drop of his spit.'

Thomas slid down Jael's spread body and gave her pussy a long, slow lick. She shuddered and groaned. 'Are you pretending I'm him?' Thomas asked, looking up over her belly, her red-slashed breasts.

Jael shook her head emphatically and said, 'Hm mm... hm mm,' from behind her gag.

'I think you are,' Thomas persisted. 'You're behind that black scarf, you can't see, and it would be so easy to let your mind drift. Fantasise that I'm Cole, Jael, go ahead.'

Thomas pulled himself up onto her. 'I don't care who you pretend I am. I'm going to pretend you're a whore I picked up on the street and brought back here. I'm going to make like I don't have to care about you, whether you get off, what you think of me afterwards. I'm going to ride you like an unbroken mare, you understand? I'm going to ride you into the ground. I'm going to break you tonight.'

He reared himself back and put a hand behind each of Jael's knees. He moved her legs back and forth to shift her hips. And then Thomas leaned into Jael and hammered down deep into her body.

She yanked against her silk restraints. Thomas knew that more than anything, Jael wanted to push her hands up against his shoulders, to help him to balance as he brutally fucked her. But he meant what he'd said; this wasn't for her. He was out to please himself.

Thomas shoved down against her bent legs as he pulled himself out for the next thrust. The muscles in his arms tensed as they bore his weight. He clenched his jaw and slammed down into her again. Jael winced as he dropped his weight into her.

It was like sliding his prick into a narrow, deep, velvet sack. Thomas squeezed the backs of her legs and pumped in and out. He had her spread so far open. He was deep inside her powerless body. He knew she couldn't participate; she could only receive his hardness.

Thomas grimaced and bit his lower lip. He reached to Jael's ankle and undid the strap that held her legs suspended. She lifted her head to let the strap loose in

140

back of her neck and dropped her feet with a thud onto the mattress. She groaned in satisfaction at this release. Thomas centred himself over her and began pounding.

His stomach was glued to hers with sweat. She pulled at her tied wrists and jerked her legs back and forth. He rubbed his chest against her maltreated breasts. She wrapped her calves around his thighs and shoved her hips at him. He stretched his body on top of hers and slid his hands up her arms to hold them flat against the bed. His fingers around her wrists, her legs around his waist, they humped.

Thomas felt the crisis. Every thrust inched him nearer to exploding his spunk into this slot. He shoved his elbows down against Jael's shoulders and twisted his torso. He hauled one leg up and jammed his knee against her bottom and slammed into her one last time.

The orgasm wrecked him. His come shot from him in a convulsion. Thomas wallowed in the lust powered by the license he had over Jael's body.

She was shoving her mound back and forth against him desperately. He knew she was trying to push herself over the same edge, to join him in climax, but he didn't want her to reach it just yet. Thomas pulled himself from her vagina and, lying on top of her still, worked to untie the knots that held her wrists.

When she was free, Jael snaked her arms around his neck and gyrated her hips, trying to get his cock back inside herself. She grunted, one of the few sounds she had made since he started screwing her. Thomas ducked his head out from under her grasp and rolled away. He snatched up the flogger from the centre of the bed, where it had landed when it slid off Jael's pillow, and stood.

'Let me see your ass,' he said breathlessly.

Automatically, Jael obeyed. In a moment she was on

all fours on the bed, then she dropped down onto her chest and spread her knees. Thomas smiled to see her present her bottom so graciously.

The flogger made a gratifying slap as it glanced off her tender skin. She rocked forward and moaned. Thomas pulled it back again and smacked the tops of her thighs. Stripes made a showing there as well, and she sobbed. He hit her thighs a little lower, and Jael buried her face in the mattress.

'Let me hear you. Now get on your back,' Thomas ordered. Without hesitation, Jael collapsed onto her side and rolled over, her thighs spread wide. 'I'm going to trust you not to move. I'll tie you again if you misbehave.' As if to show him she could control herself, Jael reached up and took the iron rungs in her hands herself.

Thomas nodded to himself and tossed the flogger onto the bed. 'I have something very special for you, Jael. Something I ordered at the stable.' He bent and opened the bottom drawer of the dresser and got it out. 'I don't think you've ever seen one of these before. And you're not going to see it yet, either. But you're going to feel it. I'll tell you what, we'll play a little game. I'll take the gag off you, and every time I hit you, you tell me what you think this is.'

Jael shook her head wildly. Thomas sneered at her blindfolded, gagged face as he slapped the end of the long rubber racing whip against his palm. 'Hear that?' he asked. 'That's what's in store for you.'

He walked to the head of the bed and put the whip beside her on the mattress. He reached behind her head to undo the gag. Jael didn't move her hands to take the scarf away from her mouth. Thomas picked up the whip and dragged its end across her nose and exposed cheek. Then he slipped the whip under the loosened gag and lifted it away from her face. 'You don't have to take guesses if you don't want to,' he said. 'But I do want to hear your screams.'

He jerked the whip into the air and let it fall with very little pressure behind it onto Jael's pussy. Its weight and the height from which it fell did the trick, though. Jael jerked and cried out. Thomas took a step closer to the foot of the bed and got a better grasp on the whip. He lifted it again and cut into her mound with it. She screamed. When Thomas pulled it back up into the air a drop of semen flew off it. His eye followed it as it travelled in an arc to land on Jael's lower lip. She tentatively stuck her tongue out, then licked it off herself. He cropped her pussy again, and she tossed her head and moaned.

'I'm being very gentle, aren't I?' Thomas asked.

'Yes, sir,' Jael answered.

'Do you know what I'm using on you?'

'No, sir.'

'I'll work on you a little more then.'

Thomas got onto the bed and straddled Jael's chest. He reached down with the whip and masturbated her with it, sliding its long thin shaft through her slit, then pulling its end up to rub against her nub. Jael sighed behind him. Thomas pulled the whip back and flicked it against the side of her vulva, in her groin. Without waiting for that pain to shoot through her, he administered another slice, an inch to the left. Methodically and at a moderate pace, he pulled the whip back a few inches and cracked it down against Jael's pussy, over and over. When he reached her groin on the other side he retraced the whip's journey and cropped her entire snatch, all over again.

Jael contorted and twisted under him, but kept her thighs spread. She dug her fingernails into Thomas's back, scratching him in a long sweep. Her first shriek steadied into a constant supplicating moan as the punishment endured.

Thomas flung the whip away. He bent down over Jael's body and put his hands under her bottom. Lifting her hips, he buried his face between her legs. She squeezed her thighs around his head, and Thomas's tongue skated over the top of the bumps and furrows that made her femininity. He took another probing lick, then settled his tongue against the top of her clitoral hood, rolled her button between his teeth, and suckled it into his mouth.

Jael jerked and struggled under him. Thomas chuckled low in his chest at her. 'Seems that this is more torture than the whipping.' He sunk his fingers into her flanks and rubbed his face from side to side, getting his lips and cheeks wet with her salty juices. He fluttered his tongue against her clit, then pulled his face away from her. He slid one hand onto her pussy and spread her open with his fingers. The little pink pearl he was looking for was hidden. Thomas knew that when he placed his tongue against it, Jael would go insane.

He found his target and pushed with the tip of his tongue. He rubbed slowly, judiciously, giving her pleasure. Jael's hands squeezed the globes of his buttocks, and then her fingers locked onto his hips. With that indication that her delight was building, Thomas slid his tongue up over the top of the tent and bared his teeth to drag them against her.

When he hit the round gem Jael jerked and squealed. 'Mmm,' Thomas moaned. He pushed his face into her pussy again and licked her, then pulled his mouth away and began masturbating her.

He pushed the heel of his hand against her pubic bone, crushing her. Jael ground back at his hand. Thomas pressed his palm down against her, cupping her entire pussy in his grasp, and moved his hand back and forth. Within moments Jael was quaking, and he felt the strong contractions and spasms start from her vagina and move even the labia he was touching.

Jael groaned, 'Yes, yes,' over and over as she swam through her long coming. When she was finished, when Thomas felt the last twinge of her secrets die, he swung his leg over her chest and turned to lie down beside her.

She didn't move to take off the blindfold. Thomas was glad to see she waited for him. He propped himself up on one elbow and tugged the scarf up over her head and threw it onto the floor.

Jael rolled towards him, her eyes still closed, and wrapped herself around him. Thomas pulled her close until her soft breasts were crushed against him. 'Didn't take much to get you off,' he said quietly.

'The whipping...' she said, and her voice died away.

'We have a lot of exciting things ahead,' Thomas said. 'I want to get on with your training. But we can't do that until you get Cole Trevor out of your system for good. It's time you got what you need from him. You feel ready?'

'Yes.'

'All right. We start tomorrow.'

Chapter Nine

Jael paced all day, getting in the housekeeper's road, milling about aimlessly, and feeling completely out of sorts. Thomas had left at ten a.m., without saying much about his destination. Jael only knew that he hadn't gone to work. And she couldn't work herself in her state of mind.

He walked in the door at six o'clock. Jael greeted him with a question and a glower. 'Where have you been?'

'Mall.'

'I thought you were going to give me something to do today.'

'Yeah, I am. But I had to set things up first. Come on, Jael, give me a break. I haven't eaten since breakfast.'

She followed Thomas into the kitchen. 'How can you eat now? The day's nearly gone, and you said last night that I could...'

'I know what I said you could do. Go out to the car and bring in the bags.'

Jael turned and walked out to the driveway. It was already nearly dark, and the weather was blustery and cold. As she walked back to the house with the department store parcels, they blew about recklessly in her hands and collided off each other noisily.

When she entered the kitchen Thomas was eating a third of a French bread, stuffed with tuna, salad cream, and cucumbers. Jael plopped everything down onto the table. Thomas winked at her and finished the bite in his mouth, then said, 'Go call him.'

'What should I say?'

'Get him to meet you at Justine's.'

'How will I manage that?'

'It's a nice lounge, upscale place. Shouldn't be too hard to tempt him to go there. I understand it's one of his favourites, actually.'

Jael narrowed her eyes at her husband and pursed her lips. Without another word she went to the office and picked up the phone. She had Cole's number memorised, and tapped it out quickly.

'Hello.'

'Hiya, Cole.'

There was a pause. 'If it isn't my own little secret admirer.'

'You made me hot last night.'

'Pretty brave of you, the way you acted with Tom right there.'

'You both had me so excited, I didn't know which way to turn.'

'What can I do for you tonight, Jael?'

'I want to see you.'

'Where?'

'Justine's.'

'What time?'

'Eight.'

'I'll be there.' He hung up.

Jael placed the receiver back on the cradle and bit the tip of her index finger thoughtfully. He agreed to that awfully quickly. She thought he had some relationship he was worried about. She shifted her weight to her other foot and gazed up into the air. Either she got him so horny he was willing to meet her in order to work it off, or there was something bigger going on. Like, he was in this with Thomas. Or he at least knew about the agreement that Thomas and she had, either because Tom told him or he figured it out himself. Or was she just being paranoid?

Jael wasn't sure that she liked the idea that her husband and object of lust were plotting against her. She thought it was Tom and her plotting about him. What if Tom was double-crossing her? She shook her head. How would he just bring it up to this guy he barely knows? No, Cole must have figured it out himself because of how she was in front of Thomas. He probably thought they have an open marriage, or something like that. She walked back to the kitchen to report to Thomas.

Thomas was looking through the bags from the mall when she came back. He glanced at her. 'How'd it go? Looks like good news.'

'He agreed. Eight o'clock.'

'Justine's, right?'

She nodded. 'Justine's.'

'Good. Now let's go upstairs. Take some of these bags. We don't have a lot of time.'

Jael and Thomas each carried some of his purchases to their bedroom. 'Take a shower,' Thomas ordered, gesturing towards the bathroom.

She came out of the bathroom, naked, within fifteen minutes. He had unpacked the bags, and the contents were arranged on the bed.

'Thomas, they're truly awful. Really, really tacky.'

He turned around and gave her a lurid grin. 'I know. I really went to the bargain basements of the teenybopper stores and some far out lingerie shops. These are all for you, baby.'

Jael gaped at the clothes in horrified amazement. 'No way, Tom! They're so not me. I can't wear stuff like that!'

'You can, and you will. I'll help.' He picked up one item of underwear. 'I don't know, Jael, this is really you. You look dazzling in red.'

Jael shook her head at him. 'It's not so much the clothes, honey, it's the place. Justine's isn't a night-club sort of thing, you know? It's where people like... well, people like you and your lawyer friends go. Suits. Lots of suits are always at Justine's.'

'So consider the splash you're going to make.'

'It's a little embarrassing, to think about walking in dressed like this. I'll look like a common streetwalker meeting a john!'

Thomas nodded slowly at her, and it dawned on Jael that that was the exact look he was going for. 'No. No, Tom,' she said. 'Not at Justine's. I don't go there very much, but sometimes I do. I don't want anybody there to see me like this. What if somebody you know is there? What would they think?' Jael mimicked a city bigwig's cigar-smoke voice and crude gestures. '"That Tom Alistair's a real dickhead, look at his wife with that other guy". Huh uh, Tom, I can't have people think that of you.'

She could tell that Thomas knew she was performing, picking at his pride in order to manipulate him. 'Nice try,' he said, and she knew the game was lost. 'I seriously doubt that anybody I know well is going to happen to be there. And if anybody I know in the slightest is there, I seriously doubt they'd recognise you in this get-up.'

'I'm sure to draw a lot of looks, though. A lot of people are going to examine me pretty closely.'

'Let me ask you, Jael, when you're walking through town and see a girl dressed provocatively, do you notice her face? I mean, you told me you played around with Robyn, and I know about Anna, so I'm assuming that you're not immune to the charms of your own gender.'

Jael smiled at him, a false, malicious little show of teeth. 'I guess not, no. I don't notice the girl's face.'

'No. Because you're looking at the way she's displaying her body. The same thing's going to happen to you tonight. Nobody's going to see Jael Alistair, well-known artist and successful attorney's wife. They're going to see a tramp.'

Jael looked down at the floor and shuffled her feet. 'I guess you're right,' she murmured.

'You know I am. Now get dressed.' Thomas handed her the article of silky decadence he'd been holding during their conversation. 'I think this should go first.'

Jael took the red corset and turned it around in her hands, examining its black laces. 'You're going to have to tie me into it,' she said softly.

'And Cole Trevor's going to have to get you out of it. That's the part that's probably more interesting to you.'

'I think wearing it's going to be the most exciting part.'

'Really? I thought you said it was sluttish.'

'It is.' Jael glanced up at him and smiled. She held her hands up in the air, and Thomas slid the corset down over her arms and chest. It settled at her waist, resting on her hips. Thomas walked behind her, dragging his fingertips across her still-exposed shoulders and upper back.

He laced the corset and drew the strings tight. 'All right to breathe?' he asked, his voice husky.

'Yes.'

He tied the laces and walked back around to look at her from the front. 'Beautiful. You really are superbly gorgeous in red. Look at yourself.'

Jael shyly walked to the dressing mirror and took in the eyeful that she'd become. The black curls of her pubic hair matched the lace that trailed down the corset's spines. Her dark hair fell in waves around her shoulders and brushed the top of the corset's bodice. She turned back to Thomas.

He pulled her to him and wrapped his arms around her. He held her for a long moment, and Jael put her arms around his waist and buried her face in his chest. She breathed his scent of aftershave cream and cologne and noticed the faint trace of cigarette smoke that lingered in his mohair waistcoat.

Thomas released her and moved to the bed. 'These go next,' he said, handing her a pair of thigh-high black fishnet stockings.

Jael sat down on the chair and pulled them on. It didn't take her long to realise that they weren't really thigh-high, though. 'Are they supposed to hit just above my knee?' she asked, looking up at him.

Thomas was looking at her with genuine lust sparking out of his eyes. 'Yeah. You'll see why in a minute. Put this on.' He tossed her a black fake leather micro-miniskirt.

'Where are my panties?' she asked.

'You're not getting any.'

Jael looked at him, then held up the tiny pencil-straight skirt he expected her to wear. She shrugged one shoulder and stepped gingerly into the skirt and pulled it up over her hips.

The micro-mini ended about three inches before the band of the fishnet stockings began. Jael looked at the white skin that showed between the fields of black, and glanced at Thomas for his approval.

'Perfect,' he breathed. 'Here's the top.' He handed her a sheer, lace, black blouse. The lace was the cheapest sort, scratchy and stiff. Jael pulled it on and looked at the puffed out shoulders and the tight sleeves. She started to button it.

'Don't do that!' Thomas growled. 'Just do the bottom two and tuck it into your skirt.' Jael did as she was told.

He handed her the shoes: a pair of red, satin, three-inch stiletto spikes. The length of the heels echoed the band of exposed flesh on her thighs, and Jael rather liked the attention to small detail that Thomas displayed in his choices.

'Stand in front of the mirror,' he said. She moved to where he indicated and gazed at herself.

Thomas stood behind her and picked up her long hair with one hand. He bent his face low over her neck and breathing hard, began kissing her. His lips travelled up and down the side of the throat, and Jael moaned and grabbed his hand. She put it on her breast, and Thomas squeezed, the lace rustling under his grasping fingers. She felt the stubble on his chin rubbing against her, burning her, his roughness so welcome.

He pulled his face away. 'We're left with this hair and your make up,' he said in a gravelly voice. 'You can't leave your hair hanging down. It's too nice, too well styled for this kind of outfit. Pull it up in a rope, coiled kind of thing on the back of your head, and fasten it with one of those cheap little pinchy combs.'

Jael looked up at him and smiled. 'You have a really technical vocabulary.'

'It's all girl stuff to me,' he said, and kissed the top of her head. 'You know what I mean. You have some of those cheap combs, I see you wearing them when you work.'

'But my hair's too long for the kind of style you mean. How about a really high ponytail?'

'Fine. Just so long as it looks common. Common as

dirt.'

Jael nodded. 'The make up?' she asked.

'You're the artist. Completely overdo it. Make it all wrong.'

'It'll match this outfit, that's for sure.'

'Get to work,' Thomas said. He smacked her bottom and she walked into the bathroom in front of him.

Jael fixed her hair, and when she turned her head sideways to see how it looked, she was pleased to see that her long dark ponytail had turned itself into one big loose corkscrew.

'I have to admit, it looks charming rather than whorish,' Thomas said, standing in the doorway. 'You can take the girl out of her classy wardrobe, but you can't take the class out of the girl.'

'What did you think of my make up last night, during the poker game?'

'I want it more dramatic tonight. That was still... tasteful.'

'That was completely over the top!'

'Maybe according to your nature-girl, granola standards, but not according to my taste when I'm looking at trashy women.'

'I didn't know you looked at trashy women.'

'I like a bit of the rough. I kind of like the way the street-tough look has come into fashion.'

Jael shook her head in mock disbelief and began applying her make up with a heavy hand. She put a thick smudged black line on the top of each eyelid, and then, instead of putting a line under each eye, she put it on the tiny space just inside her lower lashes.

'How's that look?' she asked.

'Perfectly cheap,' Thomas said, grinning. 'How'd you do that?'

'You sometimes forget, dear, that I grew up in the backwoods, on the wrong side of the tracks.'

'It's serving you in good stead now.'

They both fell silent as she continued her work. When Jael turned towards Thomas, she was pleased to see him startle at the appearance of this strange woman in his house.

As if reading her mind, he said, 'What'd you do with my wife?'

'I'm leaving her here tonight.'

'It's useless to a degree, though, Jael.'

'What is?'

'You're still so pretty. It's a hard job, making you look coarse.'

'But what do you think?'

Thomas folded his arms across his chest. 'I think you're ready to get fucked.'

Her breath was shaky suddenly. 'Can I really have him tonight?'

Thomas tilted his head and looked down at her very seriously. 'You have to come back with a buttered bun. If you can't get Cole Trevor to do it, there'll be consequences. But if that happens, you have to find another man to have before you come home. And you have to tell me the truth about who you bedded.'

'What will the consequences be, if I can't lay him?'

'If you fuck somebody else, who you don't want, simply because I told you to, the consequence will be your submission to me.'

Chapter Ten

'Yeah, Cole as in "frozen." Or in "black as coal."'

'But you're tanned just right. And your eyes are... What colour are they?' she simpered to him.

Her friend butted in. 'Sort of a grey-green.'

'Sometimes they turn blue,' Cole said, smiling to himself and knocking the ash off his cigarette into the tray at his elbow.

'Depends on the light, I bet,' the first woman said in what she must have imagined was a seductive voice.

'Yeah, well, I meant "black as coal," as in my heart,' Cole said, looking up at her. He narrowed his eyes and smiled thinly.

'I don't believe that,' she breathed.

'Believe it,' he answered.

'Who told you that?'

Cole took a drag off his cigarette. 'Every woman who's ever had the... dubious luck to get involved with me.' He exhaled.

'Is that a lot?'

'A fair number. But I wouldn't call myself a high-mileage model.' He smiled at her again. 'Before this goes any further, I should tell you that I'm meeting somebody here tonight.'

'I don't mind. I could meet you somewhere later.'

'Not one for subtlety, are you?'

Her friend spoke up again, and while the first one was chastened, Cole turned to look at the talking one.

'If you have a friend, maybe we all could get together,'

she said.

'Yeah, that might be fun,' Cole answered, shrugging one shoulder. He took another drag off his cigarette and looked towards the door, then exhaled with a 'Pah.'

The first one looked him in the eye when he glanced back at her. She adopted a brassy stare. 'No, I'm not one for taking my time, if that's what you mean. When I see what I want, I go for it.'

Cole spun back and forth a bit on his barstool. 'Hey, thanks for coming over and talking to me, but I have a date tonight.'

'Is this a blow-off?'

'No,' he said slowly, letting his voice coast upwards. Then he talked more quickly. 'It's a fact.'

'If she doesn't show...'

Cole laughed. 'She'll show, ' he said, shaking his head. 'She wouldn't dare not to.'

'What does that mean?'

'It just means that she's a woman who knows my limits. She'll be here, don't worry.'

'Mind if I hang around to see the competition?'

'She's not competition. She's my... my date.'

And Jael walked in.

She traipsed like one self-assured, but if anything, she seemed unclear about everything around her. Cole looked her over in a lukewarm way, then turned his attention completely back to the two women with him.

'That's not your date?' the first one asked.

'Nope.'

'She looks pretty loose, though, doesn't she?'

Cole cocked his head and looked deep into her eyes. 'Just because you're wearing a business suit, doesn't mean that you don't have something of a pig in you, too.'

She looked shocked, completely taken aback. 'Bastard!' she spit, but then she laughed, as if to cover up her irritation.

'No, now, look,' Cole said. He smiled thinly again and stubbed out his cigarette. He motioned towards Jael, then folded his fingers together and rested them on his lap. 'Let me point something out to you here. That woman looks the way she looks, but she's behaving herself nicely. Glanced around, found a seat, I guess she'll order a drink – very demure. You're dressed in a well-to-do way – very well turned out, I might add – but you're over here, making time with me.'

'This is what men and women do!' she protested.

'Maybe. But I don't like to mess around with a woman until she knows my measure.'

'What do you mean by that?'

Cole sighed. 'I like to be introduced to people, that's all. I very rarely pick up women in bars. I don't mean anything by that. It's just the way it is.'

'So what would I have to do to trade numbers with you?'

Cole smiled and shook his head. 'You see me as a challenge, don't you? You don't care about me, you care about getting me to respond. This is all about you.' He raised his eyebrows and turned to pick up his pack of cigarettes.

'You're a real jerk, you know that?'

'Yup. But I bet if I ask for your number, you give it to me.' He looked her up and down; a once-over.

She smirked at him. 'I'll give you my number, but you can only call me tonight. If you call me any time after this, I won't know who you are.'

Cole nodded his head knowingly, then looked down into the flame of his disposable lighter. He let the fire go

157

out, then tapped the lighter twice on the bar. He stretched his arm forward and pulled the cuff of his jacket and dress shirt off his wrist. 'All right,' he said after he'd taken a drag. 'Write it on my hand. Then I have until tomorrow morning.' He flipped his palm up and held it there.

She looked down at his proffered hand. Cole looked down, too, and felt satisfied at the affluence plain in his cufflinks and heavy gold watchband. He looked up at her, smiling his wager. She put her handbag down on the stool next to him and got out a pen.

The woman held his fingers in her manicured ones, and Cole enjoyed the pressure she consciously exerted. She stroked his fingers before she put her number in bold, thick, black strokes, tracing over each numeral.

Cole used the opportunity to look over at Jael through the wisp of smoke rising from his cigarette. She was sitting in the perfect spot to watch his every move, and watch him she did. He was entertained by the look on her face. She was right on the border of angry, he could tell. Good, he thought. Good place to sit. And good that he was making her upset. But she didn't know the half of it.

'I don't need a tattoo,' he said suddenly, pulling his hand back. He looked down at the number. 'Thanks. I'll keep it in mind tonight.' He turned his back on the two women and picked up his scotch and soda.

Too easy, he thought, when he knew they had walked away. All of them. He turned around and looked at Jael. She was sitting with her back to the wall, in a corner booth. He caught her eye and turned back around in his barstool.

Cole took a sip of his drink and assessed the room. It wasn't very busy, since it was still early on a Friday night.

There were a few local television types; Cole knew them from his work as an advertising executive. He nodded to one man and raised his drink a little. Once he had the newscaster's attention, Cole turned around, as if musing, and looked at Jael. He knew the man's eyes would follow his.

Trying to hide? Cole questioned her silently. She looked at him meaningfully, then quickly turned her face away. Cole looked back over at the newscaster, who had made sure that the men at his table were looking at Jael now. Cole heard their low catcalls and wolf whistles, and he smiled to himself before turning back around to face the bar.

He stretched his arm, exposing the face of his watch, and bent his elbow to glance down at it. Ten after eight, he thought. Punctual, Jael. Very good. She needed to wait a bit for him, though; let everybody get a good look at her.

He turned and stared at her again. She sat, looking out the window on her left very studiously. Cole looked at the city lights beyond and thought, Wish you were home? Wish you hadn't let Tom dress you up and send you out? She glanced towards him, then seemed to be embarrassed that he'd caught her. From the pink rising to her cheeks and staying there, Cole knew that she was well aware of the men's reactions to her, as well.

Then Jael did something he didn't expect. She stood abruptly, and slowly, so slowly, sauntered by him where he sat at the corner of the bar, and up its long side. Cole grinned, then ducked his head to hide his reaction. She was parading herself.

He tracked her progress across the room. Cole watched as Jael turned her head and looked at the table full of men. He could only guess that she smiled saucily at them, judging from the way they shifted in their seats and muttered amongst themselves. One held up his beer and said loudly, 'To the lady.' They all laughed.

She, for her part, nodded at them, and Cole could just hear her low voice say, 'Thank you.'

He was pleased at her valour. Still, not the voice that went with the outfit, he thought, lifting his drink to his lips. But that outfit didn't go with the bar. Good work, Jael. She was inappropriate.

Cole leaned around the corner and inspected Jael from bottom to top as she strolled towards the restaurant part of the establishment. Her shapely calves stood in relief under her fishnet stockings, above her red stiletto spikes. Her bottom, rounded like a loaf of risen bread, swayed under her tight skirt, and the leg she showed there was breathtaking in its effect. Her thighs tapered, and the skirt was so short, Cole could easily imagine – as could everyone else in the bar – that she had a lovely space between her thighs, right under her pussy. Well chosen, he thought, and couldn't help but nod in approval at her husband's dress sense that had readied her for this journey.

She disappeared into the darkness of the eatery. 'Damn,' he cursed grimly to himself. 'Game's up. Wait until she comes back.' Cole drained his glass and waited for her to return into the bar's dim lights.

Within minutes, she did. But now she stopped and asked the bartender something. Cole watched her as she walked towards the foyer. Going to the toilet, he thought. Making him wait. He smiled and shook his head at her gamesmanship, but there was no indication from her that she'd seen anyone familiar in the dining room.

He watched the foyer's doorway for her now. She came back through, and her dark lipstick looked even thicker than it had been, her eyes looked more sultry. When she made her way back to her table Cole stood and pocketed his cigarettes and lighter. He took a deep breath and walked towards her.

Jael looked up at him, and Cole stopped in his tracks and caught his breath. She was truly the most beautiful woman he had ever seen. Her cheap clothes and mask of make up didn't hide it. She wasn't obvious, nothing about her was freakishly perfect, but there was something that caught the eye and held it. The pearly sheen to her skin, the glossy darkness of her hair, the translucent blue of her eyes, her small straight nose, full red lips, heart-shaped face, diminutive jaw. He couldn't pick one thing that enthralled him more than the rest, for Jael Alistair was greatly more than the sum of her parts. The first time he had seen her, standing in the kitchen at her house, Cole had been deflated by the shock of her beauty, then entranced, then desirous, then jittery. It had all happened in minutes, and he remembered thinking through the fog of his perceptions: this must be what love at first sight is like. But he had brushed that sentiment off, and even now he held it at bay, preferring to think of her as a woman who might consent to be used.

The thoughts rushed uninvited across Cole's mind. Forget about it, he told himself sternly before taking another step closer to her. Keep your freedom. But he knew that this was the one time he'd have trouble.

He stood beside her table and pushed his hands down into his trouser pockets. 'Jael,' he said softly.

'Hi, Cole,' she said, staring into his eyes.

He took another deep breath, steadying himself. He cocked his head to look at her legs under the table and leered when he looked back at her face. 'Sorry Jael, but I have to get going.'

'What?'

'I'm busy tonight. I only showed because I didn't want to stand you up. I couldn't call your house to catch you, could I? Of course,' he continued, letting his eyes trace over the bodice of her red corset under the tawdry black lace, 'looks like Tom wasn't home, anyway, when you got ready.'

He glanced at her face. Did she buy the idea that he didn't know what was going on with her and her husband's kink, and himself as their supposed plaything? But the flash that went through her eyes like an electrical storm told him she was onto other subjects.

'Then what the hell am I doing here?' she asked. She grabbed the collar of her blouse and plucked it outwards in contempt.

'Look, Jael, I have a life outside this little game with you. I have to get to it.'

'Is it your girlfriend?'

'Something like that.' He scowled at her. 'I hardly owe you an explanation.'

'No, you don't, but if you're so attached to the love of your life, why are you collecting phone numbers in a bar?'

Cole put his knuckles on the table and leaned over her, menacing. 'It's none of your business, but maybe I'm going to call that chick I was talking to. Maybe that's what came up. Maybe I'd rather be with her tonight than go through some charade with you.'

'A "charade"? That's what this is?'

'Why are you dressed like this?' He grabbed her blouse in the same place and pulled it out. 'You're the one who looks ready for Halloween.'

Jael jerked her shoulder and turned herself away from him. He let his fingertips slide over her breast, and she pushed his hand away in a huff. 'You agreed pretty quickly to meet me here tonight. I thought something was going to happen between us. I thought we had something, you and me,' she said, stressing the last word.

'Don't be a jealous little slag, Jael.'

She glared up at him, then beckoned for him to sit down opposite her. 'I'd rather not,' Cole said.

'You and I need to talk,' she answered.

'Here? Now? I know a lot of the people over at that table...'

'The table of assholes? Figures, you'd know them.'

'Watch your mouth, Jael. But with the way you look, you'll understand if I hesitate to seem like I know you.'

'Oh, that's why you're standing here, talking to me now. Makes sense.' She rolled her eyes.

'Nothing any one of them wouldn't love to try.'

'Have a seat, Cole.'

He turned away and set his jaw, thinking for a minute. Things moved quickly with her, she was difficult to contain, let alone overpower. Mind of her own. He glanced back at her and realised that with the way she looked, she didn't mind making a scene and becoming even more an object of derision and stares. He sat down and leaned one elbow on the table.

'We'll play it your way. But I'm going to talk, Jael, and you're going to listen. You've been throwing yourself at me for a while now, acting like a slut. It's a bit much to see you show up here, looking like one. I never thought you'd be caught dead looking like this.'

She stared at him, and he could tell she was wrestling with herself over whether or not to tell the truth: that Tom had dressed her like the commonest of tramps.

'I'm not a slut,' she said softly.

Admirable, he thought. Loyalty. Then he spoke.

163

'You're not? Let's see. You whore yourself in front of me and a poker game of men. You call me so I can beat off to your voice. You rub yourself all over me, right under your husband's nose. You show up here, looking like a fuck pig. And not too long ago you were coming to me with your hands smelling of pussy, after you squirmed on the end of Anna's dildo. Speaking of whom,' Cole kept on, standing and buttoning his jacket, 'Fred's here.'

The look of utter, unmitigated shame stamped on Jael's face was priceless. Cole could barely hide his glee that he had hit the mark with such good pace and aim. He knew she was trying desperately to quell the images of herself on that videotape.

She stammered, stumbling over her distress and words. 'Fred? Fred – what's Fred doing here?'

'Actually, Jael, I knew from the minute I agreed to meet you that I wasn't going to stick around. And I figured that after you paid your cab fare to get here and ride some cock, I'd hand you over to somebody who's interested in giving it to you.'

Cole pushed his jaw out and straightened his tie, then arranged the French cuffs of his shirt to please himself. Jael seemed unable to react to a word he said, and that was just as well. Nipped that scene in the bud, he congratulated himself as he turned and walked away. He paced to the dining room and stuck his head around the corner. Fred was sitting where he was supposed to, back in the corner, well out of sight. Cole nodded at him and retraced his steps through the bar.

But the sight of Jael sitting there, stunned like a deer that was blinded by the headlights, then glanced off the hood of the car and dying, moved him. He backed up a few steps and stopped. The bartender approached. 'See that woman over there, by herself? Send her a highball. Strong one.' He tossed a five-dollar bill down and left.

Chapter Eleven

She blinked her eyes, forcing the tears to stay behind the layers of mascara. One trickled down, and she reached up with a knuckle to wipe it away. Bastard, bastard, she thought incoherently. She hated him. She bit the inside of her lower lip, hard, and glared out the window. The nightlights of the city, the headlights and taillights of the traffic, were all a blur before her weeping eyes.

She heard a throat clear behind her. 'Cole, please...' she said with a sob in her voice as she turned around. But it wasn't Cole Trevor. It was Frederick. 'Oh God, what do you want?' she asked.

'Cole let me know you were out here.'

'And now I'm leaving.' Jael stood quickly and pushed Frederick out of her way with her shoulder. She barely kept herself from running for the door, and prayed there was a taxi rank nearby so she wouldn't have to come back in here to use the payphone.

She pushed the exit open roughly. She thought he wanted her. She thought they'd leave there together. She'd pictured it in her mind, that they'd get in his car and go somewhere, to his house, and she would finally know what he was like. She would finally learn his body. She wanted him. The sobs contracted her chest, and she let one out through her panting mouth. How could he do this? How could he hurt her like this, and leave her with Fred? How could he let her know that he knew everything about her and Anna, and that Fred knew all about this meeting? She hated him. She wanted to go home. And to forget everything, she wanted to forget everything and tell Thomas it was all off, that she never wanted to see Cole Trevor again, that he would never step foot in her home again. She hated him, she wished he was dead, she prayed to heaven to let him die that night.

Jael stood in the parking lot and looked around. It was a moment before she grasped the fact that Justine's was up in a neighbourhood by itself, miles from nowhere, miles, certainly, from the nearest taxi rank. 'Shit, I hope he crashes and dies tonight,' she said rabidly as she spun to go back into the lounge.

Frederick caught her upper arm. 'Jael,' he said quietly. 'Hey, I'll take you home.'

She articulated each word clearly and vehemently. 'Leave me alone.' She threw her hands into the air and cried out, 'God, how does he know I took a cab to get here? How does he know I don't drive?' Her voice cracked as she spoke of Cole Trevor again.

'Jael, everybody knows you don't drive. It's weird. Listen,' Frederick said, walking with her, step for step. 'If you want to go home, I'll take you. It's no big deal. Why don't you let me drive you? It'll be all right.'

Jael stopped and shut her eyes for a split second before turning to face him. 'It's not going to be all right. Obviously, Fred, you know everything that's going on right now. Believe me, nothing's going to be…' Her voice died away. And she heard Thomas's command: "You have to come back with a buttered bun… you have to find another man to have before you come home."

'All right,' she said in an undertone, nearly a whisper. 'Where's your car?'

'Over here,' Fred said, taking her upper arm again, gently, and guiding her. Jael tried to quiet her breathing. She had to think about what she was doing, she told

167

herself. She had to figure out a way to make him think she wanted him. She glanced at Frederick, and was forlorn to find him shuffling along like a scarecrow. He was no substitute for Cole Trevor.

Frederick walked her to the passenger side of the Jeep. As she stood there, waiting for him to retrieve his keys from his pocket, she took a long hard look around. She wondered if Cole was sitting in his car, watching. It would be like him. But the car park served Justine's acclaimed restaurant as well as the bar, and it was packed. There was no way to pick out Cole's luxury sedan from the throng of expensive cars like it.

Disappointed, and angry with herself for caring what Cole did or thought, Jael looked at Frederick. It was on the tip of her tongue to ask what was taking so long, but then she noticed his behaviour. He was putting the key in the lock, or at least trying to. His hand was shaking like ripples on water.

'You all right?' she asked.

'Yeah, yeah,' Frederick answered. He got the key to work. 'Here you go,' he said, and took her hand to help her up into the seat.

Jael slid in gracefully, but she knew that when she parted her legs, Frederick could see high up onto the bare flesh exposed under her micro-mini. She stole a peek at his face. He wore the same slack-jawed expression he had last night at her house when she appeared in the kitchen in her leather finery. It was a predictable reaction, anyway, she thought. Frederick closed her door carefully, as if he were afraid of jarring her.

She leaned over and opened his door for him. The gesture on her part was natural, but when she was bent over, she realised her posture's potential. As Fred pulled the door farther open, she stayed in her position. She knew the interior light was illuminating her chest, making him think of the treasures that lay under the red satin and black lace of her corset.

Frederick got in as she slowly sat up, and Jael found herself in a close, intimate space with a man who was nearly a stranger to her. He closed his door after he had the key in the ignition. 'You look handsome tonight,' Jael made herself say. She looked over at Frederick. He shot her a quick smile, almost an apologetic one. But even though he was shy and skittish and bumbling, the atmosphere was sparked with his hot lust when he chanced the smallest look at her. Jael felt his masculine drive and pushed her tongue a little between her lips before she turned her head to look out the window.

'Thanks,' he finally said, as they made their way to Justine's entrance. He pulled out onto the highway and turned to take a back way home.

Should she come clean with him, since he obviously knew everything about Cole and her? Before Jael had a chance to make up her mind, Frederick cleared his throat.

'Jael?'

'Hmm?'

'You're a very beautiful young lady.'

'Thanks, Frederick.'

'No, really, I'm sure a lot of guys tell you that, but I mean it.'

'I'm sure you do. And actually, a lot of guys don't tell me that.'

'I'm really flattered to have the chance to take you home.'

Jael smiled. 'It's not that big a deal, Frederick. But thanks for offering to do it in such a gentlemanly way. I don't look too genteel myself tonight, I know.'

'You look... ravishing. Really, I mean it.'

Jael looked out her side window, then over at Frederick. 'Thanks,' she said. 'It's good to know I'm not the butt of a joke for everybody.'

'I take you very seriously, Jael. I don't know what's going on between you and Cole...'

'You have a pretty damned good idea.'

'All right, so I do. But whatever happened tonight with Cole doesn't mean anything to me.'

'But how did you happen to be there? You were with him, I assume.'

'I'm not at liberty to say, Jael.'

She frowned and stared at his profile, lit by the dashboard lights. 'Cole called you and told you to meet him at Justine's, didn't he? Did he let you know I was going to be there, too?'

'I knew you'd be there, yeah.'

She nodded and sighed. 'I can't believe he told me to come out here, and knew from the beginning he was going to dump me. On you.'

'You haven't been dumped on me. I would have volunteered for this. Especially after... that tape.' Jael cringed, and she knew Frederick felt her cold reaction, but he went on. 'I saw the tape, you know. I watch it a lot.'

'I really feel punished for doing that.'

'What do you mean?'

'I feel like I've been bullied and harassed about it since it happened.'

'Don't worry about it. I love it. Anna loves it. Cole loves it. Tom loved it, too.'

Jael heard the note of dark need slide into his voice as the conversation took this turn. This was the mood she had to have him in, she thought. She had to bring Thomas the semen-filled pussy he wanted.

'Which part did you like best?' she asked quietly.

'Oh, man,' Frederick said. He opened his hand over the steering wheel and ran the centre of his palm down the leather-encased curve. 'I like it when the two of you are completely on the couch, when she's on top of you, and I can see your whole body from the side.'

Jael made herself laugh softly. 'I thought you'd say that. That's my favourite part, too.'

'You've seen it, then?'

'Thomas showed it to me.'

'Did you like fucking Anna?'

Jael knew this was the moment to really turn it on. She steeled herself and forced the words to come out of her mouth. 'I'd like to do more dyke stuff with her.'

'What do you mean?'

'Well, riding cock is riding cock, isn't it? I would rather have her eat me, play with my tits, kiss… you know, lesbian stuff.'

'Mmm, I'd like to see that. How many times do you think you came while Anna was doing you?'

Jael giggled, disarmingly, she hoped. 'Oh, Frederick, I have no idea. Lots and lots. I lost count.'

'Have you ever thought about coming over and maybe using the strap-on? Being on the other end of things with her?'

Jael rotated her shoulders a little, rubbing her back against the seat. 'I don't know. That might be fun. I've never fucked like a man before.'

'You've fucked lots of men before, though, I bet.'

She looked over at him. 'Why do you ask?'

Frederick glanced at her and licked his lips. 'Do you like it from men as hard as Anna was giving it to you?'

She bit the inside of her lower lip before she answered.

'I like it rough, yes.'

'Man, Jael, you have to come over to see us. Anna just got a double-headed dildo for two women to buck on at once. I'd love it if you'd be the first one to try it out with her.'

Jael looked out at the dark night around them. They were on the outskirts of town. It was now or never.

'Hey, Frederick,' she said in a subdued, dusky tone.

'Hey, what?'

'I know you have to be as hard as a pipe right now. Would you want to have me?'

'God, Jael, I thought you'd never ask. Let me find a place...'

He stopped talking as she slid over close to him and nuzzled his neck. She had to get herself turned on. She kissed the side of his throat, then drew his earlobe between her lips and nibbled at it.

Fred's hand shot straight between her parted thighs. When his fingers touched her exposed pubic hair he groaned in deep satisfaction. 'No panties,' he said, as if to himself. He swivelled his elbow to slide his hand down the inside of her leg. He slipped his fingers into the top of her stockings, then pulled back up to go into her skirt again.

Jael lay down on her back, her head on his thigh, with her legs far apart. Frederick leaned to the side, towards her, and began rubbing at her briskly with two fingers. This was going to be worse than she'd figured, she thought, wrinkling her nose and closing her eyes as she lay under his outstretched arm. He was fixated on her crotch. And he wasn't very good at it. But she jerked her hips up and down and moaned in her throat.

Frederick pulled out from between her legs in order to use both hands to steer the Jeep down onto a dirt lane.

Jael sat up to see where they were going. 'Is this a park?' she asked.

'Yeah. Kids come here. It'll be all right.'

'Unless the police show.'

'Don't worry.' He stopped and turned off the ignition, and before Jael could question him, he hopped out. 'Open your door,' he said before closing his own.

Jael did as she was told and turned to sit facing out. Frederick hurried around the front of the Jeep and came to stand in front of her. 'I've always wanted to do this to you,' he said, in a voice low with longing.

She took a deep breath. The night air, wafting into the Jeep's cabin, was frigid. Jael folded her arms across her chest, in dismay once again with her clothing.

Come on, come on, she thought as Frederick fumbled with his trousers. How many times had he gotten that thing out before? She spread her knees and shut her eyes.

She heard Frederick unzip and the whisper his twills made as he pushed them down a bit. Jael reached down to stroke him, her knees around his hips. He ducked to put his head and shoulders in the Jeep, then reached towards her. He ran his thumbs over her exposed chest, then slipped his fingers down into the top of her corset to caress her breasts.

He then put one hand on the dash and the other on the back of her seat as his long torso leaned over her. Jael slid her free hand across his chest and under his jacket as she wrapped herself around his warmth. She stroked his erection with a firm grip and regular cadence, pulling the skin up over the head each time. Frederick bent his head to suck at her neck. He slipped his hands up the sides of her legs, over her fishnet stockings, and she lifted herself up as he squeezed his palms under her buttocks. She stroked his cock harder. The sooner she got this over with, the better. Jael closed her eyes to block out as much as she could.

Frederick tightened his fingers around her bottom and effortlessly pulled her to the edge of the seat. He pushed her miniskirt back. Jael lifted her hips again and Frederick slid the skirt up around her waist, then moved in close between her thighs.

Jael took the head of his rod and rubbed it against herself, trying to get wet so he at least wouldn't hurt her. His hard-on, rigid in her hand, parted her innermost lips wide. Greedily, she rubbed him against her swelling, trying to bring on the steady pain of sexual need.

But Frederick wasn't going to wait for her. He bent his knees to get the angles right, and reached to push his cock, with her hand still around it, down to her hole. He pulled his hands up over the bunched-up skirt, then slipped his palms down over it, onto her buttocks. The heels of his long hands were in the small of her back, pressing her towards him. Jael heaved herself upwards, Frederick pulled her close, and his cock split her open.

'Oh, *God…*' she groaned as the length of his greedy shaft jammed past her dry opening and into the moist interior.

'Oh,' Frederick grunted, shoving into her one last inch. Jael recoiled from the stretch and burn of his hard cock taking her.

'You're hurting me!' she whimpered.

'We'll manage,' Frederick answered in a lusty voice. 'Just shut up and let me fuck you.'

Jael moaned pitifully and dug her fingernails into his neck as he pulled his prick out, then drove it forward and pulled her close again. 'It doesn't hurt that bad,' Frederick whispered. 'Fuck me back. You'll soon get wet.'

Jael didn't know how to tell him that he nearly repulsed her, that she couldn't get excited for him, that her body wouldn't respond to him as it would to... Cole. But what about Cole? He had left her at Justine's, and he was the one who had put her in this painful predicament now. And Thomas. She just knew that Thomas was in on this whole thing. So the two of them, Cole and Thomas, had decided that Frederick was going to get a turn at her. Fine.

Recklessly, she grabbed Frederick's shirttails and yanked them up so there was nothing between their bodies. She leaned back and put her hands behind her, on the seat, and tilted her hips up. Her wide-open slit was completely available to him. With her thighs spread around his hips she felt his muscles, tensed and hard. She rubbed the top of her pussy against his wiry pubic hair. With the motion, she felt his long wide cock stir inside her.

'That's it, baby, enjoy it,' Fred moaned. 'You got me so hard. And I haven't even started ploughing into you.'

'Then fuck me,' she said. 'Fuck me hard.'

She wrapped her calves around his bottom, holding herself impaled on his staff. Frederick bent over her body, his hands still under her, and began driving.

The speed and power of his thrusts jarred Jael back and forth on his cock. But because he was so hungry to feel her pussy around his club, she guessed, he wouldn't pull himself out very far. He was holding himself in tight, jerking back and forth, forcing her to take his size.

'I'm coming,' he groaned. Jael opened her eyes and looked at his agonised expression. Frederick began circling his hips, grinding against her, and she knew he was going to jam a load into her, and not a moment too soon.

With a mighty heave, Frederick yanked himself out. 'I want this to last,' he mumbled.

'Mmm, I'm so glad,' Jael lied between gritted teeth.

'Get out of the car,' he said, backing away from her.

Jael slid off the edge of the seat and landed in the dirt in her high heels. Frederick swooped down and picked her up. She put her arm around his shoulders, feeling the smooth leather of his coat. He held her close. 'It's cold,' he said, glancing down at her. 'We'll do it out here, where we have some space, for just a little bit. Then we'll get back in the Jeep and do it some more.'

'Think you can last that long, tiger?'

'I know I can.' Frederick took a few steps away from the Jeep, into the trees alongside the dirt track. He put Jael back on her feet.

She turned to face him, and found that he'd pulled his trousers up a bit and was reaching into his pocket. He looked at her from under his eyebrows as he slowly pulled his hand out. She squinted through the darkness at what he held between two fingers.

'Is that a cock ring?' she asked.

Frederick grinned at her. 'It is.'

Jael smiled, trying desperately to pretend that this was all a fun game. 'I've never played with one of those before,' she said in a tone that was light, but obviously forced.

'First time for everything,' Frederick answered. 'Here's how it works.' He pushed his trousers and shorts down and got out his equipment. 'You open it like this,' he said, showing Jael. 'Then put it around my balls and the bottom of my dick. Here.' He handed it to her.

She took it and held it up into the starlight, inspecting it. It opened on a hinge and clicked shut. 'I suppose this is going to make you last and last?' she said, looking up into Frederick's eyes.

'Yeah, you bet.'

'All right.' She knelt in front of him, and as she manipulated the ring in the way he'd told her, Frederick ran his fingers back through her hair. 'You don't like this too much, do you, Jael?'

She looked up at him. 'I just hadn't planned on being with you tonight.'

He slipped his fingers under the elastic of her ponytail and tugged it, then picked up her loosened hair and dragged the band off the end. When her hair was free, Jael shook her head. Frederick buried his hands in her long tresses and pushed her face towards his stiff-standing cock.

'I don't know if I can do this,' she said. 'Letting you fuck me is one thing, but this...'

He didn't answer, but kept a steady pressure on the back of her head. Jael parted her lips and opened her jaw wide. His erection was flavoured with her salty seasoning, and she breathed in the aroma that had come from between her own legs as Frederick slid his shaft between her lips.

She moved her head back and forth, giving him a thorough mouth-fuck on all sides, at least as much as she could stomach to do. This was an intimate act, one that Jael had never performed casually. Frederick kept forcing himself back into her throat, and his attempts seemed to turn him on even more.

'Come on, get on me,' he said, as he backed away from her and sat on the ground. 'I want to see what you look like on top.'

Jael stood up and moved towards him. She realised he was going to make her do everything he possibly could – and the more she showed her distaste for him, the nastier

177

he was going to get.

To appease him, she reached back and unzipped her skirt. 'You'd might as well see all of me,' she said softly.

'I guess taking off those little clothes won't make much of a difference to you,' he muttered.

'No, but it'll make a lot of difference to you. And I aim to please.'

Frederick smiled at her and stroked his hard-on. Jael slipped the skirt down around her hips and stepped out of it, then dropped her lacy blouse off her shoulders. She looked down to see herself in only a corset, stockings, and spikes.

She glanced up at Frederick from under the veil created by her long, dark hair. 'Like what you see?' she asked, pouting.

'Very much,' he said. He lay back, and Jael knew he wanted her astride him. She walked the few paces to him and stepped over his recumbent body. Frederick was staring up at her, and Jael watched his eyes travel from her shoes, up her legs, to stop at her pussy. When his sights were locked on the target, Jael squatted down over his rod.

She reached down and gripped his penis. She knew her hole was already distended from taking him in the car, and she suspected her pussy had even managed to get wet by now. With one easy motion she docked his glans in her entrance. She pulled the skin of his cock back as tightly as she could and sat down on him until the sticky hair over her vulva met her fist.

Jael stretched out her other hand and put it on Frederick's chest. She leaned her weight on him and began pile-driving up and down, still with his cock skin stretched back tight by her grip. She wanted to get him off fast and put a stop to this. Frederick reached up and squeezed her upper arms. He groaned low in his throat, and Jael knew that her technique was giving him the perfect sensation.

It was time to take him in full and deep. She took her fist away as her pussy engulfed him, and she slid down until Frederick was lodged high in her cleft. His stomach muscles spasmed, and he sat up with a deep groan, then collapsed back. Jael was still squatting over him. She put both hands on his chest and began to bob up and down on his rigid mace.

The cock ring bumped against her clit every time she took him to the hilt. Jael ground down against him, turning her hips this way and that, rubbing her button against this new toy. The pleasures, she had to admit, were manifold. There was Frederick's rod of engorged but malleable flesh stuck up her, then the hard unforgiving ring against her. She threw her head back and took a deep breath of the frosty air. It felt so good, the nearly winter night on her shoulders and the glowing radiation between her legs.

Shutting her eyes tight, Jael could almost imagine that this was Cole's body spearing her. If only, if only, she chanted to herself as she bobbed up and down on Frederick's staff. Each grinding movement brought this man that much closer to his orgasm, and to giving her the evidence she needed to take to her husband and Master.

But Frederick grabbed her wrists roughly. As he crushed them Jael opened her eyes in shock and darted a glance down to his face. He was staring up at her. He was smug.

'Enjoying our ride?' he asked.

Jael broke her gaze from his eyes and looked down. 'Yes,' she said softly.

'This was fun, but I want to get back on top.' With that, he pulled Jael towards him by her wrists, and as she leaned forward, his penis slid from her crack.

He stood up and walked to the Jeep. Jael gathered her clothing from the ground and followed him. He got in the driver's side and started the engine in order to turn on the heater and blast it. Jael held her hands up into the front and rubbed them together gratefully. 'I didn't realise how chilly it is,' she said.

Frederick didn't answer. He got out of the Jeep, then immediately got in the back with her. She looked down at his lap. 'You're still rock hard,' she said.

'I know. But let's get your tits out of this corset. I want to feel you,' he said. Frederick pulled his jacket off, then unbuttoned the top of his dress shirt and yanked it over his head. He kicked off his boots and shimmied out of his trousers and underwear.

She reached down into her corset with one hand and pushed the bodice down until it was tucked under her breasts. Frederick watched her, his eyes flaming with passion. Jael dropped her hands onto her stocking-covered thighs and looked at him.

He leaned forward and took one of her succulent breasts in his mouth. His tongue circled her nipple and the bud tingled and stiffened, in spite of herself. She kept her hands in her lap as Frederick broadened his tongue and licked a trail across her chest to her other breast. He laved that nipple as well, then pulled his face back to look at her.

'Ready for more?' he asked.

She couldn't look at him. But she nodded and lay back on the seat. Frederick put one hand on her hip and slid her down until their genitals were rubbing. The head of his erection pushed against her aggressively. Jael slung her thighs over his and waited for his entry.

He rammed in. His body was stretched above hers. Jael looked at the ceiling of the Jeep over his shoulder, refusing to meet his eyes. He leaned down until he was completely on top of her, his arms around her body. Her breasts squashed against his chest, and he slammed into her over and over.

Jael felt only the driving strength of his body, no matter how she tried to disengage her mind. 'I'll fuck you till you're cross-eyed,' Frederick grunted.

Indeed, his relentless fucking made it feel like his cock was burrowing inside her to stay forever. Jael pushed her feet into the air over his bottom, until her heels hit the Jeep's ceiling, and dropped her legs open wide so he could get even deeper. 'You're so small,' he breathed, and reached back to take her ankles in his hands. Effortlessly, he placed her heels on his shoulders and crouched over her. She slipped her feet up around his neck, and Frederick put his hands on the tops of her thighs. Jael held her breath, taking the punishment that his bending and fucking caused. Then he dropped her legs back around his hips and began brutally scouring his ramrod in and out of her again. Jael did feel that he'd fucked her until she was cross-eyed – slack-jawed and cross-eyed. He was grunting and panting. She put her hands around his neck and felt the sweat run.

'Take the ring off,' she whispered.

'I want to fuck you all night.'

'No, Frederick, take it off. I want you to give me a big bellyful of spunk. I need to feel you come inside me.'

Now Jael was going to take Thomas the buttered bun he craved. The knowledge that she was able to do his bidding, to give him what he needed from her, choked her with satisfaction. She dropped her hand to her mouth and bit the back of it in order to keep her emotions in check.

Frederick didn't seem to notice her sudden upsurge of feeling. He was reaching back, working the cock ring. It opened and released his heavy bollocks and the root of his prick. He dropped it onto the floor and without further ado, stuffed his rod up her again. Jael began working her mound against him for his pleasure. He fucked her angrily, brutishly in return. The hard-on he had kept for so long was working to fire its burning load into her.

His face contorted suddenly, and he twisted sideways with a shout. Jael pulled her knees back, letting him pump the come out. Frederick butted into her a few more times, gasping and grimacing. She smiled. She had gotten him off well.

Frederick pulled out and collapsed on top of her. After a few moments he sat up and reached down to the floor to get his clothes. Jael did the same. They dressed in silence. Each of them got out of the backseat and into the front, and he backed up and got onto the road. They drove to Marlborough without talking.

Frederick turned into Jael's drive and coasted to the front door. She opened the Jeep door, and when the interior light came on, she looked over at him. 'Thanks for the ride.'

Frederick licked his lips. 'I meant what I said, Jael. Come on over and see Anna and me sometime. Now we've both had a taste of you, we'd like a full course.'

Jael looked away. She nodded, then glanced back at him. 'I'll have to ask Thomas,' she said.

Frederick looked closely at her. A slow smile broke across his face. 'Good,' he answered softly. 'That's a good idea. You do that.'

Jael got out of the Jeep slowly, and watched as he drove

away.

'I just balled Frederick,' she said quietly. The thought filled her with misery as she turned to go in, out of the cold.

Chapter Twelve

He'd given the dogs the run of the house so they'd let him know when Jael arrived. They both came padding in, tails wagging excitedly and thumping against the side of his desk and the bookcase. Thomas glanced at his watch. 'Eleven thirty,' he said. 'Quite late.'

He cleared his papers away and put his feet up on the desk, leaning back into the darkness of the office. He waited.

Jael came looking for him, as he knew she would. He heard her heels tap on the flagstones of the hall, and she appeared in the doorway.

'Put the dogs in their room,' he said in a low voice.

'Do they need to go out?'

'No.'

Jael made a clicking sound, and the two Setters turned like one red top to follow her. Thomas listened to the conservatory door open, then close after the sounds of their eight feet. Jael came back and resumed her place just inside the room.

'Is it running down your thighs?' he asked.

'Yes.'

'Come over here and get on the floor.'

Jael walked over to him, and Thomas watched her as she became visible in the dim light. Her eyeliner was smeared, the mascara had flaked onto her white cheeks, her lipstick was gone except for a tinge around her mouth. 'You look like you've been gang-banged,' he said. She knelt in front of him. 'Did you come?' he asked.

'No,' she whispered.

Thomas leaned forward quickly and his chair made a clunk as he put his feet on the floor, barely missing Jael's knees. He opened the long drawer of his desk and took out two clothespins. He placed them on the green blotter, then leaned back into his chair again. He gazed at her uncertain, degraded face before he spoke.

'And why not?'

Jael pulled both her lips into her mouth and bit them before she spoke. 'I don't think I like him.'

'You think you don't?'

'No, sir, I know I don't.'

Thomas opened the drawer again and put the clothespins away. Two big black binder clips came out in their place.

'I don't care whether you like him or not, really. But I want to know: why didn't you come?'

'I couldn't.'

Thomas leaned over to her and reached into her corset. He shoved the material down with the back of his hand and took out one of her breasts. He stroked her nipple with his thumb until it became firm. When it was tumid under his touch, he picked up one of the binders and flicked back its two metal arms. He pinched them together, and the clip opened. He held it down in front of her nipple and looked up into her big, blue eyes.

'You are not to act like a timid schoolgirl when you're supposed to be having fun. You are to use men. Like the slut you are. Use them. Now you'll wear these to the bedroom, then wait for me.' He put the binder on her nipple and slowly let it clamp shut.

Jael winced. She looked down at her breast. Thomas put the other one on her. 'How's it feel?' he asked.

'A steady, sure pain.'

'Go upstairs.'

She stood in front of him. He watched her back end sway when she turned around. Her hair was hanging down and tangled. She looked like a whore after a rough couple of tricks, he thought. Then he asked the question he knew she was waiting for and that would humiliate her, whatever her answer.

'Was it him?'

Jael stopped and put her hand on the doorframe. Without looking at him, she shook her head.

'Leave,' he said.

She walked up the stairs. Was he upset with her? she wondered in a panic. But she had fucked Frederick for him. Only for him.

Jael walked into the bedroom and stood in front of the dressing mirror. She was filled with disgust as she assessed the damage. Her red shoes were mud-splattered, and when she turned her foot to look at the heels, she saw that the dirt had gone halfway up each spike. The knees of her stockings were filthy and torn into gaping holes that made their way up the fronts of her thighs. Small pieces of dead grass were stuck in the fishnet on her shins. She touched the stockings' bands on the insides of her thighs and found that both of them were damp – with Frederick's spunk, she assumed.

The fake leather micro-mini was creased. Her tacky lace shirt was wrinkled and covered with specks of seeds. And her face. She looked at herself. She was altered. A hollowness gaped behind her eyes. That was because she was frightened by Thomas's reaction, she told herself. Not because of anything she'd done. But she couldn't deny the change. 'I don't know what's going on,' she admitted quietly. 'But something's happened.'

Thomas rounded the corner of the bedroom and saw Jael standing in front of the mirror, engrossed in her reflection. 'Take off your clamps. What are you thinking?'

She turned to face him as she took off the binder clips and handed them to him. 'You changed me.'

'I did nothing. I was here all night. You were out with another man.' Thomas took the clips and put them on the dresser.

'But it was at your bidding. I was able to fulfil your wishes tonight. I left here, dressed by your hand. I went to a place you chose and behaved the way you wanted. I came home in the condition you asked for. And when he shot his load inside me, Thomas, I was so happy that I was doing what you wanted, that I was bringing my body back to you as you wanted me. My own orgasms were nothing compared to what I felt when I realised that.'

He heard the note of desperation in her voice as she tried to come to terms with what had happened to her tonight. 'Look at yourself, Jael,' he said. 'Do you see what you're becoming?'

She turned and looked into the mirror. Thomas looked at her reflection, then at his own. The contrast between them as man and woman had never been greater.

'I'm becoming yours,' she answered in a low, humble tone. 'By following your commands, I'm becoming yours.'

'I'm creating you in the image I want.'

'I'm glad to become your creature. Whatever you desire, I want to be it.'

'You need to become this thing, Jael. You're the one who needed this, you're the reason I've taken charge of you like this.'

'My needs are disappearing, Thomas. I'm beginning

to feel as if I was born to do my Master's bidding.'

His expression softened as he looked at her serious little face in the mirror. 'I have something for you, my sweet,' he said. He reached into his pocket and pulled out a bundle of intertwined gold chains. She turned, and they both looked down at his outstretched palm. Jael began to pull them apart.

Thomas watched as she separated the three gifts. She held two, the longest and shortest, in her hands, and left the other with him. He motioned for her to turn around and look at herself again.

He unclasped the necklace and held it in front of her. She tilted her chin into the air, and Thomas placed it against her throat, then brought it back around her hair and fastened it. He pulled her hair over it and looked at the effect of the delicate gold against her white skin, and was pleased.

'Undress,' he said softly.

Jael put the chains over the posts that suspended the mirror between them and pulled off her blouse. The skirt fell, and she rolled the stockings down, stepped out of her shoes, and pulled the stockings off. She lifted up her hair when she'd righted herself, and Thomas untied the corset. 'You didn't take this off,' he said.

'No,' she answered. 'How do you know?'

'I laced it in a particular way,' he whispered, and put his fingers into the ties to loosen them. When it had relaxed around Jael's body, he pulled it up over her stretched arms and her head and dropped it onto the floor.

She stood naked before him. Thomas tilted his head and looked down at her back. There were thumbprints bruised into her bottom and the skin on the backs of her thighs. He looked at her front in the glass. Her knees were scraped and red.

'Was he hard on you?' Thomas asked.

'Yes.'

'He took you over and over.'

'Yes.'

'He did things to your body, Jael, but I own more than that. I own your soul. I own your will.'

'Yes.'

Thomas reached and took the longest chain from where it hung. He put it around her waist. He took the shortest one and bent down to put it around her left ankle. He stood behind her again.

'I just collared you, Jael. You are collared, possessed, owned. Everything you do, think, feel; it's all accountable to me. I encompass your body and mind. Do you understand?'

'Yes.'

'And, Jael, I thank you for letting me own you. Now bend over the bed.'

Jael walked to the bed proudly, ready to take whatever pain Thomas meted out to her. She was conscious of her used body, exploited by Frederick for his needs and Thomas for his. The knowledge that she could satisfy both of them so differently made her feel the value of her servitude.

She put the fronts of her thighs against the bed and bent until her chest was on the mattress. She spread her arms out and turned her face towards Thomas. He was standing at the foot of the bed, watching her.

Her eyes locked with his. 'Did he hit you?' Thomas asked.

'No.'

'That's my province,' he said.

'Beat me,' Jael whispered.

Thomas pulled his hand back and glanced his palm off

her bottom. It was a hard smack, one of the harshest he'd given her. Jael flinched as her body recoiled against the bed. Before she had a chance to recover, he hit her again. Jael gasped as the pain of her reddened bottom coursed through her. He hit her again, and she moaned. She heard the sound of him undoing his belt roughly, the hiss of it sliding out of the belt loops. She turned and looked back at him, and Thomas was wrapping the ends of the belt around his fist. A short loop extended from his grasp, and Jael clutched the soft duvet under her hands. She watched as he took a stance, legs at shoulder width, the hand he would use to strike her on the side he had turned away. His fist, encased in the belt's leather, had never looked so big.

Jael felt the wetness gel between her legs again, and her clitoris was buzzing. 'I need you,' she whispered.

Then Thomas thrashed her like a dog. His hand pulled back over and over, and the crack of the leather against her bare bottom and upper thighs sounded again and again. She screamed after the first two lashes stung into her flesh and the pain spread up her back like fire. At the third whipping she tossed her head wildly and set her jaw against screaming again. At the fourth strike she rose up and grabbed her breasts. She squeezed her nipples as hard as she could, torturing them, tormenting them the way Thomas abused her lower body. The fifth hit scorched her upper thighs, and she climbed up onto the bed, her bottom in the air, exposing her well-used pussy to Thomas. 'Please, please, fuck me,' she groaned. His answer was to beat her again. 'Make me bleed,' she moaned, and buried her face in the warm eiderdown.

Then nothing. She braced herself, waiting for a seventh stroke to finish her. But it didn't come. She stilled her sobbing breaths and listened. Thomas was still behind her. He was panting. Slowly, she lifted her head and looked at him over her shoulder.

His expression was bestial. Thomas was unleashed, animal, brutal and savage. 'Get out of here,' he growled, almost unintelligibly. 'Get away from me, Jael.'

She took him at his word and forced her legs, stiff with pain, to crawl the short distance across the bed. She managed to climb down by turning and resting her weight on her hip. Limping and lame, she staggered into the bathroom and shut the door tightly behind her.

Jael stood in the dark, her hands on the sink, staring down. Then she lifted her face to look at herself in the mirror. The weak light from the night sky outside made her look like a phantom. She leaned forwards, getting closer to her reflection, and stared into her own pain-ridden eyes.

She fumbled for the switch, and the bathroom was flooded by the lustre of the sconce lighting. Slowly, she turned before the mirror and hitched up her hip to get a good look at her backside.

The marks were in full bloom. She could see the evidence of each individual scourge Thomas had lavished on her. She was covered in stripes, and every single one still blistered with agony. The redness spread from the sides of each to join with the sharp redness that formed the boundary of the next. Her entire bottom was flowering in every shade of crimson.

A restrained, quiet knock sounded on the door. Jael bent her head low and turned to open it. She looked up at him. Thomas stood, his forearm on the wall outside, his head resting on his arm. His face was ashen.

'I reached my own limit, Jael,' he said softly.

'You didn't reach mine. I'd give you anything,' she answered.

'I know. We're both changing. Learning new things about ourselves... and each other.'

'I know. I like what I'm becoming, Thomas. But only with you over me.'

'But you still have something of your own that you need. You didn't get it yet.'

'Cole Trevor.'

'Yes. But I've decided. We're going to work our way up to that.'

Chapter Thirteen

Jael opened the door to get out of Lisa's car. 'Thanks for running me to the store,' Jael said. 'I appreciate it.'

'Don't mention it,' Lisa said. 'Anything special for tomorrow?'

Jael wrinkled her nose and thought for a moment. 'Yeah, can you make something vegetarian for dinner? I'm worried that Thomas is eating too much meat. I think he's living on fast food at work.'

Lisa laughed. 'Is he putting on weight?'

'No,' Jael answered, smiling at her housekeeper. 'But he gets this guilty look every time we pass a burger joint. Like he's lusting after his usual two all-beef patties and a shake.'

'Okay,' Lisa said. 'I'll whip up something.'

'You do that,' Jael said, and a grin far bigger than what was appropriate spread across her face. 'Right then,' she said, swinging her legs out and carrying her grocery sack with her. 'See you tomorrow.'

'Bye bye,' Lisa said.

Jael walked up to the house and let herself in the front door. She tossed her keys into the air and caught them and started whistling to herself.

The sound of voices stopped her. She furrowed her brow and glanced around, trying to make sense out of the murmurs. They seemed to be coming from the TV room.

Furtively, she put her bag of groceries on the floor and took a few steps through the sunroom to stand inside the doorway. She gasped and put her hand over her mouth when she heard Frederick's voice.

'I don't know, Tom. I don't think she's ready. She's still into some pretty simple stuff.'

'Her tastes got more Byzantine after she came home that night.'

'You guys have it backwards. Jael's not the problem. We know that, pretty much, she's ready for whatever he dishes out. The thing is, it doesn't seem that he'll go near her.' It was Anna's voice.

'He doesn't have to do anything elaborate. I'm not asking him to take part in her training. Just a good, simple romp in the hay would sort her out and let me get on with things.'

Frederick answered. 'But by handing her over to him, you are asking him to be part of the process.'

'And believe me,' Anna said. 'He knows that. He knows he has something that both of you want.'

'I didn't think he was going to mess around with her when I sent her to Justine's. That's why I told her to screw whoever she could find. He's enjoying the way he's found to dominate me through her, for Christ sake.'

'You're probably right about that,' Frederick said. 'And look how he told me to meet him and her there. And look how he brought the four of us together.'

Anna picked up his thought. 'He's orchestrating everything, and he loves it. There's no way he's going to put a stop to this entire scene by even touching Jael. Besides, whatever you say, Tom, I don't think she's ready for him. I have to agree with Frederick. I know you want him out of her system, but you have to take her degree of submission to you into account. I just don't think she's ready to take him on, even as part of her service to you. Something about her when she's around him... I don't know.'

'What are you saying?' Thomas asked.

'I respect you, Tom, I know you have a good relationship with her, and I think both of you believe he's part of the game the two of you are playing with each other. So don't take this the wrong way. But I just don't think Jael realises what's going on with her and Cole. And maybe that's why he won't give in. He can't trust himself with her. He feels something, too.'

'What do you mean, "he feels something, too"? That's ridiculous, Anna,' Thomas said.

'She's just saying, Tom, be careful,' Frederick said. 'You don't want to wreck things by pushing Jael too far too fast. Or by letting her run too far ahead.'

'She has to crawl before she can walk,' Anna said, and all three laughed.

'That's why I asked you two to come over this afternoon. I knew she was taking off with Lisa to run some errands, and I knew she was giving Lisa the rest of the afternoon off. So I figured we'd have some time to spend with her.'

Jael walked in angrily. 'What's going on?' she said. But her furore dissipated when she saw the arrangement of the room.

The furniture was in a semi-circle, all focussed on one new addition: an X-frame against the wall. A big black gym bag crouched next to the frame.

'Had a new decorator in, Jael,' Thomas said. 'Hope you like it.'

'What is that thing?' Jael asked, pointing feebly towards the X-frame.

'Horizontal and helpless is a bit of a cliché, my dear. We thought that you, vertical and helpless, would be a bit more fun.'

As if moving with one mind, the three stood and walked towards Jael. She stood fixed to the floor. Thomas went behind her and pulled her jacket off her shoulders and tossed it aside. Anna went to work on the buttons of her blouse, and Frederick knelt and tugged her tight leggings down. Thomas knelt behind her and lifted each of her feet in turn to take off her boots, and Frederick finished removing her trousers. Anna threw the blouse towards the jacket and slid her fingers into the band of Jael's G-string panties. She moved them down over Jael's hips for Frederick to take off.

'No bra?' Thomas asked. 'Not that you need it.'

'Shut up,' Jael said quietly. 'I want to know what's going on here.'

'Ooh, mouthy,' Anna said, grinning wickedly at Thomas. 'I thought you said her training was coming along very well.'

Jael heard Thomas sigh behind her. 'Don't be foolish, Anna. She's just a beast. It's fight or flight. She's not moving, so she has to come at us with whatever weapon she has.' He ran his hands down Jael's arms, then back up and onto her breasts. 'There's not much tooth or nail here, though, is there? Just soft smoothness, waiting to be used.'

'I see she wears her collars all the time,' Anna said, gesturing towards Jael's three chains.

'We're working on them as a communication tool,' Thomas said. 'Jael's felt very submissive lately. Ever since the night she got them, as a matter of fact, so she wears all three. She'll wear them in different combinations in order to let me know her state of subjugated mind.'

'I like it,' Anna said, nodding her approval. 'But you're right, Tom, she is waiting to be used. Let's get to work.'

Anna went to the black bag as Frederick and Thomas led Jael towards the X-frame. Jael stepped up to it, and they spread out her limbs and fastened her ankles and wrists to it.

Anna walked over, holding something pink. 'This will be fun,' she said, a note of pure joy in her voice. She held the jelly-like toy in front of Jael's face.

'What is it?' Jael asked in a guarded tone.

'A scorpion. With a sting in its tail, of course,' Anna said, giggling. 'This is going to be great.' She put the scorpion up against Jael's vulva and reached in with her other hand to spread Jael's lips around the plastic scorpion's body. Then Anna bent down and reached up behind Jael. She took the scorpion's tail in her fingers and gently slid it into Jael's anus.

Jael winced and struggled. 'Boy, she does hate that,' Anna said to Thomas. 'You were right.'

'Do they know everything, Tom?' Jael asked in a breathless panic.

'Pretty much, yup,' Thomas answered.

'I can't believe you'd tell—'

'Be quiet!' Anna snapped. 'We're here to play, not reason with you.' Anna pulled the scorpion's elastic around Jael's waist and tied its ends together. 'You won't know what hit you,' she said, then moved in close and pressed her lips against Jael's.

The full rose of Anna's fleshy mouth pitched Jael into a fever. She closed her eyes and ran her tongue along Anna's lips. Anna responded by grasping Jael's hair and pulling her head sideways to kiss her harder. Jael wrested her mouth away. 'Touch me,' she moaned.

Anna bent and picked up the scorpion's control that lay at Jael's feet. 'We'll all have our way with you before the day's out, Jael,' she said. 'We'll start with your pleasure, before we get our own.'

She walked a few paces away and sat down on the floor, looking up at Jael's bound body. Frederick joined Anna, and Thomas sat on her other side. Jael gazed at them. They were all dressed in their ordinary clothes, as if the other couple had just stopped by to say hello. Thomas looked amazingly like himself. He was composed, serene, the lord of the manor. But they all had a glint in their eye that was unlike anything Jael had ever seen on another human's face. And now, it confronted her three times: the expressions of people who were about to share her body in turns.

Anna turned on the scorpion with a twist of the dial on the control she held. It began vibrating against Jael's pussy. At first she wasn't sure what she felt. But as the sensations began to join – the scorpion's claws over her vulva, its body nestled against her moistness, its tail pushed into her bottom – she writhed a bit.

'Looks good,' Thomas said. 'Doesn't take long, either.'

'No, this is one of my favourites,' Anna said. 'I like using this on my girls. Of course, I learned about it from somebody else.'

'Who?' Thomas asked.

'Cole,' Anna said. She looked up into Jael's eyes with a cruel expression. 'He staked me out on my bed and used one on me.'

Jael looked away, and the stab of pain that went through her chest numbed the feeling between her legs. She yearned to stop her ears as Thomas's voice pressed on.

'What's he like in bed? What's his favourite position, for one thing?' he asked.

Anna handed Jael's control to Frederick. He cranked it up a notch. 'Cole Trevor,' Anna mused in a sexy voice. 'Cole Trevor likes anything where he's on top. But when he's on the bottom, he's actually pretty funny.' She threw her head back and laughed. 'He makes sure you know that he's not amused. I was on top, fucking like mad, rubbing the back of my vagina with that hot prick of his. I was almost screaming, it was so good.' Frederick turned the scorpion on still higher while Anna kept talking. 'But I looked down at him and there he was, his hands behind his head, stretched out, half-asleep. Then I noticed his bottom half wasn't into it either, so I looked back and his legs were straight out, relaxed. I started bouncing up and down harder, trying to get a reaction from him. He opened his eyes and said, "Anna, there's no need for that."'

Thomas laughed. 'I like my own way. I'm not happy until I'm completely on top, driving my cock in and out.'

Frederick passed the controls to Thomas. He glanced up at Jael, and she locked eyes with him, begging him tearfully not to do this, but all he did was turn the dial back to slow the vibrations down. 'Anything else we should know about Cole, Anna?'

'Mmm, his voice when he's telling you what to do. His voice is just the most sexy thing I've ever heard. So low, it rumbles right through you when he talks just above a whisper and tells you how much he likes your pussy.'

'I think Jael likes his voice,' Thomas said. 'She'd like it better if he were talking about her snatch, too.' He turned the dial and the scorpion hummed against her and in her.

'She might like something else he does, too. Cole and I tend to just fuck when we get together. We're both Dominants, so it could get tricky, otherwise. But there's one thing he loves that I enjoy doing because it pleases him so much.'

'What's that?' Thomas asked. He stood up and walked

towards Jael.

She looked at him through the tears that blurred her vision. 'Why?' she asked softly.

'Because you need to be broken,' he answered. He pushed his finger under the scorpion and felt her. Jael knew she was soaking and that the scorpion was teasing her towards orgasm in spite of – or maybe because of – the conversation going on in front of her. Thomas's finger slid along the slick of her pussy. He pulled it back out and licked it. 'Tell us more, Anna,' he said as he turned around and sat down again. He gave the controls to her.

Anna wound the dial back until the scorpion was nearly still. Then she turned it higher and higher as she spoke. 'Cole has one little kink that I'm fond of. He likes his woman to wear strings of long beads. You wear them to bed with him. He likes you to stand over him or kneel on the bed beside him and run them back and forth between your legs while he watches.'

Jael twisted and shut her eyes tight, wishing to make Anna's words go away. Images of Anna with Cole filled Jael's mind and hurt her. But the agitation of the scorpion against and inside her secret parts was too much. Thinking about Cole's body...

'Anna,' she gasped. 'What's he like? What's his body like?'

'Do you mean his cock?' Anna asked mischievously, winding the scorpion back down to a low whirr. 'Let's just say, Jael, that he's well up to the task. Any task you have in mind for him. He has a good, wide, sturdy cock. Meaty. Big balls that swing and slap against you. Feels nice when he's really pumping.'

Jael tried desperately to wriggle against the scorpion and make herself come as Anna blasted it back onto full speed. But Jael's arms and legs were too constricted by the X-frame to give her much free movement. Every time she bounced her bottom back against the framework the scorpion's tail dug into her, and the vibration there reached up just a little higher. Jael began pushing herself back and forth rhythmically, trying to get any relief while she thought about Cole between her thighs.

But the picture of him between Anna's legs stayed with her. Jael opened her eyes and glared at Anna, the woman who had seduced both her and Cole, but would do nothing to bring them together.

'I believe she's in some kind of frenzy,' Thomas said. Anna met Jael's challenge with a superior, distant look as she made the scorpion go quiet again.

'And I believe she's finished with my toy,' Anna said.

She stood and walked to Jael and yanked the elastic bind that held the scorpion to her. With another jerk, Anna pulled the scorpion's jagged tail from Jael's bottom, making Jael wince and bite her lower lip.

'Get her down, men,' Anna said. Thomas and Frederick unclasped Jael's hands and feet and caught her as she moved forward. With one shove Thomas had her on her hands and knees on the floor.

'Now let's have a guessing game,' Anna continued. 'Everybody, get your prick out.'

Jael turned and saw Thomas and Frederick getting undressed behind her. Anna was taking her clothes off as well, and she went over by the gym bag to do it. Jael turned her head away and found herself aching for the feel of cock. She'd had both the men, plus Anna's dildo, and she knew that any one of them would suffice right now to bring her the release she needed.

The three others seemed to be having a conference. Jael watched them whispering to each other. Anna was holding both Thomas's and Frederick's erections and was stroking them while she spoke softly.

The sight made Jael sick. 'Thomas,' she said. 'Thomas, please, don't…'

'What's the matter, Jael? It's all right for you to get off with my husband, but it's not all right for me to touch yours? That's hardly fair, is it? Or do you mean that you just want both of them for yourself right now? Is that it?' Anna bent down and pulled a wooden hairbrush out of the gym bag. 'I'm giving the orders today though, Jael, so there's no point in begging Thomas. And here are the rules for our new game. We're all going to take turns fucking you doggy-style, like the bitch in heat you are. We're going to touch you with only our cocks. You have to guess who's banging your box from behind, and every time you get it wrong, you get spanked with this.' Anna walked over and slapped the back of the hairbrush down onto Jael's backside. The brush whistled through the air before it bit into her skin, and Jael moaned. 'Now that you know what it feels like, you'll have a little incentive to guess correctly.'

'Or not,' Thomas said. 'Jael likes being beaten. She's learning to love pain.'

'Either way, we'll have a merry time,' Anna answered. Jael turned and watched Anna go back to the bag on the floor and pull out a blindfold and her strap-on. 'Your trusty old friend, Jael,' she said as she stepped into the harness. 'Frederick, go make sure this is on her quite firmly.' She tossed the black blindfold to her husband, and he moved over to Jael.

He bent down in front of her, and Jael looked up at his hard-on bobbing massively before her. 'I can't wait,' Frederick whispered to her. He put the blindfold over her eyes, then put his finger under her chin and tilted her face up towards him. 'You look beautiful in bondage,' he whispered.

'That's enough making love to her,' Anna said. 'Get back here.'

Jael heard Frederick walk around behind her, and suddenly she knew she was going to be gang-banged brutally. 'I don't want this,' she pleaded. 'I don't like this. Thomas, send them away. I'm not into this, being the punching bag for the three of you.'

'You heard Anna,' Thomas answered. 'No use in asking me to save you.'

Jael reached up to take the blindfold off, but a pair of strong hands grabbed her wrists. 'We're going to have to take turns holding her down,' Anna said. 'This gets more fun by the minute.'

'Thomas, no!' Jael cried, trying to pull her hands out of her captor's grip. 'This is wrong, it's all sick, I don't want it!'

Thomas's voice was close to her ear. 'Jael, if it's really too much, say "battle zone". That'll be your safeword, and that'll stop the proceedings. But why not give it a go first?'

Jael stilled to hear his reasonable tone, his articulate self-composure. 'Guide me through it, Thomas,' she whispered.

'Let's fuck,' Anna said.

Someone pushed Jael's thighs apart, and her captor put her hands flat on the floor on either side of her head, her elbows in the air.

Jael balanced her choice to opt out of this with the fact that Thomas obviously relished the idea of everybody doing it to her, one after the other. But he'd been standing over there, Anna masturbating him, as if that were perfectly ordinary and all right. And it wasn't all right; Jael didn't want him to do things with other women. The

203

agreement had never been that Thomas would do as he pleased, the agreement was that he would put her through her lewd paces.

A cock slid into her. Her train of thought was broken, and the choice of whether or not to start was now made for her. 'Uh,' she heard a man grunt as he slowly dragged his hard-on in and out of her. Must be Thomas or Frederick, she thought. Jael pushed her bottom up and back, but whoever it was eluded her attempt to get more contact. She flexed her vaginal muscles around the invading penis. 'Fuck me harder,' she moaned, trying to see by the style who it was. That didn't work either. The cock just slid back and forth, maddeningly controlled. She thought quickly. If it were Frederick he'd be banging away. It had to be Tom.

'Thomas,' she said quietly. 'It's Thomas.'

Jael heard the hairbrush cut through the air before it struck her. She yelped and jumped forward, but someone grabbed her hair and pulled back, keeping her in place.

'Wrong, it was Anna,' Anna's voice pronounced. 'I'm ashamed of you Jael, that you can't tell the difference between this plastic job and the real thing.'

'How do I know you're telling the truth?' Jael asked plaintively.

'Trust me,' Anna answered. 'Next?'

Her pussy received another shoving cock. 'Mmm,' Anna moaned. Jael couldn't concentrate on the body behind her for the sudden thought that Thomas was giving it to Anna somewhere in the room. 'I don't know... it's Frederick,' she said vehemently. Another smack shrieked through the air and landed on the other side of her bottom.

'Hit her again,' Thomas said, and another blow landed right where the first had. 'Now guess again,' he said.

'It has to be Thomas,' she said, shaking her head in

confusion. Another smack of the brush. 'Anna!' Jael cried out.

'Finally,' Anna said.

'I didn't know you were going to take more than one turn apiece,' Jael said, a sob in her voice that she couldn't control.

'We're going to do whatever we please, little girl,' Thomas said. 'Who's next?'

A third penis was up her slot. For some reason Jael was able to discern that this one was actually attached to a body. She felt sure this was Thomas or Frederick, and she aimed to find out just who for sure.

She began pumping her hips up and down, in time with the thrusts behind her. 'Oh,' she groaned. 'That feels so good.' Anna cleared her throat, and Jael tried to keep the smile from her face. That was a wife's warning to a husband, make no mistake about it. It was Frederick. She pushed back, lifting her chest just up off the carpeting. A pair of big hands landed on her hips, and she began grinding in little tight circles back against him. He went still, and she could tell he was trying to control himself and not give the game away. But she fucked on, intent on giving her other two plagues – Anna and Thomas – a real show.

Now she was banging back against Frederick. 'Never had me like this before, did you?' she goaded breathlessly. 'You didn't have a chance to take me from behind before I made you come.'

'Uh,' Frederick grunted.

'Get off her,' Anna warned.

Frederick slammed into Jael and sent her flat onto her chest in answer. He began driving like a piston, his body a machine behind her, and the shaft of his penis was well-oiled by her lubricant. She shoved her bottom up hard and high, giving him permission to pump in as deeply as he could. He recognised the signal, and she rocked back against him to stay close as he began ramming her with all his strength.

'Frederick!' Anna warned. But Jael knew he didn't hear anything but the pants of his own breathing, the wet squish of his penis slipping in and out of her hole, the slap of skin on skin.

Then he yanked himself from her. 'No!' Jael moaned, her mind reeling from the sudden loss of deep, deep pleasure. She felt the hot streaks of come as Frederick shot his load all over her bottom and lower back.

'Get the hell out of here,' Anna said angrily. She threw something at Frederick, and Jael assumed it was the strap-on from the object's obvious weight when it landed. 'Just get the hell out, Frederick. No more for you. I'll deal with you later.'

Jael listened as Frederick, still puffing from his orgasm, stood up and walked away. The rustle of his clothes told her he really was leaving. As his footsteps took him towards the door, Jael felt someone licking her backside.

She rotated her hips in wide, slow, sensuous circles as the tongue worked its way up onto her back. The blindfold came off, and Jael blinked. Thomas was standing in front of her. The licking went on. 'Mmm, Anna,' Jael moaned. 'Do that a little lower and more towards the middle.'

'No such luck, darling,' Anna said. 'I just wanted to get you in the mood for what's going to happen next.' Anna rocked back onto her knees and tugged at Jael to sit up, too. 'Put your legs out in front of you,' Anna purred. Jael did.

Thomas wrapped a length of cord around her ankles, and Anna grabbed her hands and tied her wrists together in front. Jael watched them. 'That's all?' she asked quietly when they both backed away.

'Oh, no blindfold, if that's what you mean,' Anna said. 'That's for me.'

She and Thomas moved in front of Jael, and Thomas slipped the blindfold over Anna's face. She stood there while he went to the gym bag and brought back a roll of duct tape and a utility knife. Deftly, he pulled off a length, cut it, and tore it off. He put that over Anna's mouth.

'Beautiful, don't you think?' he asked Jael, turning around and smiling at her. 'I love to see a woman in stages of helplessness.'

Jael didn't answer.

Thomas walked behind Anna and pulled her arms back, bending her elbows, and told her, 'Keep them like that.' He got a length of cord and wound it around her elbows. 'Now Jael, please pay attention,' he said, as if giving her instructions. He bent his head and lifted one of Anna's big breasts to his mouth. He sucked the nipple in between his lips with a slurp, and Anna threw her head back and moaned behind the gag. Jael turned her face away. Thomas let Anna's breast drop and said, 'Jael, I told you to watch.'

'I can't, Thomas. Battle zone. It's too much for me.'

'The hell it is. There's nothing even happening to you. It's happening to Anna.' Thomas laughed at her. 'You can't safeword for somebody else, Jael.'

'You have me tied here, forcing me to watch you with her. I can't.'

'But I just watched you get Frederick's rocks off. You seemed to enjoy that. I plan on enjoying myself with Anna's body. Now, if I catch you looking away again, Jael, I'm going to have to punish you. Don't make me do it.'

Jael looked back at him, and he cupped Anna's other

breast and suckled on it. Anna was clearly loving the effects on Jael as much as she was wallowing in the sensations of Thomas's mouth on her tits.

'Here, Anna,' Tom said when he left the other nipple alone. 'Turn a bit.' He guided her until she was fully facing his wife. 'I want Jael to take a good look at the kind of body I fantasise about.'

'Stop it, Tom,' Jael said.

'No, Jael, you like Fred's cock. Anybody knows that. And you can't think enough about Cole Trevor. This is what I think about.'

'I don't want you to think about her.'

'Just look, Jael.' He dragged his fingertips around Anna's nipples, then back and forth over one breast, then the other. 'Look at how having her arms pinned back like this makes her ribs expand. That, in turn, pushes her tits out. Makes them look even bigger, doesn't it? Juicier. Sexier. Pretty good for sliding a cock between, I'd say.'

Jael looked away.

'I told you not to even blink,' Thomas growled. 'Now you're in for it.' He paced to the gym bag, and Jael watched his rigid cock bounce with each step.

'You're that hard for her, aren't you?' she asked.

'Yes.' Thomas spat the word at Jael. He got a dog collar, lead, a black latex bra and a pair of black leather high-heeled pumps from the bag. He brought the articles to her and knelt down to put the collar around her neck. He snapped the lead to it and put its handle over his wrist before he untied her wrists and moved to free her ankles. He reached to grab the shoes and slipped each one over Jael's feet. When he was finished, she held her arms out in front of herself, trying to obey what she knew his orders would be. Thomas slapped her cheek when he saw. 'Don't ever assume,' he said in a low voice. She lowered her arms slowly. 'Now hold them out,' he said. She did so. He slipped the bra over her arms and fastened it in back.

'Now, heel,' he said, standing up and jerking the chain. Jael spun on her bottom to follow before he hurt her neck. She tried to stand, but Thomas caught her and shoved her down. 'Like the animal you are, bitch,' he said. 'Stay down where you belong.' Jael hung her head and crawled behind him.

Thomas took her in front of Anna. 'Sit,' he said. Jael sat back on her haunches. 'Now watch.' He handled Anna's breasts again, picking them both up, moaning at their weight in his hands, sucking one nipple, then the other, kissing down the sides of one into Anna's armpit before backtracking and doing the other. 'Cole no doubt enjoyed the same thing,' Thomas said after several minutes of his loving Anna's breasts had gone by.

'I don't care about Cole. I only want you,' Jael answered.

'Shut up, Jael. Don't say things we all know aren't true. I can truthfully say, though, that I don't care about Anna the way I care about you, Jael. I give you my cruelty.'

'I love your cruelty.'

He pushed her away with his foot, then spun and walked back to the gym bag. Jael had no choice but to crawl after him as quickly as she could. Thomas reached into the bag and took something out. When he turned towards her, she saw it was a rolled up newspaper.

Thomas beat her with it. He hit her back and bottom and thighs, over and over, punctuating his words. 'I'm sick of your noise,' he said. Jael whimpered. 'I can see I've been too easy with you,' he said as he dropped the newspaper and took a ball gag out of the bag. Jael looked up at him, pleading silently. 'Open that hole,' Thomas said, and she did. He slipped the ball into her mouth and buckled its delicate leather straps together at the back of her head. Thomas then paced back over to Anna, dragging Jael after him.

'Do you want to kiss Anna's nether lips?' he asked Jael.

She paused, but then nodded.

'Only if you sit up and beg for it.'

Jael rocked back and dangled her hands in front of her chest like a dog's loose paws. She opened her mouth and panted, staring up at Thomas with a sorrowful look.

'Go ahead, kiss her pussy,' he said. He jerked the chain to make Jael move towards Anna.

Jael stood on all fours and stretched her neck to press her lips against Anna's pubic hair. 'Would you like to see it better?' Thomas asked. Jael paused again, but nodded once more.

Thomas knelt down beside Jael and parted Anna's labia. Jael stared at the other woman's genitals. 'See how red she is? I think she wants to be fucked. And here's her button.' Thomas grabbed it between his finger and thumb. 'Mmm, I know she wants to be fucked now,' he said after a few seconds. He slid his fingers back over Anna's wet lips, and she bent her knees to give him clear access. He pulled his fingers out and showed them to Jael. 'See how wet she is? She needs it. Now, Jael, would you like to get even with Anna for all the squealing she's made you do?'

Jael nodded. Thomas stood up and walked behind Anna to untie her elbows. Gently, he took her arm and led her towards the sofa and had her sit down with her hips on the edge. Anna reclined on it and waited. Thomas picked up the strap-on and pulled Jael to her feet. He helped her put on the dildo before he led her over in front of Anna.

Thomas took the blindfold off Anna, then, and said, 'Go ahead Jael, have your way.'

Jael looked at Thomas, then back at Anna. She could only imagine how she looked herself. Jael glanced down at the high heels that completed her slave-wench ensemble. And she picked up one foot and placed it between Anna's legs.

'Oh, yes,' Thomas whispered. Jael leaned her weight into Anna's crotch and began moving her foot up and down. Thomas dropped Jael's lead and bent down quickly. He separated Anna's lips towards her vagina and took the spike of Jael's heel. Gently, he slid it into Anna. When he was finished, Jael began slipping the heel in and out of the prone woman in front of her.

She looked over at Thomas. He was stroking his cock at the sight. Jael put her hands on her hips and swayed back and forth, moving her shoulders provocatively as she fucked Anna with her foot. But Thomas wasn't looking at Jael. He only had eyes for her rival.

Jael was helpless when Thomas pushed her away and leaned over Anna. Anna's back arched and she moaned, and Jael knew that Thomas had penetrated her. She watched the way his hips and buttocks worked, his tight muscles, the way he pumped himself against this other woman.

'Oh,' Thomas groaned, panting. Anna's legs were spread as far as she could make them go, and from the way she grasped Thomas's bottom to pull him in, Jael could tell that Anna wanted him even deeper.

Jael was paralysed. There was her husband actively fucking another woman right in front of her. It didn't matter that Frederick did her, she thought, her breath catching in her throat with a sob; she was their plaything. Thomas was in control of that. He could have stopped

Frederick if he'd wanted to. But there was nothing she could do to stop this. Nothing.

Tears ran down her cheeks as Anna clawed at Thomas and bucked underneath him, trying to scream behind the duct tape that held her mouth shut.

Thomas seemed to sense that something was wrong. He stopped banging Anna so single-mindedly and spun his head to look at Jael. She put her hands up to the ball gag and tried to drag it from her mouth. Thomas pulled out of Anna and stood up, breathless from his efforts between her quivering thighs.

'Now, do you really feel like getting even?' he asked Jael, a little breathlessly. She nodded vigorously and stepped up.

'I have her good and wet for you,' Thomas said, getting behind Jael. Jael leaned over Anna, just as he had been, and took the big dildo in her hand. Staring down into Anna's gleaming, smug eyes, Jael jammed the fake prick in.

Thomas grabbed Jael's hips and began pressing against her. His hands were telling her how to work her hips like a man. Jael paid attention and found a tight, pounding rhythm with Thomas's help. Anna grabbed onto Jael's bottom, just as she'd grasped Thomas's, and arched her back and moaned. Jael lowered her head, watched the sweat trickling between her breasts and down into the latex, and humped like an animal.

Anna was working up to it, Jael could tell. Her legs were thrashing and kicking, she was moaning deep in her chest, her eyes were shut, her body was taut. Jael worked at her, making sure the dildo's length dragged against Anna's clit with every deep stroke.

'You coming?' Thomas panted. Anna tossed her head in answer and groaned behind the tape.

But just when Anna's fingers dug the hardest into Jael's flesh, Jael yanked the toy out of Anna's body, wrested her hips from Thomas's tight grip, raised her fist, and swung it through the air to backhand Anna.

Thomas caught her wrist. 'You little tramp!' he blurted furiously. He stuck his fingers down into her collar and dragged her away from Anna, yanking her hair as he did. Anna pulled the duct tape off her own mouth and glared at the pair.

'She needs lessons, Thomas,' Anna hissed. 'Bring her over here. I think I know how to give her one. We'll do the thing that seems to upset her the most.'

Thomas handed Anna the lead and sat down on the sofa. 'Get on the floor,' Anna said, jerking the lead for Jael to drop onto her hands and knees. When Jael was humbled before them, Anna sat down on Thomas, facing him. His cock was so stiff and solid, Anna just had to move her hips towards him to engulf his body with her own.

Jael hung her head, but Thomas reached down and grabbed her hair, pulling her face up.

'Watch this,' he said, his face covered with a sheen of sweat as he pushed his hips up underneath every downward stroke that Anna took.

Anna started to come quickly. She wrapped Jael's lead around both her fists and dragged her even closer. Jael was forced to kneel, then to lean her face down into Thomas's and Anna's joined genitals. With a scream of blissful suffering, Anna took her orgasm. She jerked Jael's lead over and over, and when Thomas groaned and grabbed her hair in one hand and Anna's thigh with the other, Jael knew that she was within inches of the place where he was pumping his spunk into another woman.

Anna rolled off Thomas, to recline next to him. She dragged Jael across his lap. 'Eat your dear Master out of me, Jael,' she ordered. Thomas undid the buckles that held the ball gag in Jael's mouth, and as soon as her tongue was free, Jael bent to work on Anna's steamy cleft, to reclaim Thomas from her body. She licked Anna's split, pushing her tongue into the vagina just enough to savour the bleach-like taste of Thomas's come as it flowed down towards her open mouth. Then she ran her tongue between Anna's wet vulva to her tumid clitoris. It was still fat and heavy with excitement. It ought to be easy enough to please her and maybe get a pardon, Jael thought. She used her palm to pull the dark hair up away from her target and took Anna's greedy clit between her lips.

Jael knew she had an agile little tongue, and she also knew how to make the delicate strokes against a woman that would drive her over the brink. Jael was sure of her ability to prod a woman towards rapture in a way that a rough ride on a cock didn't. Jael feasted on Anna like a glutton, groaning in her own chest, her low voice matching Anna's alto that was rising in volume as she greeted the climax that Jael treated her to.

Anna clutched the back of Jael's head, mashing Jael's face up against her pussy as she came. When she was finished, she rudely pushed Jael away.

But Jael was in a frenzy for sexual contact of her own. She hankered to give herself the heady delight of an orgasm, if no one else would. Jael rolled onto her back and reached down, eager to meet Thomas and Anna on the other side of this threesome. But Thomas stopped her. He kicked her hands away from herself, and before she could protest, he had her on her stomach and was tying her hands behind her back. He turned around and tied her ankles, then Jael felt him bend her knees and pull on the cord between her hands. He seemed to be tying all of her limbs together with another rope, and when he stood up and she was left on her stomach, bent like a bow, she gasped.

Anna had dressed in the time it had taken Thomas to truss Jael. The two of them walked around the room and gathered up the strewn toys and clothes, and Thomas pulled on his trousers. They paced out of the room together.

Jael lay on the floor, in pain. Her back was on the verge of spasm, and she felt unable to hold her neck like this for much longer. Just as she was ready to call for help, Thomas walked back into the room.

But he didn't move to untie her. Rather, he stood in front of her and folded his arms across his bare chest. 'You'll sleep on the floor at the foot of the bed tonight,' he said clearly. 'You made me look like a lenient and indulgent Master in front of Anna. And for your pains at being a badly behaved slave, you can give up hopes of meeting with your beloved Cole any time soon. You don't have the training that would let me trust you if I let you fulfil the kind of desire you have for him.'

Thomas bent down and untied her ropes. He dropped them on her back and walked away, leaving Jael to lie on her stomach in the middle of the floor, used, frustrated, debased, and filled with despair.

Chapter Fourteen

She heard Thomas walk into the room, and she slowly spun the chair around to face him.

'I looked everywhere for you!' he exclaimed. 'You heard me yelling for you. You even heard me set my briefcase inside this door, and you didn't answer!'

Jael shrugged and completed the entire turn, to wind up facing the computer again. Thomas walked up behind her and she knew from the way the chair tilted back that he had put his arms on the back of it.

'What you doing?' he asked playfully.

Jael moved the mouse and clicked to go to the next link. 'Nothing,' she mumbled.

'Sweetheart, I need to talk to you.'

'All right, Thomas, talk.'

'We're hosting the poker game tonight.'

A thrill went through her, but it was short-lived, by her own choice. She stamped it down, swallowed it, made herself take a normal breath, and said nothing.

'Jael, turn around and look at me.' Thomas stood up straight and gave the chair a push. Jael let it spin around and looked up at him.

'When was the last time you worked?'

'I don't know. Don't worry about it, it's my sculpture.'

'I do worry about it. I can't help it. Every day, you're moping around...'

'I'm not moping.'

'All right, you're hanging around the house. Doing nothing. I ask Lisa, she says you do nothing the entire

216

time she's here. I went to the barn, looking for you, and I'm concerned. That sculpture is to be in those gardens on the first day of spring. You're no further on it than you were two months ago. Have you hit some kind of a block? Do you need to talk to somebody?'

'I don't need any help from *you*,' Jael said, unfolding her legs and putting one foot on the floor to push herself towards the computer again. Thomas stopped her.

'Why did you emphasise that last word? As if to say that I, especially, am the person who's causing you trouble. Jael, I told you to look at me.'

She looked up at him defiantly. But the care in his lively blue eyes was real. 'Your eyes are the same colour as a gas flame's right now,' she said insolently.

'It's because you have me worked up. You know how I get over you. You got like this before, Jael, you couldn't do anything, and then you went and talked to that doctor, and everything was fine, you were able to work. Maybe the same treatment is in order.'

'No, it's not. It's not the same problem.'

'Then what's the problem?'

She stared up at him.

'Is it Cole Trevor?' he asked quietly. She looked down and nodded her head.

'Can you put it into words?'

At that request, Jael hid her face in her hands and shook. She felt her shoulders quaking, but she dammed the tears. She dropped her hands, but stared at her lap as she spoke. 'I feel like I'm dying of starvation. The longer I go without him, the weaker I am. I see him everywhere. I hear his voice. I'm afraid that I'm actually going out of my mind.'

Thomas took a deep breath. 'Maybe we'll just have him over tonight.'

'What do you mean?'

'We can play a few good hands together, just the three of us.'

Jael gaped at him, then turned her face away, not wanting him to see the reaction that she knew was budding in her soul. 'Thomas, won't you be upset at seeing me while I want him?'

'I'll find a way for you to be with him, but it's going to rely on you. All right?'

Jael bent her head. 'I'll do anything you say.'

Thomas grunted. 'Maybe. Now let me call him.'

He walked around to his desk and picked up the phone. He stared at Jael as he hit one of the speed-dial numbers. In a moment, he said, 'Cole? This is Tom Alistair. Hope I'm not catching you at a bad time... Hey, how about some poker...? I thought it could be just the three of us... You, me, and Jael... Eight o'clock... See you then.'

Jael's face remained impassive throughout the short discussion. When Thomas hung up he continued looking at her, as if he were waiting for some indication of deep emotion from her, some sign of what was to come.

But Jael kept herself to herself.

'Go upstairs. Get dressed. I want you in that pair of off-white drawstring trousers...' Jael's eyes widened, and she knew that Thomas read her expression of trauma and dismay. 'Don't sass me, Jael, and don't point out how awful they are. I know damned well they're the nastiest things you have. God, they look terrible on you, Jael. Whatever made you buy them?'

'They were on a discount rack for two dollars. I only use them for work...'

'Nonsense, I've seen you wear them in public.'

'Only the art store, where I know everybody...'

Thomas held up his hand. 'It's all neither here nor there. Let us not get distracted. A shirt – what can you wear for a shirt? That's tough. Any shirt that's on you is near your face, and that makes it ten times prettier than it really is.' He smiled at Jael, and she smiled back demurely. 'And off-white is hard to mismatch. Oh, I have it!' Thomas clapped his hands once and grinned at her. 'Wear that sort of sandy, stone-grey waistcoat.'

'No way, Tom, that combination is too ugly for words.'

'Jael,' Thomas said, suddenly looking very seriously, 'I said what I want. That's all there is to it.'

Jael bent her head and remembered that she still wore all three gold chains. 'Yes, sir,' she whispered, before she stood and headed upstairs.

'No shoes, no socks,' he shouted up after her. 'No bra, no panties. Pull your hair up off your neck, pile it on top of your head. Make it look pretty. But no make up.'

He met her in the bedroom as she was getting dressed. 'Wait on the bench on the landing.'

'Yes,' she said softly.

When she was finished doing her hair, she walked out to the bench and sat down. She wasn't wearing a watch, so it was hard to tell how much time was passing – or wasn't passing, as it felt to Jael. She didn't know where Thomas was after he went by from lighting the fire in the library. But then, she heard the doorbell.

'It's him,' she whispered to herself. 'He's here.' She strained to hear them. Their voices were coming closer. She sat silently, hardly daring to breathe. They walked by the bottom of the staircase, and she watched them go into the library together. She heard Thomas ask Cole what he wanted to drink, and was pleased that Cole chose brandy. But their voices died down to a murmur when, as she imagined, they went to sit in front of the fireplace.

After a trying period for Jael, Cole emerged from the library. Thomas came after him and walked up the hall to the side door in order to call the dogs. Jael watched Cole saunter to the foot of the stairs. He looked up and smiled at her.

'Come downstairs and say hello to me, baby,' he said in his full, resonant voice. She was startled to hear a term of endearment for her fall from his lips. He held out his hand to her.

'Thomas told me to wait, and I'll wait until he says I can join you,' she said. Cole nodded, seeming to understand everything about her statement, and strolled off down the hall. Jael leaned over, craning her neck, taking in as much of him as she could before he disappeared from view. When he was gone she leaned back. She congratulated herself. She was doing as she'd been told. The knowledge felt good to her.

When she looked to the bottom of the stairs again, Thomas was standing there. He smiled up at her like a rascal. 'I see you suffering,' he said in low tones. 'Why don't you come down and cater for us?'

Jael stood boldly and marched down the stairs. Thomas walked before her, and she followed on bare feet. When they were in the kitchen, she moved quickly and skilfully to take food from the refrigerator and prepare it for the two men in her life. Thomas brushed past her, his chest making excruciatingly close contact with her back, as he got a bottle of fine wine from the rack and opened it. Jael sliced the cheese and fruit, put it on a serving board with a variety of crackers, and placed the morsels gently on the table for Cole and Thomas before she stepped back to await her next instructions.

Cole, sitting in his standard place, looked at her, his eyes glowing like the cinders he had just walked away from in the fireplace. 'Have some wine with us, beautiful,' he said.

A tremor went through her when he addressed her with sweet words. To hide her response, she looked to Thomas for permission. He nodded his accord. 'Thank you, Thomas. Thank you, Cole,' she said, and moved to pour herself a glass.

'Sit down, Jael,' Thomas said as she took her first sip. 'It's only the three of us tonight. Loosen up, have some fun.'

'I'd rather not,' she said softly.

But both men's backs stiffened, and austere, unyielding expressions crossed their faces. Jael felt confused and flustered, not quite sure of how to explain that she felt bad in front of them because of her appearance. 'I... I don't really want you to... to look at me,' she stammered. 'I look wrong... these clothes... no make up.'

'Is that all?' Cole asked, unwinding into the indulgent attitude he'd had since she first saw him tonight. 'Maybe you'd feel better if you weren't wearing those clothes. Maybe you'd feel better in nothing. Take your clothes off.'

Jael looked to Thomas as coolly as she could. But she knew he would read the agitation, excitement and fright in her eyes.

Thomas grinned at her. 'Cole has a good idea. Take them off.'

She stood and began unbuttoning her top. She glanced at each of them, trailing her gaze back and forth. They were watchful, as if waiting for her to do something that would require their tough-minded intervention. She turned and draped the waistcoat over the back of her chair, then tugged loose the knot in the drawstring of her trousers. Cole leaned forward in his chair, and when Jael looked at him, she saw that his voracious eyes were centred on her crotch. She pulled the waist of the trousers loose and pushed them down around her hips. They fell to the floor, and she watched them because she didn't want to look at Cole as he appraised her body. Jael had always been sure of herself, in her quiet way, sure her body was the sort men liked to have in their arms. But since Thomas had started teasing her and comparing her unfavourably to Anna over these past weeks, Jael's confidence in the lure of her petite build had dwindled.

But Cole restored that faith. When, still gazing at the floor, she stepped out of the trousers and pushed them away with her foot, she heard Cole exhale heavily. She looked up to find that his very soul was insatiable for the sight of her. She looked at Thomas victoriously, and was quite content to see that he was watching Cole's reaction, as well.

Cole's voice cracked when he spoke. 'She should be shaved, Tom.'

'Maybe if things go your way, she can be all yours to shave later,' Thomas answered.

Cole smiled. 'Maybe.'

Jael felt a blush creeping over her chest and up into her face as they talked about her. She tried to focus on anything except her own nudity, so Cole's sudden movement when he stood and stepped towards her made her flinch. He smiled down at her and raised his hand slowly. He brushed her cheek with his fingertips. 'Never feel bad at giving me pleasure, Jael,' he said in a voice just above a whisper. She blossomed under his touch, but didn't meet his eye.

Cole lifted his chin and gazed down at her face. He took her chin in his fingers and tilted her head different ways in the bright kitchen lights. 'Look me in the eye,' he breathed. She did.

'Tom, I like the gentle flower look about her. I like her

222

coyness, too. Very, very pretty. Very ladylike. Refined woman. But she'll have to be a little bolder if she's under my control.'

Jael let a flash of the lust she felt for him flood her eyes, and she stared him down, smiling a lurid, bawdy invitation of a smile. 'Very good,' Cole said softly. 'I like a little bit of raunchiness in my slave.' He took his hand away from her face. 'Do you want to belong to me?'

Jael nodded and whispered, 'Yes.'

Cole nodded absentmindedly and began his inspection. He pushed her away from the table and walked around her. 'Beautiful hair,' he said, brushing it with his palm. 'Always looks good. Glossy, long. Good reins, I bet.'

Her libido ignited. Jael felt faint with not just a desire for his body to be in hers, but a need for him to take possession of her. A hot itch travelled down her spine from Cole's hand and landed heavily in her clitoris. She throbbed for him.

He caressed her neck, and he groaned a bit and lingered with his hands around her throat. Then he descended to her shoulders and squeezed them. Jael felt her fragile collarbones constricted by his tight grasp. He dug his thumbs into her shoulder blades, as if feeling to see how much fat was on her bones. As his palms slid down her upper arms and squeezed, Jael had to exercise every control over every muscle in her body to stop herself from leaning back and falling into his arms.

Cole slid his fingertips up the sides of her breasts. She gasped. His fingers walked across her flesh and squeezed her nipples. He crushed them rhythmically and hard, and Jael whispered, 'Oh, God, yes.' She couldn't help but push her bottom towards him. Cole pushed his hips against her once, then slid his hands down onto her stomach and pulled her back against him roughly.

Jael bent over, grasping the tabletop. And she looked up at Thomas as she prepared to be taken by Cole Trevor's hard cock.

Thomas leaned back in his chair. He held his glass of wine in both hands, and his hands were resting on his lower stomach. His posture was that of a man completely at ease with everything in the world. But his eyes were dark, his jaw was set, and Jael knew from the barely discernible look on his face that he did not want things to happen like this.

She stood up. 'Very good,' Cole said. She realised she had just been tested, and the idea that the two men were in league to take her to a certain point and strand her there alone mortified her. Cole left her no time to think, however. He pushed her shoulders to make her bend down again. She held onto the table in the same way, but this time he pushed two fingers into her bottom.

She sprang forward, trying to get him away from her. 'I like it up the ass, Jael,' he said calmly. 'I understand that you're not enamoured with that, so if I get hold of you, that's all I'm going to do until you learn to treat me right.' He jammed his fingers up farther.

Jael nodded frantically and said, 'You can do anything to me.'

Cole laughed as he pulled his fingers back and shoved them up again, making her feel sick. 'I know I can do anything to you,' he said. 'That's why I'm here.' He finger-fucked her bottom some more.

Jael hung her head down low between her shoulders and bit her lower lip. She hated this. Could he be serious; this was all he'd do to her? But an impulse crossed her mind. She lifted her head and arched her back and began working herself on his hand.

'That's it... that's right,' Cole whispered. 'Learn to love it.' Jael bent her knees to keep her balance and reached back with both hands to separate the cheeks of her backside. She gyrated her hips and found that the longer she encouraged Cole and helped him to befoul her like this, the more she liked it.

He pulled his fingers out of her and walked to the sink. He washed his hands slowly, standing there for several minutes, working over each finger, the backs of his hands, his palms. He dried them very conscientiously on a paper towel before he turned back towards the table where Jael stood and Thomas sat. 'All right,' he said. 'Let's get to it.'

And Jael understood. The poker game was going to be for her. She was the wager.

'I'm still her owner,' Thomas said as Cole sat down. 'I want to make things more interesting. We'll include her.'

'All right, what do you want to do?' Cole asked.

'I want her to play the first hand with us. If she wins, she can choose immediately whether or not you can play for her. If I win, I make the decision about whether or not it goes on. If you win, Cole...'

'I take possession immediately,' Cole interrupted.

'All right,' Thomas said. 'Fair enough.'

Cole pressed on. 'If I win this first hand, I get to determine the circumstances where I take her. In other words, I take immediate possession, but maybe not immediate use.'

Thomas squinted at Cole. 'All right, agreed.'

'I don't like it,' Jael began.

Cole spun to look at her. 'Shut up.' He looked at Thomas. 'If that's all the better she's trained...'

'You wanted her to be bolder, not I,' Thomas said, smiling shrewdly.

Cole looked at Jael. 'You'll be bold in my hands, between us – not in front of anybody else. At least not until I have you trained to my specifications. And never, never by running your mouth.'

Jael bowed her head, then looked up at Cole. Her appetite was whetted. Cole seemed to sense it. He moved towards her and took her face in his hands. She looked up at him, and he ran his tongue along her lips. Jael pushed the tip of her tongue out to meet him, and he tasted like wine.

'All is forgiven,' Cole murmured. 'Let's play.'

Thomas took the cards from the side of the table and dealt them as Cole and Jael sat. Jael kept glancing at Cole, barely able to take her eyes off him. She could be his, she thought, and she knew there would be a wet streak on the oak chair when she stood up. She could be his tonight.

They each figured their hands and discarded. Thomas dealt out the new cards. Jael laid down her hand. Three kings, and she won.

'I want Cole to play for me,' she said without hesitation.

Thomas dealt again. He won when the hand was finished. He looked at Jael as he made his decision, and she made sure he saw her desperation writ plain. 'I've spent some time on her,' he mused aloud.

'There'll be others,' Cole said.

Thomas looked at her again, and Jael saw that he would acquiesce to what he knew she wanted. 'You can play for her, Cole, if we agree that at some later date, I can play a hand or two to win her back, should you take both possession and use tonight.'

'Fine.'

Thomas dealt. Lady Luck smiled on Cole.

'One last hand,' he said. 'If Tom or I win it, things

could go any which way. If Tom changes his mind, that is. I guess if Jael wins it,' he continued, nodding at her, 'we just keep going because her choice doesn't matter.'

Thomas began shuffling the cards again. While Thomas was looking at the deck fluttering through his fingers, Cole leaned towards Jael and reached for her leg under the table. She saw his motions and put her knee within his reach. Cole slid his chair closer to her and tickled his fingertips up the inside of her thigh. Jael parted her legs and began panting harder the higher he went.

'One minute, Tom,' Cole said. 'Just in case I lose this next hand to you, I want to do something.'

Thomas smiled thinly at Jael. 'You might get an itch scratched,' he said. 'Go ahead, Cole.'

Cole stood and walked around her, to lean on the back of her chair with one hand. 'Put your feet up on the table and spread your legs,' he said. Jael obeyed. He reached down over her torso and pushed his fingers right between her soaked pussy lips. Cole began rubbing, and Jael melted into the sensation of him giving her pleasure. 'She gets really wet, doesn't she?' Cole said in a strained voice. Thomas didn't answer.

Jael couldn't take it. She grabbed Cole's wrist and began guiding his hand, plunging his fingers in and out of herself, moving him all over her heat. She threw her head back to rest against him. 'Oh, please,' she moaned, nearly crying. 'I need you.'

Cole laughed harshly. 'Greedy for it, too.'

Jael's head snapped up and her eyes opened at his caustic words. Thomas was staring at her. But Cole was still rubbing, concentrating on her clit, finding the hard button inside the folds of flesh and flicking it with the tip of his middle finger. Jael's eyes rolled back, and she could feel herself losing contact with the world.

227

A loud click next to her ear brought her around. She looked down, and sucked in her air when she saw the blade of a knife against her, with Cole's fist around its hilt. His other hand still masturbated her, still fed a steady line of pleasure into her pussy without ceasing. But Jael couldn't take her eyes off the knife. Cole turned the flat of the blade against her skin and traced up her stomach and between her breasts with it. Jael felt herself break into a sweat, and she dared not look at Thomas to see his reaction to this game. There were no rules suddenly, nothing that she or her husband had even considered, Jael knew. This was uncharted territory, and Cole was pushing her into a deep, dark forest of desire.

He turned the blade and ran its sharpened edge along her throat. 'Do you have dark fantasies, Jael?' he whispered in her ear.

'Yes. Yes,' she answered in a choked voice.

'Am I in them?'

'You are them.'

'Could I have power over you?'

'You have power over me.'

'I want to do everything to you, but the one final thing, Jael.'

'I want you to.' Jael gasped and sobbed, and her mind spun out of control as the knife dragged against her. How did he know? How did he know the dreams she had that she wouldn't even think about, wouldn't admit to anybody? How did he know her?

Cole's voice was directed at Thomas next, as Jael quivered and shook, her eyes shut against a deep, blood-crimson colour that had washed over her in the fright with which Cole Trevor was confronting her.

'Is she this way for you?' Cole asked.

'I told you she wanted you.'

228

'Anna and Fred told me she was gagging for it, too. But the way everybody talked, she just wanted to slide on my pole. Interesting, but not like this. Nobody said she already gave herself to me.'

Jael felt his breath on her face and opened her eyes to see him staring down at her. When she looked into his wolf-grey eyes, the orgasm closed in. Without breaking the stare, Cole ran the blade down her chest and around one nipple, and Jael exploded. She pulled her legs back and closed them around his hand, working her mound against his fingers. He had made her come with the slightest touch, with mere brushes of his skin on hers.

She fell back to earth. Cole pulled her head back by her hair and kissed her. He ran his tongue along her teeth, then pulled his mouth away and ran the point of the knife over her lips. 'I want you to come at the sound of my voice,' he growled. 'I'll train you until the knowledge that I'm in a room with you makes you crumble inside, then detonate.'

Jael gazed into his eyes and let everything she felt run from her mind to his. 'That means I'll have to love you.'

Cole stood up abruptly and clicked the switchblade back together to put it in his pocket. He sat down in his chair and stared at her. 'Look at yourself,' he said, gesturing towards her feet, still up on the table, and looking point-blank down at her exposed pussy. 'Look at the way you behave in front of your husband. I don't own you yet, Jael. And Tom, I'll tell you, I don't think I want a slave who can give herself to someone else while she's in training with me.'

Jael answered. 'I would never have to give myself to anyone else if you had me.'

'Look at me,' Cole said.

She gazed into his eyes.

'I never want you to love me. You must never love me.'

Jael's eyes filled with tears, and she put her hand to her mouth to stifle the cry that rose through her chest.

Cole watched her impassively. 'All right, Tom, let's play the last hand.'

Stoically, Tom dealt. Jael didn't bother to look at her cards. She pulled her feet off the table and folded herself up as small as possible in the chair, her arms across her stomach, bent double in the pain that Cole had just stabbed through her. How could she not love him? She loved him; she'd always loved him. She put her forehead down on the table and cried.

From Thomas's groan, Jael knew that Cole had won. Cole threw himself back in his chair, and Jael raised her face to implore him to help her. Before she could speak, though, he said, 'I do take possession. But I don't take use. I don't want her, really. Since she's already given herself to me, this presents something of a problem for you two. But a slave can serve only one Master, and right now Jael seems to be serving herself, throwing her emotions and ownership of herself wherever the fancy takes her. Like I said, though, I take possession, meaning I have the right to come over and use her whenever it's convenient for you and me, Tom.'

'You're hurting her,' Thomas said. The brusque tone of his voice belied the care Jael knew he felt for her.

'Those are the terms we agreed to. I'd take possession, leaving myself the option of not taking immediate use.'

Thomas shrugged. 'If you want it that way, fine.'

'Maybe I'll take complete possession of her later. She needs some problems worked on now, and they're not the kind I enjoy ironing out.'

'I resent that.'

'You probably do, but this is your first slave, and I guess you love her. You let her have her own mind about certain things. She hasn't given up her own desire; you haven't broken her. In fact, you fuelled it by pandering to her over me.' Cole looked at Jael. 'I may never take use of you. And you're the only one who can free yourself of being possessed by me. You're wearing Thomas's chains, I see. Remember who put those on you, and think more about his desires than your own.'

Cole left.

Chapter Fifteen

Jael sat before the fire. The dogs were stretched at her feet, lolling with each other and impervious to her torment. She'd walked them long and far tonight, under a moon that was wholly waned. The darkness, Jael thought, would help her to find herself. The physical exertion should have brought her some peace of mind, too. But now, back in the house, she felt cramped and idle and restless. Her gin and tonic balanced on the arm of the chair, and she bounced her knee up and down in agitation.

It had been days. Days since he'd been there. She hadn't slept in the same bed as Thomas since then. How could she lie with one man when another one owned her? She took a long draught of the sour drink, one that she didn't even like, and hoped that some kind of hazy relief would greet her at the bottom of the 37.5-proof glass.

Ah, but Cole was right, she admitted to herself angrily. The rotten bastard was right; she wasn't thinking about Thomas. She never realised – oh, God help her – but she really never realised that he had desires other than her. Seeing him with Anna was a short sharp shock. That's how wrapped up with herself she'd been. She wasn't even that much into Cole, not at that point. She was into herself and what she wanted. Her jealousy over Cole having a girlfriend, her jealousy over Tom being attracted to Anna. What was she thinking, that they were all supposed to let her run amok while everybody else behaved like vanilla, middle-class sorts at a Rotary meeting?

She stood up and threw the rest of the drink into the fire and watched the flames leap to destroy it. She still throbbed and ached when she thought about Cole Trevor. But all she ever wanted from him, really, was an orgasm. He gave her one. So let him go. He didn't have possession of her from now on. With that spasm, that night, he left her system. She'd go and ask Thomas what he wants. She'd give her consciousness over to him.

With that thought, Jael paced out of the room and went upstairs. Thomas was lying on his back in bed, but she could tell he was awake. Jael took off her clothes and walked towards her husband. Thomas spoke before she could.

'If you want to remove my chains, go ahead.'

'I don't want that. I only want what you want.'

'So you don't have any desire for him any more? Come on, Jael, but forgive me if I can't believe that.'

'No, Thomas, I don't want him. When we began this journey together, we did it because you thought that if I were to satisfy myself where Cole's concerned, while under your command, the desire would go away. Obeying you and doing what you wanted was supposed to be something between us, Thomas, something for us... not the ruin of us.'

He didn't answer, but she could tell from his stilled breathing that he was listening carefully to every word she said.

'Tom, taking off your chains now would change everything we have. I don't want to do that, not after the way we've become closer and mean more to each other through sharing my submission to you. Cole Trevor can't change what you and I have, not by taking possession of me. I rid myself tonight of him.'

'Get into bed,' Thomas whispered.

Jael crawled in beside him and clung to his long-familiar, well-loved warmth. He put his arms around her and kissed her forehead. 'You've been on quite a journey by yourself, my love,' he said. 'And it's not over yet. I want Cole to use you. I want you to submit to that want of mine. I want to hear his praises in honour of what a wonderful slave and good fuck you are. It will do my vanity and ego wonders, and he'll tell everybody about your talents.'

'Who's everybody?'

'Anna and Fred.'

Jael closed her eyes. 'Maybe the five of us someday, the four of you using me...' she whispered.

'Maybe,' Thomas answered.

Chapter Sixteen

He stopped outside the main entrance, and Jael opened the door to hop out.

'Follow everything to the letter,' Thomas said. 'I'll know if you don't.'

'No need to remind me,' Jael said, leaning back and puckering up for him to kiss her. He brushed his lips against her cheek, and she looked up at him. 'This makes me so happy, Thomas, to be able to do this for you. To know that you want this, that you created it, and that I get to do it for you. It's incredible.'

'Don't forget to have fun,' Thomas said, but he was smiling at her warmly.

Jael got out of the car, and he pulled away. She strutted to the wide glass doors and pulled one open to walk into the high airy spaces of the mall. 'Wonder where he'll be?' she quietly asked herself, looking briefly to the right and left. Well, he had the same list of her errands that she had, so he'd probably find her. And he'd take over from there. She grinned to herself.

It was mid-afternoon on a cold, early winter's weekday, so there weren't too many people around. That part disappointed Jael. She wanted to put on a show for a lot more people, and she still relished the long look she'd taken of herself in the mirror at home. A tight, black knit, long-sleeved top with a low V-cut neckline and, quite obviously, no bra. A tight little red and black and gold plaid skirt with no underwear, bare legs, slouch socks and a pair of brown Doc Marten work boots. Jael giggled to herself. She reached into her hair and tossed it about, feeling the thin braids all through it. She stretched one hand out in front of herself as she walked and looked at the big, cheap, silver rings she wore. No make up, though, she thought. What was it with these guys and not wanting her to wear make up? She pushed the straps of the big black bag she wore higher onto her shoulder and walked jauntily along.

As she passed a clothing store the young men who worked there crowded at the entrance and stared. One of them was brave enough to give a wolf-whistle. Jael glanced back over her shoulder and wiggled her butt for them, giving them a wide smile. Another one made like he would walk after her, but laughing, fell back. She turned and walked backwards, beckoning him to follow her. He grinned, turned red, and went back into the store.

Jael walked past some benches where some women about her age sat. They glared at her, and she read the words in their eyes. But she wiggled her bottom for them, too. She wondered if any of them were getting hot for her, and she smiled.

'Now for my first job,' she said to herself. 'A new pair of track shoes for me.' She swung into the sports goods store and sat down on a seat and stared at a male clerk. He came over, his movements jerky as he met her eye. He was nervous and intrigued at the same time, Jael could tell.

'I'll try a pair of those in a size six,' she said, pointing at the first shoe that caught her eye. He disappeared without a word and brought back a box. He knelt in front of her. Oh, it was exciting being the one higher up for a change, Jael thought and grinned. As the young man pulled off her boot she slid to the edge of the seat and spread her legs. Thomas had sat her in a chair and knelt in front of her at home, to check out the perspective, and he'd ended up eating her for twenty minutes before they left the house. Would he get hungry, too? she wondered, smiling down at the top of the guy's head.

When he looked up at her his eye couldn't help but be drawn right to her snatch. Jael squirmed a little in the seat, as if uncomfortable, and parted her legs a little more. He took a good long look.

'Okay, that's fine,' Jael said sprightly. 'Thanks for your help.' She kicked the shoe off, slid her foot back into her Doc Marten, and walked out of the store without tying it.

Her next stop was the bookstore. She glanced around for Cole, but didn't see him, so she walked straight in. The health section was just ahead on the right, and she knew what she was looking for there.

The row of sex manuals was displayed prominently. Jael stood with her feet at shoulder-width and hitched her skirt even higher up her thighs as she picked one up and perused it. Out of the corner of her eye she saw someone walking towards her, and the hair colour looked like Cole's. She glanced up, she knew with a receptive, eager look on her face, but it wasn't him. Nonetheless, she had caught the man's eye. He slowed down as Jael kept looking at him, now a little more shyly. She glanced back down at her book as he turned into the health section and stood next to her. She held open the pages of her book to show a man and woman coupling, rapturous expressions on their faces, and when she was sure she had her new friend's full attention, she reached down, went up under her skirt, and gave herself a sly, quick rub.

The man cleared his throat, and she looked up at him with a foxy smile as she slowly withdrew her hand. She put the manual back on the shelf and bent down to lace up her boot and tie it. While she was kneeling with her face at the man's hips, she looked up at him and was delighted to see him gazing down at her, pure brute need all over him. She licked her lips and let her tongue protrude before she stood up, turned on her heel, and started to walk out of the aisle.

'Excuse me,' the man said, with a clearing of his throat.

She turned around slowly to greet his stare. 'Me?' she asked.

'Yeah, you.' He cleared his throat again. 'I recognise you. Someone told me about you.'

Jael froze in place and stared at him with her eyes wide. 'What do you mean?'

'Guy about my age stopped here around ten minutes ago. Told me to look out for you.'

Concern about her appearance and Cole's opinion flooded her. 'What did he say?'

'He just said to look out for a really young woman who'd come into this aisle. She'd be dressed kind of... badly.'

'Oh.' Jael glanced down at herself. 'Obviously, he meant me.'

'So it would seem.' The man paused, looking her up and down as she regarded him from under her brows. 'He said to give you this.'

He passed her a perfectly square envelope made of heavy linen-like paper. Reluctantly, Jael took it from him.

'What's this?' she breathed.

'No idea. He gave it to me. Said to give it to you and wait around.'

Jael didn't meet his eye again, but pushed her index finger behind the envelope's sealed flap and ripped it open. She pulled out a thin piece of paper and skimmed three words: Do him here.

Involuntarily, her eyes flew up to the man's face. She wrenched her eyes back down to the paper. Do him here? Her eyes darted over the top of the bookshelf next to them. Right here?

Slowly, Jael handed the note to the man. He looked down at it, then up at her. He was clearly confused, but she could tell that those three words had thrown petrol on the burning he already had for her.

He gave the note back to her, and Jael shoved it and the envelope down into the outer pocket of her bag, then dropped the bag onto the floor with a thud.

'What're you going to do?' he asked.

'I guess I'm going to do you.'

'Just like that?'

'He wants me to.'

They both glanced around furtively. She knew that her newest partner was looking around for spectators, but Jael wanted to see if Cole was watching her. Would he trust her to do this, on her own?

'I could go for a blow-job,' the man muttered. Jael looked down to see him opening his fly.

She glanced around again, before slowly bending to kneel in front of him. When she was on her knees, she looked up. He wasn't too bad, considering he was a complete stranger, picked out for her by her Master for the day. Crouched before him in the quiet of the bookstore, watching as he got out his half-hard cock, Jael felt her pussy melt into a horny wetness.

'This is gonna be fun,' he said, staring down at her. 'Turn this way.'

Jael moved in the direction he indicated until her feet were flat against the shelf. He stood in front of her and picked up a copy of the *Kama Sutra*, replete with photographs.

Jael looked up at the cover of the book as it formed a canopy over her head. The man cleared his throat again, and she looked at the prick that was quickly growing into a pole. She licked her lips and took his length in her fist, leaving the head exposed. With a few firm strokes she had him at full mast.

She looked up at the book again, then at the mace in her hand. This was admittedly sexy, being alone with a stranger's rod. It seemed that he was going to get off on just the feeling of her mouth around his cock, without looking down at her. The anonymity of it all excited Jael. She reached up under her short skirt and massaged the hood of her clit.

At the same time, she pushed his hard-on upwards and took the head in her mouth. She pushed her tongue against the bottom of his shaft and with quick, firm strokes, moved her head up and down. She felt the hot friction between her tongue and the base of his cock's head.

He grunted above her and moved to put the book back. Suddenly, Jael was under the bright fluorescent lights of the store. She looked up at him expressively, a third of his phallus lodged in her mouth. He broke the stare and reached for another book with one hand while pushing her head down onto his erection with the other.

Jael considered pulling her mouth off him and tantalising him a little bit longer by running her tongue and lips up and down the sides of his rigid penis. But, quickly, she looked to each side and decided against it. It would be best to get this over with as soon as possible.

She relaxed her jaw and throat and let him shove her face over his hardness. She moaned a little as she took him. Her hand was still under her skirt, and she began rubbing fast and hard. Her head bobbed on his prick, keeping time with the pleasure she was giving herself.

He spread his legs a little further and shoved his hips forward. Jael gripped his thigh with her free hand, then slid her fingers around his cock and began stroking the bottom half while she sucked the top. She clenched her jaw slightly, sucked in her cheeks, and got as much resistance in her mouth as she could.

The blow-job went on and on. Jael stopped rubbing herself and reached up to cup his balls through his jeans. She moved her hand in little circles, stroking them, encouraging them to shoot their come down her open, ready throat.

It didn't seem to help. Her jaw and lips were tiring. Jael pulled her mouth back and flicked her tongue over the tip of his penis, tasting for pre-come. The amount would tell her how far she had yet to go.

There was none. Jael stroked his cock some more, trying to milk something out of him, but nothing leaked onto the probing tip of her tongue.

She pulled her mouth off him altogether and glanced to the right and left. 'This isn't working,' she whispered.

'I know. I can't move,' he said peevishly. 'I need to fuck you.'

'I hate to leave you like this, but I can't suck your cock anymore. My jaw's giving out.'

'All right,' he answered. He put his current book back on the shelf and looked down at her. 'I have to fuck you.'

Jael's first instinct was to refuse. This was a public place, after all. And she could finish this scenario at any time just by walking into the main aisle of the store and pacing into the mall.

But the order to do this guy had come directly from Cole. It would displease him if she didn't do her job, and do it right. It might displease him so much that he wouldn't even deem it fit to punish her for her transgression – he would just leave.

'All right,' she whispered, moving to get to her feet. 'Do you want to do it standing, right here?'

'Hell, no,' he answered in surprise. 'I want to bang the shit out of you. We have to find somewhere else more private.' He looked around, turning to examine the back of the store. 'There's a door. Must be storage. Come on.'

With a quick tuck and zip, he was moving away. Jael picked up her bag and followed. She kept her head bent, refusing to meet the eye of anyone who might see her.

He had already disappeared into the back. She assumed it was safe, since he hadn't come back out, and she popped in as well.

There he stood, his jeans already completely open, his cock and balls out over the top of his boxers. He moved to stack some boxes, and his erection bounced in readiness.

'Get on here,' he said, motioning. Jael walked over, turned around, and gave a sprightly little hop onto the stack.

He barely waited for her to lie back.

He grabbed her thighs roughly and dragged her to the edge of the box. Her skirt slid up, and as Jael spread her legs around his hips, he pushed towards her. His cock was in.

'Ah,' she breathed as his size cleaved her and the welcome fullness crushed up through her pelvis.

'Shh,' he ordered.

Jael got a good look at his face for the first time. His eyes were shut, his head thrown back, and he was ramming in and out of her. His hands still held onto her thighs. She knew that at that moment, she was nothing

242

but a fuck-doll to him.

His fingers tightened their grip. Jael winced as his thumbs drove into the soft skin inside her thighs. He was grunting, forcing, pumping his way in and out of her. The boxes swayed and threatened to collapse. With a deep groan, he stilled his motions, then gave her another hard thrust.

He came. Quickly he backed away from her, zipping his jeans and tugging at the button. She righted herself, slid off the boxes, and dragged her skirt down as far as she could.

Without looking at her again, he opened the door and walked out. She followed him out of the store, and they went their separate ways.

Her next stop was on the other end of the mall's expanse. Jael paced quickly, getting her pulse up, breathing deeply and enjoying the feel of the knit top against her bare nipples. The store was soon in sight, and Jael walked in to look at jeans.

'Can I help you?' the young man asked.

Jael looked at him. He was no more than a lad just graduated from high school. 'Yes,' she said. 'I want to try on a pair of button-flies.'

'Uh, we only have them in men's sizes,' the boy said, looking down at her body.

'That's okay,' Jael said, wrinkling her nose at him and giggling. 'I think I can fit.'

'Yeah, probably,' the boy said, visibly perplexed about how to respond to such an onslaught of sluttishness.

'There's one problem,' Jael said, intent on pushing her behaviour even further when he came back over with a pair of narrow-legged jeans.

'What's that?'

'I'm not wearing any underwear. Would it still be all

right for me to try them on?'

And Cole's voice sounded behind her. Jael felt herself fall into it. 'I'll get them,' he said, and handed the young man a crisp fifty-dollar bill. The boy looked from Jael to Cole, and obviously couldn't put the two of them together as a couple in his mind's eye.

'Um, is he with you, ma'am?' the clerk asked.

Jael glanced back to see Cole glaring at the hapless young man. 'I don't want her to cover up those legs while I'm looking at them, so I'll buy her the jeans to take with her,' Cole said.

Jael smiled. 'Thanks. I don't think we've met.'

Cole looked down at her. 'No, we haven't. But I've noticed you a couple times this afternoon, and you look like you could do with some company for a few hours.'

The boy stood there, gobsmacked. Cole glared at him again. 'Do your job,' he said slowly and distinctly. The clerk finally started to move. Cole and Jael followed him to the cash register.

When they were in front of him again, Jael said, 'What do I owe you for this?'

Cole took her hand and kissed it before he said, 'We can discuss that in a bit.' He took his change and the bag from the clerk and, still holding Jael's hand, walked out of the store.

When they were in the main passageway he lit a cigarette and handed it to Jael, then lit another for himself. He squinted at Jael through his smoke-laden breath. 'Really,' he said. 'I don't know how you could look like more of a fuck pig. Are you?'

'For the right man, I can be anything.'

'You inspire me to want to be the right man.'

'So what do I owe you for these jeans?'

'The right to make you look like more of a slut.'

244

'All right.'

Cole took her hand in his again, and they walked together. He nodded towards a big department store, and they stopped to stub out their cigarettes. Jael looked down at his hand as he pushed his smoke into the sand of the ashtray, and a stripe of heat raged through her pussy to think of what that hand had done to her the last time she had seen him. Cole took her hand again and veered into the department store, and the two of them strolled through men's wear towards a dressing room well back in one corner. Cole looked around, so did Jael, and when they both saw the coast was clear, they ducked in.

Jael walked quickly into the first stall, and Cole drew the curtain behind them. He motioned for her to give him the bag she carried, and he began reaching into it and taking out the things that Thomas had packed, to put them on the ledge that served as a seat. Jael watched him take out a comb, hairspray, make up, a collapsible cane, a few lengths of rope, a pair of heels, crotchless fishnet stockings that fit like chaps, without a bottom in them, a bra with the nipples cut out, and a tube of personal lubricant.

'Very nice,' Cole said, tossing the tube into the air and opening the bag under it. 'But I don't think we'll be needing it.' He closed the bag after the tube fell in.

'Stand still,' he said. Jael lifted her chin and looked at herself in the mirror as Cole began moving around her. She was shocked to see how good he was with the make up, how he knew what each and every bit was for, and when he came to stand in front of her and began applying it, she found herself getting turned on under his careful, dextrous hand. To have him look at her like an object; indeed, to have him surveying her in the same way that she judged her sculpture, was sexy. Jael became as still as a block of marble for him, willing herself to be his most perfect canvas and work.

When he moved away again, Jael saw herself in the mirror. Bright blue eyeshadow, ruby blush, oxblood lipstick, layers of mascara, black eyeliner. He stood behind her and looked at her in two dimensions, as well, then reached around and smudged the eye make up so she looked like she'd been walking the streets all night. He stayed behind her and began teasing her hair with the comb and spraying it stiff. When he was satisfied that she looked enough like a tramp, Cole picked up the heels and dropped them at her feet. He handed her the bra and stockings. 'Put these on.'

Jael bent down and took off her work boots and socks and dropped them in the bag. Cole put his thumb under her chin as she knelt, and pulled her to her feet. Then he knelt down in front of her and held out his hand. Understanding, she placed her foot into his grasp. He traced her instep with the broad of one fingernail, then traced the outside of her foot, around to her heel. Jael shivered. He put her foot down, and Jael moved to put on the stockings. She pulled up her skirt and stared at Cole as he looked at her pubic hair.

'That really does want shaving,' he said. 'Maybe some other time. Maybe you should tell Thomas to do it.'

'I don't tell Thomas what to do,' Jael answered curtly. 'But if he wants me shaved, he's certainly the one to do it.'

Cole gave her a little smile. 'I hear you're drained of all desire for me to take possession of you,' he said.

'But being here with you today and becoming what you want me to be is so different from what I usually am.'

Cole smiled again.

He stepped away from her, and Jael turned to look at herself in the mirror again. Cole reached around and unbuttoned the top two buttons of her shirt, so her cleavage was exposed.

'Much better,' he said. 'Now for the bra.'

Jael pulled the shirt off and left it hanging around her neck as she pulled the last fetish article on. Her nipples stood taut in the holes made for them, and when she pulled her shirt back on their hardness was evident.

'Perfect,' Cole said. 'Meet me in the men's room at the opposite end of the mall.' He adjusted the collar and cuffs of his well-tailored clothes and walked out.

Jael packed everything into the bag. Her hand lingered on the cane, and then she walked out after him. No one saw her emerge from the dressing room, and that gave her a moment to put on some attitude before she began sauntering through the men's department.

When she walked out into the mall she saw the man from the bookstore. He looked at her in utter disbelief, then turned to follow her, as if she were leading him with a chain. She stopped, picked her foot up, bent sideways a bit as if knocking something off the spike of her heel, and looked at him after she'd treated him to a good view of her bottom. He licked his lips and shook his head, and she smiled saucily at him before she continued down the main thoroughfare, and he gave up the chase.

Several times she glimpsed Cole standing at the entrance to stores, watching her progress. He would walk out as she went by, pace past her, and go into another store up ahead. Jael liked to know that she was under his watchful eye, but then, she saw him talking on his phone. She furrowed her brow slightly. She wondered why he wasn't paying attention to her, before she saw from the way he appraised her and spoke into the phone that he was describing her for someone. She swayed her hips for him as she passed.

The other end of the mall, her destination, was just ahead. Jael walked through and off to the left to find the short hallway that led back to the toilets. She walked down it, glanced back to make sure no one was following her, and slipped into the men's room.

One man was standing at the urinals. When he heard her high heels tap on the linoleum, he looked back in astonishment. Politely, Jael looked away until he was finished. He quickly washed his hands, but before he walked out the door, he said, 'Business meeting?' Jael winked at him and looked him up and down. He grinned at her and left.

He must have passed Cole in the hall, for no sooner had the door swung shut from his departure than Cole pulled it open and walked in. He smiled and motioned for her to give him the bag. Jael wasn't surprised to see him take a photocopied sign – Out of Order – from the bag and a roll of masking tape. He opened the door a crack and taped the sign outside.

'Public is one thing, but too public is another,' he said.

With no other warning, Cole tossed the tape onto the floor and grabbed Jael's hair. He pulled her to him, hard, and kissed her angrily. His tongue nearly went down her throat, and Jael went weak at the knees. She held onto his broad shoulders as he kept kissing her, and in answer, Cole pulled up her skirt and squeezed her bottom's cheeks. Without taking his open mouth from hers, he pulled the gaping hole of the stockings open further and smacked one of her cheeks with his open palm. Jael nearly swooned at the pleasure of the sting.

Cole pulled his mouth away from her as she collapsed

against him. Jael opened her eyes and looked up at his face. His eyes were glazed with his compulsion to fuck her, his mouth was stained with her red lipstick, and she knew that at that moment he needed her more than she needed him.

She licked her index finger and ran it around her hard nipple, on the outside of her shirt. Cole yanked the shirt up and took that exposed nipple in his mouth, drawing the skin out from behind the bra and sucking hard. Jael grabbed a handful of his dark hair and pressed his face into her breast. He began wrestling with the shirt, pulling it over her head. Jael helped him to pull it off, and Cole looked down at her chest.

'One nipple's harder than the other,' he said. 'Let's fix that.' He pinched the other between his knuckle and thumb, hard and fast little pinches, then slightly harder ones, then long squeezes.

Jael reached towards his shirt and unbuttoned it as best she could. He stopped torturing her long enough to let her get his clothes open. Jael ripped it back, exposing his golden body, and she buried her face in his curly hair. She pushed her tongue against his skin and licked from the centre of his chest to his nipple, and she sucked it between her teeth and bit it hard. Cole jerked the back of her hair down, but didn't drag her face away. She ran her tongue to the other nipple and bit him there, too. He groaned and slapped the back of her head.

Jael ran her hands all over him, all over his back and chest, feeling the muscles. She wanted him, she admitted to herself. She wanted him, wanted him, wanted him.

She reached down to undo his trousers, and Cole stopped her with a firm grasp on her wrist. 'Get in there,' he said, pushing her into the large handicapped-accessible toilet stall. She obeyed, and he kicked the bag over to her. Jael watched him as he bent down to get into it, but she saw the outer door begin to open.

'Cole,' she gasped. He took one big step into the stall with her, and she pushed the door shut behind him. In one motion he picked her up. She spread her legs around his hips, and he leaned her against the door. Jael grabbed the hook that stuck out and stared into Cole's laughing eyes.

The voices were those of two adolescent boys. 'It says it's out of order,' one boy said.

'I don't care, I'm just going to take a piss.'

'Yeah, but what if somebody comes in?'

'Man, I'm just going to piss in one of these urinal things. They can't all be broke. Somebody else is in here, anyway.'

Jael pulled herself up, using the hook, and rubbed her wet crotch on Cole's erection.

'Yeah, all right,' the second boy said. The sounds of two people urinating tinkled through the room.

Cole looked at her and reached down to unhook his trousers and undo the zip. She glanced down and saw he wore boxers, and when he shoved them down the head of his cock sprang out.

'Hey, did you hear about the virtual reality programme Andy bought?'

'No.'

'It's a chick, dude. Like, you can pick what she looks like and stuff, and she'll do anything you say. But you have to be nice to her, or she, like, calls the cops or won't let you in the next time you knock on her door and stuff.'

'Are you serious? You can fuck her? Can you see it on the screen?'

'You can see her, not yourself.'

'Oh man, I'd love to get a load of that.'

'Andy and me were playing with it the other night, and we were spanking her. She was loving it.'

Jael licked her lips when she saw that Cole did have a thick prick; Anna was right about that. Jael struggled, hanging from the door, and Cole centred himself and pushed upwards. The angles were all wrong, but she was so slick and so needy, and he was so stiff and so rampant, his erection slipped into her begging pussy.

'You going to try to flush this thing?'

'Yeah, go ahead.'

'You, this was your idea.'

One urinal flushed, then the other, and the two boys walked out.

'Didn't wash their hands, dirty little sods,' Cole whispered. And as soon as everything went quiet, he glared at Jael and slammed her back against the stall door. She moaned, and Cole began pumping, just an inch at a time, between her legs.

'God, yes,' Jael moaned. 'You're in me, yes, please, fuck me.'

'Like that?' Cole grunted.

'Yes,' Jael moaned.

'Then you're going to love what I have in mind,' he said. He stepped back a bit, pulling Jael off the door, and put her down. She groaned in agony as his penis slipped from her.

'I have to have it,' she pleaded, and even clasped her hands together as if in prayer to him.

Cole looked at her, amused. 'You're going to get it,' he said. 'I'm actually glad those kids came in. You had me almost in your control, did you know that?' He smiled craftily at her. 'I think you do know.'

He walked around Jael. 'Get back in there,' he said, as he picked up the bag. This time he got what he wanted out of it. The collapsible cane appeared, as did the lengths of cord, which he put around his neck. Cole turned Jael around with a push and lifted up her tiny skirt. She shoved her exposed cheeks towards him, knowing that the way they pushed through the openings of the stockings was very eye-catching. He pulled the cane back and hit her.

Jael lurched forward. Cole struck her again. He glanced the cane off her bottom a third time, and that seemed to be all he could bear. He groaned and extended the cane, then grabbed her wrists. He pulled her arms back and expertly tied each wrist to the cane separately, with the cane underneath. When she was secure she felt him unzip the back of her tight skirt. He tugged it down over her hips, Jael stepped out of it when it fell to the floor, and Cole kicked it away.

Cole pushed her to bend over. She heard him pulling down his trousers behind her, and then he separated her buttocks with both his hands. Jael steeled herself – he was going to bugger her, just as he said he would. But all she felt were kisses. Cole kissed her bottom, licked the cheeks, ran his tongue all over her. His fingers and thumbs pressed into her flesh, massaging her roughly, contrasting with the sweet attentiveness of his mouth.

He stood up slowly, running his hands up and down her fishnet-covered thighs. Jael felt him move in tightly against her. His swollen club bumped against her backside. He put his feet between hers, one after the other, and made her stand spread-eagled before he resumed his place behind her.

Now, she readied herself. He had everything about her open and receptive, and she was sure he would ram himself into her bottom. Jael was so ready for it, she hoped he would so she could show him the way in which she served her man.

252

Cole took the cane in his hands and rocked Jael back and forth with it. 'Hurt?' he asked.

'No,' she whispered.

'Bend your knees, baby,' he said. She did.

As soon as she did he yanked her backwards, and his cock surged into her vagina. The pleasure of having him fill her up, of Cole Trevor banging her from behind, made the breath catch in Jael's throat. She kept her arms straight, and Cole fucked her, his knees bent, pushing and pulling her back and forth with the cane. Jael gasped in rapturous misery and arched her back so her bottom was pushed out further towards him. She concentrated on her pussy running up and down on his sturdy cock; the emptiness she felt for the split second when only the head was in her, the fullness she felt as he ran his manhood back in.

Then, suddenly, Cole pulled himself out, put the wet glans of his hard-on against her anus, and jerked her backwards. They both groaned. Jael screwed her eyes shut and grimaced. 'My cock is so soaked from you,' he muttered behind her, 'my balls are dripping. Oh, I like that.' He grunted as he pushed himself the whole way into her bottom. 'Tight.'

Then he pulled out, and Jael winced in the pain of his sudden withdrawal. But before she could fully feel the pressure release from her anus, Cole was back in her pussy.

'Wetter here.' He pushed and pulled her back and forth on his rod before he yanked himself out and jammed back into her now-distended anus. 'Tighter here. Where should I go?'

Jael knew it was a rhetorical question. Cole pulled himself out and gave her a shove so that she stepped closer to the toilet. Then he pushed on the cane, lifting it

253

higher and higher so that her arms were bending backwards at the shoulders. She was forced to rest her cheek on the toilet seat as she clenched her teeth against the pain. 'If it's too much, say "plastic,"' Cole panted.

Jael bit her lower lip and vowed to take the pain with the immense pleasure of his probing, digging shaft.

Cole entered her again, still pushing steadily against the resistance of her arms. When Jael could nearly take no more, he held her suspended, and in a grunting, panting frenzy, he fucked her like mad. Jael kept her knees bent, kept herself still, felt him ramming away behind her as he balanced his thrusts against her bottom and his pushes against her arms.

Tears of anguish squeezed from Jael's eyes as he shoved her arms up one more inch in his raving passion. Her lips came together to start the safeword when Cole jerked her arms down, pulled her back hard against himself, and moaned. His legs shook as he came. He stood behind her for a long moment, still holding her bottom tight against his hips.

And then, he released her.

Jael stood up, her shoulders screaming. Cole quickly untied her wrists and she flexed her back, rounding her shoulders forwards. He squeezed her upper arms in his capable fingers and pressed a kiss into her hair on the top of her head.

Jael turned around, eager to hold and kiss him, but Cole dropped his gaze and shoved his shirt into his trousers and fastened them. She stood there, watching, as he buttoned his shirt in a preoccupied way, looking at the wall above her head. He reached into his back pocket and pulled out his wallet, opened it, and tossed a fifty-dollar bill at her.

'Fifty dollars for the jeans, fifty dollars for the fuck,'

he said.

He turned around and walked out of the toilet, ripping the sign off the door as he went. Jael hurriedly pulled herself together, shoved the bag's contents down into it, and walked out as well.

She went to the appointed entrance and stood in the corridor. Something made her look back, and she saw Cole sitting on a bench, watching her. He smiled and looked away when he found out he'd been caught. Jael smiled too, and turned back to see Thomas pull up outside.

She walked out and opened the passenger-side door. As she threw the bag onto the back seat and sat down, she saw Cole Trevor walk in front of them, within feet of the car. He looked back as he crossed the traffic lane and blew her a quick kiss.

Thomas grinned at Jael. 'You ran into each other, then?' he asked.

She smiled. 'You might say that.'

Chimera Publishing Ltd

22b Picton House
Hussar Court
Waterlooville
Hants
PO7 7SQ

www.chimerabooks.co.uk

chimera@chimerabooks.co.uk

***

Sales and Distribution in the USA and Canada

Client Distribution Services, Inc
193 Edwards Drive
Jackson
TN 38301
USA

***

Sales and Distribution in Australia

Dennis Jones & Associates Pty Ltd
19a Michellan Ct
Bayswater
Victoria
Australia 3153